MURDER YOUR DARLINGS

MURDER YOUR DARLINGS

Mark McCrum

This first world edition published 2019
in Great Britain and 2020 in the USA by
SEVERN HOUSE PUBLISHERS LTD of
Eardley House, 4 Uxbridge Street, London W8 7SY.
Trade paperback edition first published
in Great Britain and the USA 2020 by
SEVERN HOUSE PUBLISHERS LTD.

British Library Cataloguing in Publication Data
A CIP catalogue record for this title is available from the British Library.

ISBN-13: 978-0-7278-8993-5 (cased)
ISBN-13: 978-1-78029-668-5 (trade paper)
ISBN-13: 978-1-4483-0366-3 (e-book)

All Severn House titles are printed on acid-free paper.

Severn House Publishers support the Forest Stewardship Council™ [FSC™],
the leading international forest certification organisation.
All our titles that are printed on FSC certified paper carry the FSC logo.

Typeset by Palimpsest Book Production Ltd.,
Falkirk, Stirlingshire, Scotland.
Printed and bound in Great Britain by
TJ International, Padstow, Cornwall.

'If you here require a practical rule of me, I will present you with this: "Whenever you feel an impulse to perpetrate a piece of exceptionally fine writing, obey it – whole-heartedly – and delete it before sending your manuscript to press. *Murder your darlings.*"*

Sir Arthur Quiller-Couch
On the Art of Writing (1916)

'Kill your darlings, kill your darlings, even when it breaks your egocentric little scribbler's heart, kill your darlings.'

Stephen King
On Writing: A Memoir of the Craft (2000)

*his italics

S he felt a little giddy, but that was OK – just the heat, probably, or her pre-brekky *espresso*. She picked up the ladle, swung it towards the silver bowl and filled it to the brim with water, then lifted it carefully, meniscus shimmering, not spilling a gorgeous drop, over to the glowing orange coals. With a twist of her wrist she turned it, then laughed like a child as the steam foamed up into the little cabin, the heat just behind it, like sound following light.

Two more minutes, that would do it, don't be silly, deep breaths, feel that rasp of heat on the back of your throat. Ah, how she loved it! Heat, heat, heat, right through to her bones, chilled as they were from her refreshing early dip in the pool outside. And with the heat, the scent of lavender, from the blue glass bottle of Neal's Yard essential oil she had brought out with her from home. It reminded her of long-ago summer holidays in the South of France, lying in the hammock in the barn in her bikini, *après-déjeuner*, waiting for one of those nice young men to come and pay court to her. Annoying Anthony, now there was a chap she'd given a bit of a run around to. Hey ho, was it her fault he'd felt he had to kill himself? Absolutely not. His life, his decision. I wasn't that marvellous. Or was I? Later, of course, the crazy trips abroad. India in '66, Morocco in '67, long before the dreaded scourge of 'backpackers', when it had been a novelty to be a traveller, when there was adventure to be had, spliffs to be smoked, gurus and Berbers to be seduced and all the rest of it. She hadn't been that nice to boring Bobby in Essaouira, had she, or humdrum Harry in Kashmir for that matter, but what was life for if not for living, as her dear Papa always used to say. 'Look before you leap, but don't look for too long, or you may never leap.' That had been another of his *bon mots*. She had never, to be honest, met a man to match him. His wildness, tamed by his sheer, impeccable *style*.

Another wave of giddiness rocked her. What was going on? She was normally fine for as long as she wanted *dans le sauna*. OK, time to get back to reality. Far away from desert dreams to the dear little souls of 'the writing group'. What a funny bourgeois bunch they were, tedious as burnt toast most of them, but still, maybe she was learning something. Francis the tutor had a twinkle in his eye, it had to be said. Were she only thirty years younger, and still in possession of the famous 'body', who knew what might have transpired? But hey ho, *tempus fugit, Anno Domini* and all that. This was what you did in your early seventies, when flesh sagged and memory lagged. Studied the art of memoir and stuffed your creaking carcass with yummy nosh. And then – Christ, what was *that* – got dizzy in the sauna.

Carefully, putting her hands down on the natural pine planks to steady herself, she lifted her dainty old bottom off her towel and got to her feet. She was short of breath and could feel her heart racing wildly. What *was* this? Was she having a heart attack or a stroke or something? Desperate now to get out, to gulp fresh air, she reached for the door handle and realized it wasn't there. What? Where on earth? Oh my Christ, the bloody thing had come off and fallen to the floor. How had that happened? She'd used it, surely, to get in, how else would she have opened the door? But hang on, the outer one was still there. Mocking her from the other side.

She reached down to pick it up and almost fell over. Hands shaking, she got to it, grasped it, held it up to the square fixing on the door. But no. It didn't, *wouldn't* engage. Where was a decent man when you needed one? She staggered sideways on her feet, reached out with her other hand for the bench. She felt like a woman on a ship in a storm. Like she'd felt on the Santander ferry with David the Dreary, why had she wasted even a minute of her life with him? Was she about to be sick? Oh Christ, those prawns must have been off last night.

Without the handle, she couldn't get out. She could see the tantalizing little steel catch that was holding the door shut, keeping her in, like a prisoner. Even as she stared at it, it swam out of focus. The handle, too. The whole cabin was a blur. She threw herself against the glass but nothing moved. Ouch. All she'd done was hurt her shoulder. Don't panic, she told herself, as she hammered on the door with both her fists, then screamed at the top of her voice. Would they hear her? Surely they must, even though the walls were thick and the sauna was deep in the basement of the villa.

With another wave of nausea she grabbed the bench, gulped at the throat-searing dry air. OK, OK, keep calm in an emergency, that's what Daddy would have said. It's hot but not so hot, if you don't put any more water on the coals the cabin will slowly cool. You can bear it. You can drink the water from the bowl, keep hydrated. Someone will come. It's breakfast time, for God's sakes! They will miss you and be here. Fabio will come. To check. Handsome, saturnine Fabio will c—

She slid sideways past the bench to the floor. As she fell, she was aware of a blurry face in the shadows beyond the door. Shouting at her, as hands gesticulated and fingers tapped loudly on the glass. *Rat-tat-tat!* Oh mercy be, thank the heavens, was she saved? No. The fingers didn't reach downwards for the handle. They pointed up, and around, wildly, as the gaping mouth yelled on . . .

ONE

'It's not that I particularly dislike her,' read Poppy, 'although I have to say I do. It's more that she dislikes *me*. Hates me, in fact, and makes no secret of it. It's been the same since we were teenagers, though the sad thing is we were tremendous friends as children.'

A flicker of regret crossed her features, like the shadow of a cloud covering the sun; but almost before that had fully registered, Poppy had pulled herself together. She looked up from her trembling oblong of A4 and round at the attentive group, with that same mischievous, yet undeniably superior smile that had been troubling Francis all week. Not just Francis. All the guests at the villa were finding her irritating, with her grand manner and constant namedropping.

'*Tremendous* friends,' she repeated with emphasis. 'Games of hoopla. Dressing up. Running into the woods to build dens. We were most ungirly girls, really. The trouble was, of course, the house. Framley Grange. The most beautiful house in Wiltshire, people said. Though growing up, we took it totally for granted. My father had improved it, of course, beyond measure, but it had always been lovely, with the tall, spreading cedars over the great lawn at the front and the surprising wildflower meadow at the back. The twinkling trout stream beyond. The mill house that was now the summer house. The natural pool, far superior to those vulgar blue pools that were to blight the landscape later. Where we could bathe naked, *nunga punga* as my father used to say, in the argot he'd picked up as a young officer in India during the war. Ah, how we loved Framley! Even before we were old enough to realize how famous or important the constant stream of visitors often were. Cabinet ministers, judges, my father's top brass army colleagues. All lured by my father's legendary dry wit and my mother's generosity of spirit. But then, when we came to understand that it was to be I who was, in the end, to inherit the place, things started to go wrong in our sibling relationship. I could never put a finger on it directly, just little things. Minty would help herself to my party frocks without asking, for example, knowing how much that irritated me. Was I prettier than her? Perhaps I was. Was I cleverer than her? Perhaps I was. Did it seem unfair that I should get the looks and the brains and also the house? But that was life, as my dear father often used to say, shout sometimes. "There's no such thing as fairness in the human condition, whatever the bloody Commies like to think . . .'"

When she'd finished, five minutes later, there was the usual short silence. Which Francis, as writing tutor, was honour-bound to break with some comment or remark. He liked, generally, to be as positive as possible, before pointing out, perhaps, a few things that could have been done better.

'That was very strong, Poppy,' he said. 'Very strong,' he repeated, playing for time. 'The point of this exercise, which as you know I jokingly call "Murder Your Darlings", is to be as honest as possible about someone close to you – and you really succeeded in that.'

There were murmurs of agreement from around the table and Poppy beamed back, smugly.

'It's not easy, telling it how it is,' Francis continued, 'so well done. I got a very clear picture of your sister, and your father. And also of this wonderful house you lived in as a child—'

'Still live in,' said Poppy.

'Still live in, great, and you gave us some nice details of that. The cedar trees, the mill house, all very atmospheric. I almost wanted more. Did anyone else think that?'

This was always a good trick, to throw things open to the table. However good, bad or dreadful they were as writers, most of the group were coherent critics.

Liam, the scruffy, middle-aged Northern Irishman, was the first to dive in. 'Not sure I wanted more about the house, though it does sound rather splendid. Like one of those Anglo-Irish mansions the IRA used to enjoy burning out in the Republic.' He chuckled, loudly. 'But the sister, and the father. I got a sense of them, but it wasn't powerful. What did they look like? What did they *smell* like? I'd have liked a more objective picture, to be fair.'

With each disparaging word, you could see irritation spreading across Poppy's features. Though this whole exercise of writing and then reading out loud was intended to provoke criticism, none of them really liked it when it came, however politely couched it was.

'I agree,' said Zoe, the self-styled 'Hampstead Jewess', adjusting her half-moon specs on the bridge of her nose, then looking down to consult a scrawled page of notes. 'So you were honest, Poppy, almost too honest, I'd say, about how clever you're supposed to be. But there wasn't enough specific detail. You talk about your father's "legendary dry wit". But even if it was legendary, with *whom* was it legendary? And isn't "dry wit" a bit of a cliché. Wouldn't it be better to see examples of it, Francis? Show not tell, and all that.'

There was no denying Zoe, who would always drag him in to her spiky takedowns. She was usually right, which made it worse.

'It's a first draft,' he said emolliently. 'It's an exercise, and there's lots to work with here. Trying to remember specific jokes is obviously more difficult than talking about a "legendary dry wit". But that's what we have to do. As writers. We have to work hard to yes, show not tell, as Chekhov famously said. The point is, I'm holding you all to a very high standard here. I don't imagine Dan Brown would redraft a phrase like that . . .'

'"Legendary dry wit,"' repeated Poppy. 'Is that really Dan Brownish . . .?'

The scorn in her tone indicated that she saw herself as a cut above the international bestseller.

Scottish Diana, never one to allow discord, now chipped in. 'I thought it was jolly good, Poppy. If I'm allowed an opinion.'

'Of course you're allowed an opinion,' Francis said. Christ, the passive-aggression of this woman knew no bounds. Her accent reminded him of the old joke about Edinburgh ladies of a certain background, gossiping over morning coffee. 'What's it called when two cars run into each other in Morningside? A *crèche*.'

'It's so hard to be honest about one's feelings for family members,' Diana went on, fixing the group with her large, sincere, if rather troubled blue eyes. 'I mean, I found my father rather tricky to deal with at times, but I don't imagine I would ever want to write about that.'

'Why not?' asked Liam.

'Far too personal.'

Liam chortled. 'What would you want to write about,' he asked, 'as a matter of interest?'

'What do I write about, Liam?' Diana replied. 'What I see in front of me in my daily life. Little quirks of other people. Unusual stories that I overhear in tea shops and restaurants. That sort of thing. But never anything about people I know personally. And nothing too negative. There's enough negativity in the world without us having to read about it all the time, isn't there?'

'That's a point of view, for sure,' said Liam. 'What did you think, Sasha?'

He turned to the young mixed-race American, who lay on the big blue beanbag in a white top and jeans, a fuchsia scarf around her neck, frizzy golden-brown hair framing her pretty, thoughtful face, like some alien goddess dropped into this coterie of geriatrics. She had booked the course on the Internet with apparently little idea what she was letting herself in for, except that it was 'in Italy', a place she had wanted to see, she had told Francis, ever since reading E.M. Forster's *A Room With a View*.

'I thought it was great,' she said, and laughed boisterously, as she often did just after she'd spoken. 'I'm so in awe of you all, with your stories, and your experiences. I wish I had a tenth as much to write about.'

'You will, dear,' said Zoe. 'All too soon you will.'

'I'm sure you do already,' said Liam. 'You just have to access it.'

'And on that upbeat note,' said Francis, 'let's break for our mid-morning coffee.' It was exactly eleven o'clock and he had been saved by the notional bell.

The group shifted themselves at varying speeds. They left the long table under the vine and made their way out into the bright sunshine of the gravelled courtyard. The main bulk of the villa was to their right: pale-blue shuttered windows set in a façade of honey-coloured stone, undressed and wonderfully higgledy-piggledy, if you looked closely. The first door you came to led into a little piano room, where there were also shelves of fluffy toys, for the families who stayed here over the summer; then there was the main front door to the hall, with its worn black and white tile squares; the third door along led into a room with an oblong marble dining table and an open fireplace. At the far end of this was an industrial-sized Gaggia machine, where guests could make their own coffees. Here the writers formed a loose queue, politely offering to help each other with the tricky practicalities of tamping and squirting and frothing. 'Careful, Poppy!' cried Diana, as she turned on the steam wand before she was ready with the jug of milk. 'Or you'll scald yourself!'

'I'm hopeless, aren't I? Never quite got the hang of this bloody thing. And you're always so helpful, thank you.'

Once they had sorted out their cappuccinos and espressos and teas they headed back into the courtyard, to relax on the faded white deckchairs or sun themselves on the upright wooden benches that stood against the wall of the villa. Soon they were joined by the three ladies of the art group, who had been painting *al fresco* this morning, on the sloping lawn beyond the barnlike dining hall that stood at the far end of the courtyard. From this neatly mown green demesne there were wonderful rural views to wrestle with, out across the Umbrian/Tuscan countryside to the distant blue-grey outline of the Mountains of the Moon. An abandoned chapel, a study in glowing terracotta, lay above woods and sunflower fields on the high ridge to the left. Far away down the valley to the right, where the hills were covered in deep green forest, sat the grey turret of a castle. Fortunately, you couldn't see the battery chicken farm directly below the villa, though if you knew what to listen for, you could hear the awful squealing of the trapped birds first thing in the morning and last thing at night.

Francis was tempted to join in the mid-morning banter, as the writing group let off steam or asked the art group how they were getting on and the art group responded in kind. But then he decided to have five minutes in the sunshine on his own. The teaching was always more intense than he allowed for, especially if he had to keep the peace with such disparate spirits as this lot.

Snooty, self-satisfied Poppy was accompanied on this week by her quiet, dignified, if somewhat portly husband Duncan, who had told the group that he had no work in progress and nothing to write about anyway. 'Yes, you have, darling,' Poppy had cut in. 'Your memoir. His life as a diplomat,' she added, 'which is absolutely fascinating. Culminating in two postings as ambassador.' That she was writing her own memoir of their life together was not supposed to put him off, even though she had already regaled the group with some of the choicest anecdotes: the dinner party in Sierra Leone where no one had turned up, not even the guest of honour; the Bulgarian butler who had turned out to be a hitman; the not-so-discreet wife-swapping among the international diplomatic corps in Saudi Arabia.

Then there was forty-something civil servant Roz, who was looking for a new direction in her writing, and – she cackled, huskily – in life. Her best chance of that here was probably bluff, tanned, fifty-something Tony, who had joked that if he wrote honestly about his life he'd have to shoot the reader (the ladies had privately nicknamed him 'the spy'). And that was it: a group of eight, an excellent number, Francis thought, in that it was big enough to have a range of different perspectives, yet small enough that they didn't spend all morning reading back their various efforts at composition.

The oddest was undoubtedly Liam, the eccentric Irishman, such a caricature of the type that Francis would have ruled him out as a 'realistic character' in any exercise on that subject. During the introductory session yesterday, when Francis had asked them all what they were working on at present, Liam had told them that his memoir was about drugs and politics, but particularly drugs.

'So what is it?' Poppy asked. 'A been-there, done-that, got-the-T-shirt and learned-my-lesson type of memoir?'

Liam laughed. 'So what lesson am I supposed to have learned?'

'The dangers of drugs, I imagine. The harm you can do to yourself.'

'Bollocks to that!' Liam replied. 'I've never done any harm to myself. Quite the opposite. I've expanded my sensibilities.' This had led to a five-minute discourse on the *wonders* of drugs, how the world would be a better place if they were all legalized immediately; more than that, if ordinary people made a habit of taking them regularly. 'Can you imagine,' Liam said, 'if the politicians, rather than being forced to lie about how they'd never taken this or that illegal substance, admitted that they had of course, at college, or as young people, like anyone else. That they'd enjoyed them. That they continued to enjoy them, like fine wine. If they all got stoned at those conferences abroad, the G7 and Davos and such like, the world would be a better place. Just imagine if all those fellows from the EU just sat out in a sunny field in Switzerland and got wrecked on some Grade A sinsemilla. The problems of Europe would be solved in a jiffy. Dontcha think?'

Poppy had laughed at this, a measured tinkle. 'A most interesting point of view, Liam,' she said.

'It's not a feckin' point of view, Poppy, excuse my French,' he replied. 'It's the obvious truth.' His memoir wasn't so much a memoir about drugs, he went on, but a manifesto *for* drugs.

'So what do you say to the parents of the eighteen-year-old girl whose life has been cut short by a dodgy ecstasy tab?' Poppy asked.

'It's not an ecstasy *tab*,' Liam scoffed. 'It's an E. OK. A "pill"' – he drew the quotes with his chubby fingers – 'known as an "E". What I would say to them is this: if only drugs were legalized, they would be properly controlled and there would be no more "dodgy ecstasy tabs". Any more than the whisky and brandy you buy in pubs is likely to have meths in it, as it did during Prohibition. Or the abortions you get in UK hospitals are going to kill you, as they did before David Steel's law. It's the illegality that's the problem, not the drugs themselves.'

Over drinks before dinner last night, Poppy had given Francis her opinion of Liam. 'A most original person,' she'd said, tight-lipped. 'Though it can't be good for that young American girl, listening to all that nonsense about drugs.'

'She's twenty-three,' Francis replied. 'She has an M.Phil from the University of Oregon. I'm sure she knows all about drugs.'

'I just hope he hasn't brought a whole load with him,' Poppy countered.

Why do you 'hope', you bossy creature, Francis thought. 'I'm sure he hasn't,' he replied. 'Customs and all that.'

Now he lay back in the warm sunshine, closed his eyes, and eavesdropped on the chit-chat. To his right, he could hear Duncan talking to Sasha about Ghana, where some of her ancestors had come from and he had once been posted as a First Secretary. To his left, Diana, as an old Villa Giulia hand, was giving advice to newbie Roz about where and how to go, if she wanted to walk to the pretty little nearby town of Civitella this afternoon. It was, she said, her very favourite local walk, though sadly, even with the new hip she'd had put in three years ago, she was unable to do it anymore. 'We're all getting older, that's the trouble. I've been coming here for over twenty years. We were quite sprightly when we started. Hard to believe, but we were.'

When they returned to the table under the vine, it was Liam's turn to shine. 'As I mentioned to you before,' he said, 'I'm a single fellow with no siblings, so I've no immediate family to hate, apart from my ma and da, and they're dead and gone now. So I guess all I'm left with is memories.' He sighed deeply. 'I did this one as a poem.'

'OK,' Francis replied, smiling to conceal a surge of irritation. This was supposed to be a prose exercise and the Irishman knew it. Francis had already begged him to stop doing 'poems', which were hardly poems anyway, more like the modish chopped prose that so often passed for poetry these days. 'Let's hear it.'

Liam gave the group the beam of the creator sharing his work, took a deep, theatrical breath, and began:

> '*Da.*'

There was a long pause, as Liam's bright brown eyes looked slowly round the group, and his right forefinger rose up in an arc towards his nose. Then:

'*The official bastard,*' he continued in a near-whisper.

> *With his God behind him*
> *The whip always to hand*
> *Or the slipper*
> *'Take your medicine, lad.'*
>
> *Yet his struggle*
> *Not with me*
> *But*
> *With his overlord and master*
> *The British State*
> *Was the one I grew to understand*
> *And share*

How bravely he fought them
In secret
Out in the training camps
At crack of dawn
In the rain and the wind
The words of Padraic Pearse
'In bloody protest for a glorious thing'
Always in his ears

He who took his own medicine
From his
Da
Who took his
From the whip hand
Of the Black and Tans
The British dregs
In silly uniforms

But when I saw him
Laid out on the mortuary slab
My own tears came
Why had they waited all these years
For this lifeless hulk
With the all-too familiar wrinkles
Round his dead brown eyes
The white hair curling
Like wood shavings
And the cruel thin mouth

Da
On the slab
Da
On the slab
Da
On the slab
Da . . .

Liam faded away theatrically, his last '*Da*' a whisper. There was silence.

'Wow!' said Sasha, clapping. 'That was powerful, Liam.'

'Thank you, my darling.'

'It was indeed,' said Tony.

'Thank you, Liam,' said Francis. It wasn't the right moment for an honest critique so, with a studiedly thoughtful nod of approval, he threw the piece open to the group.

'It's funny,' said Poppy, after the initial round of praise was over. 'These feelings that you had, Liam. Because I loved my father. But then I suppose he never laid a finger on me, and was always very kind and supportive, whatever I was doing. And even though he was away a great deal, on army business and so forth, he always had time for us when he came back. He'd strip off that smart uniform and be a regular Papa. So we loved him, in a very uncomplicated way, unfashionable though that may seem.'

Liam gave her a quizzical look. 'Did you say he was a general, Poppy?' he asked, in his soft Irish brogue. This was pure mischief, as if Poppy had told them her father was a general once, she had told them twenty times. 'The General Anecdotes,' Roz had called them, last night, when Poppy and Duncan had retired to bed, and a group of them were sitting round drinking in the library. 'I don't mind the Diplomatic Anecdotes, they're moderately interesting, but if I have to listen to another of the effing General Anecdotes, I will quietly scream.'

'You know he was, Liam,' said Poppy, and for a moment her smile froze. Then she was back in upbeat mode. 'Is it time for lunch? I feel a glass of Pinot Grigio coming on.' She turned to Sasha and gave her a stagey wink. 'Hard work, this writing lark, isn't it?'

'It is,' Sasha agreed. She stretched out her young arms and yawned like a cat.

Back in the sunny courtyard, the guests helped themselves to wine and beer, justifying themselves noisily.

'We are on holiday.'

'Are we? I thought this was supposed to be a writing course.'

'Don't they say that an author is never on holiday?'

'Always on holiday, more like.'

Laughter.

'And what about us artists?' came a North Country accent.

'You lot are definitely always on holiday.'

'Actually painting is jolly hard work.'

Lunch at Villa Giulia was famously delicious. Scottish Diana had told Francis several times that Benedetta's food was one of the key reasons she came back year after year for Gerry and Stephanie's September writing and art fortnight. Over the summer months the villa saw many types of visitors, from would-be musicians in April, wannabe cooks in June, to parents with small children in July and August. They all raved about the nosh. Benedetta had, as the Italians put it so wonderfully, *le mani d'oro* – golden hands. 'And so charming and beautiful with it,' Diana said. 'Have you met her yet?'

'Not yet.'

'I'll introduce you.'

There was a spread of cold dishes, in which you could discern bits of past evening meals re-presented among cold meats and fresh salads. Chicken legs and pasta alongside parma ham crostini; courgette flowers in batter; glistening slices of aubergine; quarters of pear wrapped in pecorino cheese – there were perhaps thirty to choose from.

'Now what is *this*? Chickpeas and zucchini.'

'That looks alarmingly like last night's supper.'

'But all the more delicious for it,' snapped Diana, who was not one to tolerate a single word of criticism of the regime. Roz, meanwhile, was leaning over the table taking photos of all the dishes with her iPhone.

Outside, they sat and ate at two sides of a long wooden table that ran parallel to the dining room and was shaded at one end with large square white canvas parasols. Francis found a place in the sun opposite two of the art group, Mel and Belle, who were friends from North Yorkshire: Knaresborough and Wetherby. Belle was like a superannuated Betty Boop, with bouncy (presumably dyed) blonde hair and a figure that you might have called pert were she not sitting one along from Sasha. Mel, by contrast, looked like something from Middle Earth: short, square-shouldered, flat-chested, with a big nose and ruddy cheeks under hair that was an incongruous – and frankly clashing – orange.

'Knaresborough's near Harrogate, isn't it?' said Francis, making conversation.

'Exactly,' said Belle. 'I expect, as a crime writer, you've been to the crime festival, have you?'

'I have. The Old Swan Hotel. And I've had tea in Bettys.'

'You have to do that,' said Mel, 'even if it is full of Japanese these days.'

'Did someone mention Harrogate?' called Poppy. 'Such a lovely town. I had a very happy three years there.'

'With Duncan?'

'No, long before him. It was just me, as a saucy singleton, with my little business. If I hadn't had to take over Framley I'd have stayed there forever, probably.'

'What was that, Poppy? Your little business?'

'Interior decoration, garden design, that sort of thing.'

'Interior decoration, how interesting. When was this?'

'In the Seventies. Yes, in the Seventies.'

'What was it called?'

'Oh, I can't remember. Such a long time ago now.'

There was the *ping* of a spoon on a glass from one end of the table and Stephanie, their hostess and organizer, got to her feet. She was a large lady who went in for colourful floaty dresses and big hats. Gerry, her partner, was contrastingly lean, cadaverous almost, with a wild, narrow corona of black hair round a well-tanned pate. Besides being co-host, he was the art tutor. He had once been a senior teacher at a well-known West Country art school. Now he had the time and space at last to do his own work, much of which was to be seen on the walls of the villa.

'Sorry to interrupt, lovely people!' Stephanie called. 'I hope you've all had a wonderfully creative and productive morning. This is just to say that you are entirely free to do what you want this afternoon . . .'

'Lucky us,' muttered Liam loudly, winking at Sasha. This drew an audible 'shsh' from Diana.

'. . . whether that's continuing to work on your own writing or painting, reading, snoozing, going for a long walk or cycle ride in the gorgeous Italian countryside, lazing by the pool, working out in our mini-gym or taking a relaxing sauna. By the way, if you do want a sauna in the morning, just ask Fabio, our handsome handyman and gardener, and he'll be happy to switch it on for you. If you can't find him in the house, he's always in the garden—'

'On one of his infuriatingly noisy machines,' said Zoe.

'Cake,' Stephanie went on, looking firmly down at the scrap of paper trembling in her hand, 'will be put out as usual in the small dining room at four, and you can of course help yourself to tea or coffee – or alcohol, if you're feeling naughty – at any time. We meet for drinks before dinner at seven-fifteen sharp, and then after dinner tonight I'm thrilled to announce that Duncan is going to give us an illustrated talk on his beautiful house in England, Framley Place.'

'Grange!' called Poppy.

'Framley Grange, sorry. And also the magnificent garden he has created there with Poppy, his wife.'

The silence that followed this was somewhat pregnant, as everyone knew by now about Poppy's 'published' book, *The Garden That Saved A Marriage*.

'The garden that saved a marriage!' called out Poppy. 'I have copies for sale, if anyone's interested.'

'That sounds fascinating,' said Diana, loudly. 'I shall look forward to that.'

TWO

After his two glasses of wine, Francis decided to slump with his book in a deckchair on the shady side of the courtyard, the far end from the dining room, where there were three or four bedrooms in a separate building rendered in a similar honey colour to the stone of the main villa. From here you could look up the steep slope above the drive to where a quaint wooden Wendy house sat by the stepped pathway that ran up through the mass of ornamental bamboo that lay below the tall shady trees. He was half-listening to the group as they made their plans to go out or head back to their rooms for a siesta, meanwhile watching Sasha, who was offering a counterpoint to the otherwise sedate atmosphere by doing cartwheels along the yard-wide cross of paving stones that divided the gravel courtyard into four neat segments. She had changed into purple harem pants and a clinging white T-shirt, a perfect match for her golden-skinned Rubenesque figure.

From inside, upstairs, came repeated halting attempts at Gershwin's 'Summertime'. It was Poppy, doing her saxophone practice. Jesus Christ, could you count the ways in which the woman was irritating? (Admirable though it was of course that a septuagenarian should be learning a musical instrument for the first time.)

All too soon Francis's attempts at a snooze were more decisively interrupted by a bony jab in the midriff. The wrinkled yellow forefinger belonged to Zoe. She was *so* sorry to interrupt, had he been asleep, apologies, though with that racket going on, she thought it was unlikely. For a moment Francis thought she was back with some tedious tech query; yesterday she'd got into a complete tizz about how to get files into an order on a memory stick. But no: was it possible that he could have a quick look at her memoir at some point during the next few days? Was this in the remit of what he'd agreed to do? he wondered, as he stared at the fat wad of A4 being held out before him. Teaching for a fortnight, Stephanie had said when she'd recruited him at that literary festival in Dorset where he'd been running a masterclass on 'creative crime writing'. There had been, in the verbal contract, nothing about editorial services. Could he give twitchy Zoe a frank 'no way'? And if he made an exception here, how many of the others might descend upon him with their *oeuvres*-in-progress?

'Thank you, Zoe, that's great,' he heard himself say, as he took it from her. 'I'll look forward to having a read.'

He returned to his room, at the back of the villa on the first floor, cursing his pusillanimity. OK, so if it was truly dreadful, he could always comment on a chapter or two. On the other hand, Zoe's exercise writing was as spiky and perceptive as her conversation. When he'd told the group that keeping a daily journal was a good way to improve your style and powers of observation, she had retorted that she'd kept one since she was nineteen. So maybe he was in for a pleasant surprise.

The bedrooms were all named after Italian artists. His was Masaccio, the obscurity matching, he thought, the quality of the room, which was smaller than most of the others, with a single bed and an overhead light that, despite the heavy brass chain that held it up, let out only the feeblest glow. It had a tiny en suite, with an ancient enamel hip bath which he found it hard to fit into, even with his knees up; and all too easy to slip in, when he attempted to stand and use the wobbly shower mounted above. The main room had a view of sorts, down over the valley, but it was rather obscured by trees, not at all like the splendid prospect in Gerry and Stephanie's suite – Tintoretto – at the far end of the villa. Still, fair enough, they lived here, and what was he? Only the visiting tutor.

He sat down on the bed with Zoe's stash of manuscript. But it seemed a shame to be reading in the gloom on such a beautiful afternoon, so he decided to leave the task for later and take himself off for a walk. He remembered Diana's instructions to Roz, and crunched off up the gravelled drive of the villa, through the tall, wrought-iron gates, along past the closed doors of the silent village, and out on to a road lined with tall, deep-green cypresses. Here, to the right, was the village football pitch, a scruffy, weed-strewn compound fifty metres or so below the main road.

Beyond that, the track dropped down steeply past a couple of more modern houses into the valley. At the bottom, by a tumbledown terracotta-brick barn, surrounded by a slew of rusting old farm machinery, was a bridge over a waterless stream bed, and on the far side a field of dried-up sunflowers, their seed heads black, the withered leaves a purplish grey. He wondered why they hadn't been cut earlier, when they were fresh and colourful. Would the seeds, perhaps, be harvested later? Or was this just the abandonment and decay of a remote rural place?

Francis walked on, up the unmade road on the far side of the valley, kicking up white dust as he went; then into olive groves, where crickets hummed noisily in the early afternoon heat and the backs of the grey-green leaves flashed silvery-white in the light breeze. Here he came out on to a stony track which led along the ridge to the ruined church, and a restored but empty house right next to it. Both were locked, though there were children's toys visible on the kitchen floor through the window of the house.

Ten minutes later, Civitella came in sight across flat vivid green fields of tobacco. The old town of white, ochre and pinkish brown houses with narrow terracotta tiled roofs rose steeply up an almost conical hill. From the coach ride that had brought most of the party in from the airport on Saturday, Francis knew that a new town lay beyond, down in the valley. But from this side only a scattering of modern houses and a small supermarket spoilt the picturesqueness of the view.

Arriving eventually at the bottom of the hill, Francis stopped for a glass of water in a little café with a stripy green and yellow awning, then climbed up the steep cobbled lane that wound its way to the top, where, by a tall white church tower, there was an open courtyard with a fine view over the countryside all around, including the fields he had just walked through. There was no one up here but a woman in a flowery skirt, leaning against the low wall taking photographs.

It was Roz.

This was one of those awkward moments, where you couldn't just say: 'Hi, great to see you, bye.' Francis felt obliged to chat to his student, and then, in due course, to walk back down with her to the café at the bottom of the hill, where they were the only visitors, apart from a Japanese woman with huge sunglasses and a stylish black hat. They decided to have a coffee together, while Roz sampled a couple of the cakes under the glass counter, taking photos of them with her iPhone and then making notes in a little black Moleskine book she pulled from her bag.

'I have a blog,' she said, when Francis asked her if this was research for her writing.

'About food?'

'And travel. Please don't mention it to Gerry and Stephanie. I like to be under the radar. Once people get wind, they start doing things differently. Being super-nice and banging on about their philosophy.' She raised her eyebrows. 'Which isn't really the point.'

They strolled on, down the hill, and paid six euros to see Perugino's famous *Martyrdom of Saint Sebastian* in the little Civitella museum. After which, of course, they were bound to walk back together.

They laughed a bit about Italian painting, as Francis confessed how little he knew of the period of art history when the Italians had been pre-eminent. Though he could see that this naked man in a loincloth strung up and surrounded by archers was beautifully painted, he had no real understanding of its context.

'Me neither,' said Roz. 'But I have to say I prefer it to those dreary paintings of Gerry's. Amazing that here he is, surrounded by all this incredible beauty of landscape and light, and all he wants to paint is panels of grey and brown.'

'Exactly what Poppy said.'

'Not to his face?'

'Yes.'

'That woman! She seems dedicated to pissing off as many people as she can. It's extraordinary.'

But no, Roz went on, as they walked back down the narrow tarmac road that skirted the fields, she was enjoying herself on the course. After a fashion. Though she hadn't realized the vibe would be quite so, er, old. Francis chuckled. He neither. He explained how he'd been recruited by Stephanie at the lit fest. This was his first time out here.

'So have you done this sort of thing before?' Roz asked.

'Oh yes, quite a bit. Arvon courses, and that kind of thing. You have to, these days, to keep going as a writer. Unless you're very successful with your books.'

'But you enjoy it?'

'It has its moments.'

'Despite the difficulties.'

'Such as?'

They both said 'Poppy' at the same moment, and in the same tentative tone. The synchronicity made them laugh.

'I really oughtn't to bitch about my students,' said Francis.

'No, you shouldn't. Certainly not about a fellow "published writer".' Roz cackled. 'Not to mention interior decorator, horse-woman, cook, musician, pilot . . .'

'Her relationship with her husband puzzles me,' Francis said. 'He seems like such a decent, thoughtful, dare I say distinguished character. And she . . .'

'Is a pain in the arse, crashing snob, preposterous name-dropper, absurd fantasist.'

'I can't be seen to agree with that. Although, I was intrigued that she was a personal friend of Jilly Cooper.'

'She helped, if not came up with, the plot of *Riders*, or *Shaggers*, or whatever the silly book's called.'

'And she knows John Julius Gnaw-witch, whoever he is.'

'A chum who's so close she doesn't know how to pronounce his name.'

'Don't forget Billy Connolly.'

'And Princess Anne.'

They laughed. 'I suppose all relationships are a mystery,' Francis went on. 'There are archetypes lurking in the background one never knows about. And physical attraction is a very odd thing. What Duncan saw in her originally I have no idea.'

'Her lovely blonde hair,' said Roz, 'which must come from the most expensive bottle Harrods can supply. Or perhaps her gym-toned figure, only improved by riding to hounds. Or maybe it was just her money – or her fabulous house. So what about you?' she asked, as they turned off the main road and up the lane that led back over the hill past the church. 'Do you have a little lady at home – or perhaps a little man?'

'Neither, I'm afraid. Not at the moment, anyway.'

It was an evasive response, but Francis didn't particularly want to have to explain his personal life, or kick-start the inevitable sequence of questions that would end up with him talking about Kate, his wife of many years before, who had drowned in a freak accident in Egypt. Nor did he want to justify a life where he was single but not celibate, with random moments of intimacy that he liked to keep in their own box, away from his established circle of friends. He was in no hurry to start receiving those invitations that read 'Francis *and* . . .' Francis *and* someone he might soon tire of, Francis *and* someone he would then have to pretend he liked more than he did. He had been down that road, too many times for comfort. Meanwhile, his married friends, particularly the women, were so keen for him to 'find someone', now that he was in his late forties. As if partnership with an appropriate other was the answer to all human woes. Weirdly, often, the more appalling their own relationship was, the more they wanted him to be settled. Sometimes they could even put a self-righteously moral spin on his singleness. 'You do lead a rather selfish life,' one of them had told him the other day; and he, thin-skinned as he knew he was, had felt hurt. But was it selfish to want to be on your own? There were plenty of extremely selfish people within the monogamous arrangements that society generally approved of; they were just fortunate enough to have saintly partners.

'How about you?' he asked.

'I'm single,' she replied. 'More or less. It gets harder, I think, as you get older. You get fussier, certainly as a woman. But then again, I'm not bothered about kids. Whatever my mother likes to think.'

'No. Much overrated,' Francis agreed. 'But that's one thing you're not allowed to say these days. That kids tie you down, quite often they destroy your relationship.'

'Is that what you think?'

'Partly. It's what I've observed with my friends. It often strikes me that the ones with the best relationships are the ones who've not had children.'

'I guess with your own children it's different,' Roz said.

'It must be.'

They walked on in silence for a bit, both lost in their own thoughts.

'No,' Roz continued eventually. 'I never met the right chap, as my father would say. So here I am, at forty-two, looking for love on a residential course full of geriatrics.'

'Is Tony geriatric?'

She laughed. Was she blushing? 'No,' she said. 'But he must

be well past fifty. And so not my type, Francis! Actually, I think he's probably gay.'

They were back in time for the pre-prandial drinks in the little side dining room, where the Gaggia now sat silent, and open bottles of wine stood alongside bowls of crisps and nuts and olives on the marble tabletop. The guests had mostly dressed for dinner, nothing too extravagant, but smart-casual plus. In this pool of elderly faces Roz stood out, comparatively youthful in her black and red striped top and tight, A-line black skirt. But even she seemed middle-aged in comparison to Sasha, who was doing yoga poses in the middle of the courtyard, now in a sleeveless black catsuit, though her favourite fuchsia scarf was still draped around her neck.

'Poor child,' said Liam, as they stood watching.

'I'm not sure "child" is the right word,' said Zoe crisply. 'She's a grown-up woman. Why exactly is she poor anyway?'

'Stuck with us lot of geriatrics.'

'Speak for yourself,' said Roz.

'I can't think what she's doing here,' said Poppy. 'Really.'

'She's learning her craft, like the rest of us,' said Tony. 'I rather admire her. Most girls her age would want to be on a Club 18-30 holiday or whatever.'

'Do they still exist?' said Zoe.

'This is the trouble with the Internet,' said Diana. 'You never know quite what you're getting, do you? I ordered a little armchair the other day. Brown leather. It looked wonderful online, but such inferior quality when it arrived, I had to send it back. A waste of everyone's time.'

'She can hardly go home now,' said Poppy.

'I don't think she wants to,' said Tony. 'She's probably taking notes and will put us all in a brilliant novel.'

'Doubtless,' muttered Liam, wandering out to join her. After a little natter, during which Sasha threw back her head and laughed loudly, he was to be seen attempting an awkward pose himself.

'I do hope,' said Poppy, 'he doesn't think he's in with a chance.'

Francis turned to Duncan, who was standing next to him, watching quietly. 'Have you had a good day?' he asked.

'Not bad,' the ambassador replied. 'I enjoyed this morning, though I do appreciate I must be your worst pupil.'

'Not at all,' said Francis.

'I'm not exactly loose, creatively. Comes of years and years of writing measured diplomatic dispatches, I'm afraid.'

Francis asked, tentatively, about his ambassadorial postings. Sierra Leone and then Bulgaria, Duncan confirmed, as an actual Head of Mission. 'Not the most illustrious destinations, but both very interesting in their way. Of course we were directly involved in Sierra Leone, as I'm sure you know.'

Rather than expose his ignorance, Francis decided he would declare a relevant interest: his natural father, who had come from Botswana. Was that so? Duncan said, fixing him with a look of close study, as if his skin colour had suddenly acquired an extra interest. Botswana was a remarkable country, he went on. One of Africa's success stories. 'Whether that has anything to do with the fact that the tribal boundaries coincide almost exactly with the colonial ones is a moot point.'

'I hadn't thought of that,' Francis replied. He'd never visited the country, even though his father still lived there, and he'd spent nine months after college teaching in a school in Swaziland, which was only a few hundred miles away.

'Not Waterford?' said Duncan.

'Got it in one.'

'A famous institution. The Mandela children were educated there, I believe.'

'They were.'

One of the Italian cooks came in and nodded at Stephanie, who promptly pinged her glass.

'*Aperitivos* over!' she cried. 'Dinner is served.'

Everyone gulped down their drinks and made their way out of the French doors into the courtyard beyond. The walls of the villa were now glowing ochre-yellow in the gloaming, alongside the warm pink stucco of the barn-like dining room, where patches had peeled off like huge jigsaw pieces to reveal dull grey stone beneath. The two big flat metal crosses up by the eaves were 'earthquake crosses' Stephanie had told Francis, who hadn't even realized they were in the zone. 'On the edge of it,' she'd replied, crossing her fingers. 'Luckily we've only had a couple of tremors in twenty-five years.' She caught his look. 'Even in 2016. That was the bigger of the two.'

Inside, a long table was laid, glass and cutlery glinting. A log fire spat and crackled in a cast-iron stove at the far end. There was a discreet musical chairs-style jostling for places, as people tactfully positioned themselves next to those they would be happy talking to for four long courses. Keeping an eye on Poppy – whom he really did not want to be trapped with – Francis wondered how oblivious she was to her own unpopularity. He was so busy avoiding her that before he knew it there was only one place left for him, between Mel from the art group and Diana. Not that he minded getting to know dwarfish Mel a bit better. But it was Diana who was ready and waiting for him, her beady blue eyes fixed on his. Her thick white hair seemed almost blonde – in this light anyway. He offered her a glass of wine, which she eagerly accepted.

'Are you enjoying yourself?' she asked, as she took a hefty sip and sat back. 'So far?'

'Yes, very much.'

She gave him a very candid look, up and down, as if appraising him at the start of a job interview. 'I think you're doing pretty well.'

'Thank you.'

'Better than some of the tutors we've had.'

'Thank you again.'

'Though maybe not quite so good as one or two of our stars. You probably won't like me saying this,' she went on, 'but I'm not a huge fan of what you do.'

What did she mean?

'Crime writing,' she explained. 'Nothing personal, you seem like a very nice fellow, but it always seems to me that there's enough nastiness in life as it is, without the need to make it up as well. I have to say, it does puzzle me. Whenever you switch on the TV, there seems to be yet another programme about a psychopath or a serial killer. I just wonder why everyone's so interested. In real life, these people are thankfully few and far between. If we can't hang them, as we should, I'd prefer them to be locked up and nothing more to be said. But there we all are, glamorizing them at some level. I'd rather watch a nice nature programme.'

Francis couldn't resist. 'About animals tearing each other up?'

'Yes, but they're animals. They act on instinct.'

'Which is OK, is it? I find some of those David Attenborough programmes pretty alarming. Sweet little seals being attacked by sharks.'

'It's the circle of life. You should see my darling cat Horatio when he catches a vole. He tosses it from paw to paw, with a truly wicked gleam in his eyes.'

'And you don't mind that?'

'He's a cat. That's what he does. That's what he's supposed to do.'

'In God's well-appointed universe?'

'He died in June,' Diana said. As she looked down, he noticed she was gulping.

'I'm sorry,' he said.

She pulled out an embroidered cotton handkerchief from her substantial bosom and wiped away a visible tear. 'Thank you. He has left rather a void.' She sniffed, then smiled. 'We all have to go sometime, don't we?'

One advantage of this age-group, Francis thought, was that they knew – by and large – how to behave at this sort of occasion. After the tasty little asparagus tartlet starter new plates appeared along with great bowls of pasta in a creamy orange tomato sauce. Diana turned decisively to her other side to engage the ambassador, twinkling as she offered him a glass of wine and broke into his existing conversation. Francis followed suit, turning the other way to Mel from the art group. She wasn't doing the writing, she said with a laugh, because she wasn't any good at it. She did try, sometimes, bits of poetry, but she knew it was rubbish.

'Maybe it isn't,' said Francis.

'No, I can assure you, it is. I'm not that great shakes at art either. But I enjoy it. Splashing around with acrylics. He's not a bad teacher, is Gerry. Quite strict about drawing, which I like. Though you'd never guess from his paintings, would you? He said a funny thing yesterday. "Imagine your children were going to die if you didn't get your line exactly right."'

'I guess that concentrates the mind.'

'And I'm here with my friend Belle, who I've known and worked with half my life, so we have fun together. Away from our other halves. Well, my other half. Belle's Michael sadly passed last year.'

'I'm sorry to hear that,' Francis said politely. 'So are you still working together?'

'Oh yes, very much so. We have a little interior decoration business based in Knaresborough.'

'Like Poppy . . .'

Mel rolled her eyes.

'You don't think she was serious?' Francis added.

'Knaresborough's only four miles from Harrogate and I never heard of her – or her business. Perhaps we had different clients.'

'And what does your husband do?'

'As little as possible,' Mel cackled. 'No, really, Brian's officially useless.'

Before Francis could stop her, she was off. About how Brian spent all his time on the golf course, never fixed anything in the house, never did any washing up, on the few occasions he did, messed it up completely, leaving the dishes greasy and little bits of food in the drain. Then he ate in a very unattractive way, talking while he was eating, so you could see his food in his open mouth. Then he got half his dinner down his front anyway, so she was constantly having to wash his pullovers.

'I'm surprised you're still together,' Francis said with a laugh.

'So am I,' Mel replied. If she wasn't so lazy, she'd probably have given him his marching orders by now. Mind you, they had two children. Grown up, but with their own families, who lived nearby. Changing everything around now would be very disruptive.

After the pasta came the *secondo*: big flat earthenware dishes of lamb chops roasted with rosemary, sauté potatoes, gleaming green runner beans. Duncan had given up on Diana, so Francis was back with her.

'Another glass?' he offered.

'I shouldn't, but I will. This is my holiday. I look forward to it all year.' She smiled round at the two long rows of glowing faces. 'I've been coming here for over twenty years. Hard to believe, but it's true.'

She had first come, she went on, when she'd split up with her partner, who'd run off with a client. 'God knows what he saw in her. I suppose she was in London and I was stuck up in Suffolk. But the truth was I never imagined, for one minute, that David would leave me. We had such a good life together. A beautiful half-timbered house, five acres, tennis court, swimming pool, all the trimmings. It was a wreck when we bought it, but we did it up together – a real project, as you can imagine – and David was so proud of what we'd done with it. Then glorious summer holidays, year after year, down in the convertible to France. We used to take three weeks and drive the Route Nationales, you know, keep off the motorways, such fun. Whizzing along, warm air in our faces, poplars on either side. Stop wherever we found ourselves, as you could in those days. Even those trucker stops, Les Routiers they were called, had wonderful food. Skiing in February. Christmas in a nice hotel somewhere. And then suddenly there I was – alone. It was quite a shock to the system, I can tell you. Come the summer I had absolutely no idea what to do about a holiday. But then, after a few ghastly solo years, looking at penguins in Patagonia and so forth, I heard about this place. And came. It was the second year that Stephanie and Gerry did it. It turned out to be just the tonic I needed. So I've been coming ever since.'

The irony was, she went on – flushed and rather tipsy now, Francis thought – that once her ex's floozy had got him she didn't want him; she soon discovered what a selfish pig he was. 'Of course he wanted to come back, but it was too late by then. The trust had gone. He quickly found a replacement. Men do, I'm afraid – no disrespect to you, Francis. And she – Number Two, I called her, or Miss Piggy, she looked like one, I'm sorry – kept him on a very short leash. Much shorter than I ever had. Ha ha! He had to live with that, the silly fool.'

'How did you know all this?'

'Oh, he never moved very far away. From Saxmundham, where we'd been. I stayed because I love it round there. I moved into a dear wee fisherman's cottage in Aldeburgh, another wreck, but I soon fixed that up. D'you know Aldeburgh? Pretty little seaside town, albeit our beach is mostly pebbles. I saw him on a bench there once. He didn't come over. I was tempted to say hello, but I didn't want to get into a fight, because he was never very happy about our settlement. I'm afraid I took him to the cleaners.'

She was sad, though, because they'd had such a wonderful relationship when it was going strong. 'A proper partnership. He helped me and I helped him.'

'And is he still alive?'

'Oh yes, he's still chuntering on. She's got her work cut out, these days, Miss P, because he's not very well, by all accounts. Dementia,' she hissed. 'Very sad. But not for me.' Her eyes twinkled.

'Did you have children?'

'Never wanted them. We were working too hard and having too much fun. I sometimes regret it now, when I see my friends with their grandchildren. It's a nice insurance policy for your old age. But Francis, one thing you realize when you get to my time of life is this: that some things were meant to be, and some weren't. There's no avoiding that.'

Just as he thought she might start weeping into her green beans, someone made a light remark and the conversation became general. Tony ('the spy') was opposite Mel, and next to him, opposite Francis, was the third member of the art course, a thin, elegant, straight-backed woman called Angela, who reminded him power-fully of the Old Lady in the *Babar* stories. She bared her gleaming white teeth at him in a frequent smile, even though the ambient din made it hard to exchange words.

A great chocolatey pudding arrived. The waitresses came round, bending over the diners to get their orders for coffee and tea. Then came the *ping* of Stephanie's spoon. 'Duncan, *Sir* Duncan, I should say,' she giggled, 'is now going to give us a talk about his amazing house – in Wiltshire – and its even more amazing garden.' It seemed as if Stephanie had been imbibing freely too. She hadn't mentioned the ambassador's title publicly before, though she had come up behind Francis earlier and whispered loudly, 'You do know he's a sir.'

The guests all trundled off to bed as soon as Sir Duncan's PowerPoint presentation was over. Perhaps envy had done for them, because Framley Grange lived up to Stephanie's gushing epithets. It was a perfect English manor house with a perfect English garden. The little audience gasped quietly as yet another fabulous image revealed yet another pergola, arbour, grotto, herb garden or carefully planned lavender walkway. Afterwards Francis found himself on a sofa in the little library where the talk had been. Roz was with him, and they each had a glass of grappa – her idea.

'He's certainly got a beautiful place there,' said Francis. 'You'd wonder why he'd ever want to leave.'

'Oh, everyone needs to get away, don't they? Even the queen. Although, come to think of it, she never really gets away . . .'

'How d'you mean?'

'If she's abroad she's working, isn't she? Shaking hands with heads of state and so forth, being nice the whole time, very exhausting. And then, when she takes a break at home she's stuck in one of her houses.'

'Stuck?'

'Think of it. She never turns up at some place completely out of the blue where she's never been before and has no idea what it's going to be like. And there's maybe a welcome cake on the side and a pint of semi-skimmed in the fridge. That's my definition of a holiday.'

'OK.'

'It's all, "Hello, Balmoral, haven't I been here before? Oh yes, I have, and we will have the stag for dinner, thank you. Hello, Sandringham, oh how very nice to see you, how's your lovely wife and kids been keeping these past eleven months—"'

'So why did you decide to come?' Francis asked, cutting off this bizarre and frankly tipsy riff. 'Were you really looking for love?'

Roz grinned. 'Oh, I don't know. I needed a new direction. I've been doing the same kind of writing for years. Business writing, basically. It's all a bit formal, though I have got my little blog as well, as you know. I had the idea that coming out here, in the groves of Tuscany, I could release my inner creative juju.'

'And have you?'

'Maybe. With your help.' She reached over and patted his thigh, then looked at him in a way that made him wonder whether she might be about to come on to him. And that wouldn't have been unwelcome, because there was something about her, and the way she held your gaze, that was undeniably sexy. Although obviously not right here, scrutinized by the entire writing course for the rest of the week.

'Anyway,' she went on, 'I was telling a bit of a fib earlier.'

'Oh?'

'I'm not really single.'

'No?'

'I've got someone. But he's a secret. Has to be, because he's married.'

'Aha.'

'I do love him, and want him, every day in every way, but you know, there's this wife.'

'I see.'

'Who's frankly a total pain in the arse. I don't know why he's with her. Anyway, I'm talking too much now. Just wanted to get that off my chest.'

'No worries.'

She gave him a look of deep scrutiny. 'You're very anodyne, Francis, you know that.'

'How do you mean?'

'You do know what anodyne means?'

'Harmless . . . neutral . . .'

'Exactly. I mean, it's hard to make you react. You're constantly chipping in with these nice little comments, interspersed with not-so-discreet leading questions. So I spill my guts out but I never really find out about you.'

'That's your choice.'

'There you go again. Jokey and evasive.'

'I think it might be time for me to go to bed.'

'You see. You can't take it. When the chips are down you're up and off. Anyway. He's basically a bastard. He's got her. And he's got me. Though not for much longer.' She sighed deeply. 'I'm not in the longevity business anyway.'

It was an odd remark to make, Francis thought, as he made his way up the worn stone stairs and along the tiled corridor, past a string of Gerry's depressing abstracts, to poky Masaccio. Out through the slatted shutters the moon had risen above the mountainous horizon, a bruised circle, almost full. It flooded the long valley below with silver light, casting blue-black shadows from the trees under his window. He remembered Chekhov's famous advice, the bedrock of many a creative writing course, which Zoe had alluded to in her take-down of Poppy in class that morning. 'Don't tell me the moon is shining; show me the glint of light on broken glass.' Though of course the great Russian had never said that exactly, had he? He stood there for a minute or two, sipping at the large glass of water he'd brought up, to which he'd added a pre-emptive Alka-Seltzer. It was all very beautiful and he had drunk too much. Certainly for a tutor who had to be on form tomorrow, adjudicating between all these restless egos.

THREE

Francis woke early. Was it the wine he'd had at dinner? The grappa with Roz? He didn't know, but he was wide awake and buzzing while it was still pitch-dark. He switched on his dim bedside light and read for a bit, before trying to fall back to sleep again. But the gods of slumber were not in a mood to return this morning, even though Francis knew that his teaching would be sharper and more patient if he was properly rested. Eventually it was dawn. Through his narrow oblong window he could see the sky starting to glow pink. He got up and looked out. Beyond the dark silhouettes of trees, white mist sat in the valley. He decided to get up and out into the landscape. He put on yesterday's clothes and pulled a fleece on top. Even through the window he could feel the chill of the morning air.

He clicked his bedroom door gently shut behind him. Downstairs, the heavy wooden front door of the villa was locked, but the big iron key was there on the inside. He let himself out, then tiptoed across the gravel towards the slatted wooden table below the vine where later he would be holding his morning class. Today he had a couple of excellent exercises for the group, including his session on dialogue, which Roz had told him she was longing to get stuck into, as dialogue was something she struggled with. 'You and so many others,' Francis had said, 'but after you've done my workshop on it you'll be totally freed up.'

'Can't wait,' she'd replied.

At the end of this long table was a swing chair, which hung from a bolt in the roof, where you could sit back and read. Indeed, there was often a polite stand-off for this choice spot; you would see one of the guests tiptoeing away from the lunch table to put their books on its comfy teal blue cushions to claim it for their afternoon snooze. Beyond that was a cast-iron gate, which opened on to a set of stone steps running down the side of the house to a ragged formal garden, with gravel pathways between unkempt beds of flowering plants. Stephanie and Gerry kept their villa in good shape, but the gardens weren't quite as well-maintained. Whatever the lean and hungry-looking Fabio did on that noisy tractor of his, it wasn't weeding.

A path paved with variegated flat stones led down to an arch in the perimeter wall. Through a battered wooden door, another, pebbled path led down past a stand-alone outhouse with a terracotta tiled roof to an old tennis court, below which the grass slope dropped away into the valley. Here, to one side, Francis found a wooden bench, glistening silver with dew. He wiped it roughly with the back of his hand, then sat, taking in the silence and the view.

It was, undoubtedly, magical. The sun in the east had spread a sultry crimson blush right across the panorama of sky and was now touching the highest slopes of the distant mountains with yellow-pink light, even before it had risen above the dark, forested ridge to the right. Below him, white-grey mist swirled up the valley, puffing into clouds which broke loose and were tinged with pink as they rose higher, up, up, like escaped balloons, into the empyrean. He took out his notebook and tried to work out how he could possibly describe such a scene; it was something he liked to do, a writer's exercise, attempting to nail beauty, always the hardest thing. But even as his Uniball Eye poised over the lined blue paper of his Smythson notebook and he jotted down the inadequate words *pink glow spreading across, fading to left*, he heard, very distinctly in the silence, a scream. It came from the villa, and it came from a woman.

He got to his feet and ran. Back up the way he'd come, clattering up the steps into the courtyard, round through the front door and into the hall. To find . . . nothing. There was no sound on the stairs. Upstairs, the doors in the long corridor were all shut. Surely he hadn't imagined it?

He paused for a full half minute, not sure what to do. He could hardly start searching the bedrooms one by one, could he? Unless the scream was repeated, he was stuck. Was he? What if by failing to act he had allowed something terrible to happen? But how could he act? How embarrassing would it be if it had just been someone having a nightmare? He decided he would go back to Masaccio and read until breakfast. If there was a follow-up he would be right there; hopefully able to get out into the corridor in time and work out exactly which room it was coming from.

He sat on his bed for a minute or two listening to the silence. 'I'm not in the longevity business.' Roz's strange remark ran round his head as he picked up the pile of paper that was Zoe's manuscript. To distract himself from his worst imaginings, he scanned the chapter titles and saw that this was a Jewish memoir. Hardly a surprise, as Zoe described herself as such. But he hadn't reckoned on this: grandparents escaping from Polish pogroms, close relatives dying in concentration camps, a harrowing personal story behind the soignée, well-to-do, old lady that she was now.

By eight o'clock he was ravenous. He went downstairs to find Diana alone at the long table in the courtyard, her statuesque face soaking up the early sunshine. 'Statuesque' really was the word, he thought, as he avoided tripping on the two stone steps up into the dining room, where he helped himself to a slice of cold ham and a warm crispy roll. Diana's fine old features, framed by her bangs of white hair, looked like something carved from stone – the Sphinx perhaps.

'Isn't this glorious?' she said, as he slid into a chair opposite her.

'It is.'

'Aren't we lucky? There are so many people in the world who don't have this.'

'This is true,' Francis agreed, forking in his first mouthful of ham.

'The world's in such a shocking state these days. All those poor refugees, being driven from pillar to post with nothing but their bare possessions. Not that there's anything much I can do about it, at my age. But I do *care*.' Diana slathered the tip of her croissant with jam from her plate, gave it rather a savage bite, then washed it down with the dregs of her coffee. 'This fig jam is so good. No, there are some days I can hardly bear to switch on the television. Those desolate, desperate faces. Still, we're on holiday now. Time to put our bigger worries on the back burner.'

'Yes.' He wondered if he should mention the scream. But if Diana had heard it, surely she would bring it up?

She fixed him with her most inclusive smile. 'I thought for a moment there my traditional position as the first down to breakfast was going to be usurped.'

'By me?'

'No. By that Roz person. She was here before me yesterday – and in this very seat.'

'Breaking all the rules,' teased Francis.

'There are no rules, don't be silly. That's one of the things I like about this holiday. You can do as you please. If you want to lie in the middle of the courtyard and do sit-ups no one's going to stop you.'

'Like Sasha and her cartwheels.'

'Quite.' Very carefully, between thumb and forefinger, Diana picked two croissant flakes off her pursed lips. For one reason or another – he hoped it wasn't just straightforward racism – Diana disapproved of Sasha.

Tony joined them, dressed up in a smart blue linen jacket and silk tie. He was terribly sorry, he said to Francis, but he had something he had to do today in Perugia, so he was going to miss the morning's exercises, much to his chagrin.

Francis shrugged. 'It's all entirely optional.'

'That's the lovely thing about this place,' said Diana. 'We were just saying. One does as one pleases.'

'By the way,' said Tony. 'Did anybody hear a strange scream earlier?'

'Yes,' said Francis, with a bolt of relief that he hadn't imagined it.

'A scream,' said Diana. 'What kind of scream?'

'It was, like,' Francis said hesitantly, 'a woman.'

'It wasn't like a woman,' said Tony crisply. 'It was a woman. What I heard, anyway.'

'I was outside,' Francis said, 'by the tennis court. But I came running back. To find total silence.'

'Yes, that's what I thought was odd. It woke me, and I was going to get up and see what was going on. Then – nothing. So I'm afraid I fell straight back to sleep again.'

'I didn't hear anything,' Diana said. 'Perhaps you were both imagining it. But then again, I always sleep very soundly. Until my alarm goes off at seven thirty. And then I'm wide awake. I'm very lucky like that, because a lot of people my age have problems sleeping.'

A little later they were joined by Zoe, who had also heard the scream. 'I was wondering if I should get up and have a look, but then it went quiet, so I thought it was probably just someone having a nightmare.'

'I certainly didn't hear it,' Diana repeated crossly, almost as if the three of them had made it up.

They were joined at that moment by Mel and Belle, who were giggling like schoolgirls.

'What is she like?' said Mel, 'with her nightmares. She woke me up at God knows what time this morning, yelling her head off.'

'Who did?' asked Diana, unnecessarily.

'Belle. She has these nightmares, don't you, pet?'

'Ah,' said Tony. 'So there's our explanation. We were starting to worry.'

They were all relieved that the scream had a reason. Belle did this from time to time apparently. 'And the strange thing is,' she said, 'I never remember the dream at all.'

'She never even wakes up,' said Mel. 'What a weirdo.'

'Morning, team! Enjoying the glorious Italian sunshine?' It was Poppy, rather flushed. 'I've had such a lovely swim and sauna. Now I'm ready for my yummy brekky.'

'Is it open so early?' Diana asked. 'The pool? It never used to be uncovered before breakfast.'

Poppy tapped her nose. 'I had a discreet word with that nice handyman chap.'

'Fabio.'

'That's the feller. So sweet, under those murderous Italiano looks. He agreed to unroll the cover for me. And fire up the sauna. Which I do love, first thing. A bit of heat to the old bones.' Diana said nothing, but this didn't stop Poppy answering her unspoken question. 'It's how you speak to people, I suppose.'

She tripped off smugly into the dining room and Diana scowled; though, only for a moment, before the all-forgiving smile reappeared. 'He's such a kind man, Fabio,' she said. 'He'd do anything for anyone. "Murderous looks", honestly. He's just a typical countryman. He's Romanian, in any case, not Italian. Not that'

– she dropped her voice to a whisper – '*she* would ever listen for long enough to find that out. I do think asking for the pool to be opened specially just for one person before breakfast is a bit much.'

'No Roz today?' Poppy observed, cheerfully, at nine thirty, when the writing group took their places under the vine.

'She wasn't at breakfast,' Diana noted.

'I'm sure she's allowed a lie-in,' Liam said.

'Shall we wake her?' said Poppy.

'Don't be ridiculous,' said Zoe. 'She's a grown woman.'

Francis was sorry that she wasn't there for that morning's first exercise, which he called 'My Life In . . .' The idea was to describe your past in terms of one repeated object: the cars you'd driven at different times of your life; the houses you'd lived in; the shoes you'd worn. Poppy surprised them by doing 'knickers'.

'Not such a boring old stick as you thought,' she said when she'd finished detailing five different sets of underwear, including the taffeta petticoat with which she'd wooed her first husband.

'None of us think you're boring, Poppy,' said Sasha.

'Thank you, Sasha. I'm glad to have one friend.'

Francis was unable to get out of his head the image of Poppy's first pair of knickers, electric pink, which she'd worn in the early Sixties as a Beatle-loving teenager – or so she said. Later, in her 'naughty phase', when she'd been Up North for a while – she pronounced it *Oop North* – and 'very much a free spirit', she'd gone in for basques and then, when the underwear came on the market in the 1990s, Agent Provocateur.

'I thought your piece was brilliant,' said Sasha. 'No offence, but it's sometimes hard for someone of my age to see you lot—'

'Us *lot*,' echoed Diana, scornfully.

'Sorry, you older people.'

'It's getting worse,' said Zoe, with a cackle.

'As like, young. I mean, don't get me wrong, I'm so much in awe of your experience. It's like you all have so many stories to tell and I feel like this inexperienced child.'

'You are, dear, a little,' said Diana.

'That's a bit harsh,' said Zoe.

* * *

'Have you seen Roz?' Francis said to Stephanie, as they stood in the sunshine at the mid-morning coffee break. 'I was just a bit concerned, because she told me she was looking forward to my session on dialogue. And I'm just about to start it.'

'I shouldn't worry,' said Stephanie. 'The fact is the guests do often seem terribly enthusiastic about something and then don't follow it up. She's probably just having a lie-in. Or gone for a walk. I'll get Gerry to pop up to her room in a bit and see that all is well.'

But Roz's room was locked, and she wasn't at lunch, where her absence was further remarked on.

'Perhaps she's having a secret liaison with handsome Tony,' said Mel.

'Don't be ridiculous,' said Zoe. 'We saw him drive off on his own.'

'Maybe she was waiting at the bottom of the hill, by the cypress trees.'

'Mel's a fantasist,' Belle explained. 'Her favourite reading is Mills and Boon.'

'And what's wrong with Mills and Boon?' said Mel. 'They outsell all the posher books by miles. At least you know what you're getting.'

'Is that the point of fiction?' said Zoe. 'Knowing what you're getting. Personally, I like to be challenged.'

Afterwards, as others sorted themselves out with deckchairs and espressos, Francis, Stephanie and Gerry went up and knocked loudly on Roz's door. There was no reply.

'Time for the master key, I think,' said Gerry. He didn't seem particularly alarmed, though Francis's imagination was running wild. Surely he wasn't going to be treated to a repeat of the chilling drama at the Mold-on-Wold literary festival, four years before, when the celebrated critic Bryce Peabody had been found dead in his bed in a room just down the corridor in the very same hotel where Francis was staying?

But when they unlocked the door and pushed it open the room was empty. Roz's bed was made and in the wardrobe her clothes were all hanging or neatly folded.

'All present and correct.'

'She'll have gone for a walk,' said Stephanie. 'Or a cycle ride. I'll check the bikes.'

'It's just odd that we didn't see her at breakfast,' said Francis. 'And we were in the courtyard all morning.'

'She might have slipped out the back,' Stephanie said. 'If you go down past the sauna and the tennis court, no one need see you.'

'Interesting choice of reading,' said Gerry, pointing at the book by her bedside. It was *Suicide Club*, by Rachel Heng.

'Don't be silly, Gerry,' Stephanie said. She turned to Francis. 'In eighteen years, we've only ever had one incident on this course. Zoe having an asthma attack last year and having to be rushed to hospital in Perugia.'

'We were worried she might stage another,' Gerry added. 'She loved the Italian consultant so much.'

'Gerry, that's naughty. Asthma is a horrid illness. You don't "stage" an attack.'

'Of course you don't,' he replied. 'Unless you're Zoe.'

'Gerry!'

At four thirty that afternoon, as per the week's photocopied schedule, there was a 'Teatime Symposium', chaired by Stephanie, on the subject of Time. Francis had planned to skip it and read Zoe's memoir by the pool, but at four o'clock a great bank of grey cloud marched up from the distant mountains to cover the sun. The temperature dropped, and a few spots of rain plopped down on to the dry brown grass. With the weather having removed the temptation to be idle, curiosity overcame him. He went back into the villa and found quite a large group in the library, spreading themselves round the armchairs and sofas, dark silhouettes against the bright day beyond the window frames. With the exception of Liam and himself, they were all ladies. There was still no sign of Roz.

'If she's not here at *aperitivo* time,' Stephanie said, 'we'll send out search parties.' Part of Francis was quietly approving of her relaxed attitude to her guests' welfare, but only part of him. But it wasn't for him to overreact, was it? His hostess had been running these courses for twenty-five years.

'So . . . Time,' Stephanie went on, removing her gold-framed specs to smile warmly and inclusively round at the attendees. 'How do we mark it? And why is it that Time can go so slowly at one moment – and then so fast at another? I always find this out here, on these lovely creative weeks. For ages, everything seems to be dawdling along – there's plenty of time to do everything we want to do and then, suddenly, it's the last night and you're all packing. Does anyone else feel this?'

There was a general murmur of assent.

'Definitely,' said Mel. 'It's like time crawls until Tuesday, and you think, I've got ages here, time to do loads of painting, and then suddenly, you're right, it's like, now we've only got till Friday, no time at all.'

'I remember my father used to say—' Poppy began.

'The general,' Liam cut in. Francis was surprised to see him at this rather genteel discussion; he wouldn't have imagined it was his cup of tea at all. Perhaps it was the presence of the ever-curious Sasha that had encouraged him to join.

'The general, exactly.' Poppy stalled him with one of her brightest smiles. 'You may laugh at my father, Liam, but he was a very interesting man. And a brave one. Anyway, in the war – that's the Second World War, Sasha—'

'Not the First,' said Liam.

'As a young soldier,' Poppy continued, 'he spent some time in Burma and used to repeat to us girls something the Chinese said about time travelling at two speeds. Maybe it was Confucius or someone, I can't remember the exact quote, it was like a short poem, or haiku perhaps—'

'Haiku's Japanese,' said Liam.

'I do know that, Liam. But there is a Chinese equivalent. The two cultures are very close.'

'That's why they hate each other, like the English and the Irish.'

'*I* don't hate the Irish, Liam. Not most of them, anyway. Well, that was the gist of it. What Mel and Stephanie just said. Put, obviously, in a rather more elegant and finished way. But the same sentiment: sometimes time takes so long, and sometimes it just races past.'

'You can't remember the quote,' said Liam.

'No, I can't,' said Poppy.

'This is so true,' said Belle, cutting in tactfully. 'About time travelling at two speeds. And perhaps another point about it is that when we're young we tend to rather take time for granted.'

'Definitely,' said Diana. 'Young people do.'

'Do they?' Sasha cut in. 'I mean, no offence, but I think about every day that passes. What was it the man said, "Live every day as if it's your last." I think that's a great attitude to have.'

'Oh dear,' sighed Zoe, loudly. 'You have such a lot to learn.'

'What's that supposed to mean?'

'It means, my dear, that you have so many, many, *many* days before you until you face your last one. I wish we could all say the same.'

'Until Michael – my husband – passed, late last year,' Belle said, 'I never really thought about my life ending. Now I think about it every day. What it will be like, when and how it will happen.'

'Every third thought,' said Liam.

'What's that supposed to mean?' asked Mel.

'It's a quote, from Shakespeare's *Tempest*: "Every third thought shall be my grave." Meaning, once you get to Prospero's age . . . you remember who Prospero was, Mel?'

'Er, no,' she said, looking down. 'Should I?'

'Funnily enough,' Poppy cut in, 'I saw the great Sir John Gielgud in the role in the 1970s. A legendary performance.'

'You don't say,' said Liam. 'Was he a personal friend?'

'Don't be silly.' If looks could kill, Francis thought, Liam would be a goner.

'No, Mel,' the Irishman went on, 'Prospero was an old king in a Shakespeare play . . .

'Aren't they all?'

Poppy's tight-lipped moue was matched by Liam's bark of laughter. 'The quote,' he went on, 'means that once you get to a certain age, every third thought you have is about death.'

'I don't,' said Mel. 'I hardly think about it at all.'

'Of course we all *have* these thoughts,' Diana cut in. 'But in my view it's best not to give in to them. Unlike Belle, my husband is still alive, but unfortunately – for me – he's with another woman. So when he left me, thirty years ago now, it was like a little death in a way. One life was over. Our life, the life we'd had together. And I was very sad about that for a while, and thought about it a lot, maybe not every third thought, but every fifth. And then one day, I remember it well, it was a lovely April day, one of those days when you wake up and the sun is shining and everything's

green and the flowers are out, and you just think: I simply can't
be depressed about this one minute longer. So I hauled myself out
of bed and got dressed and went down to the beach, at Aldeburgh,
where I live, and treated myself to lunch at a café there, with a
nice glass of wine and all that sort of thing, and I made a resolution. That I was going to enjoy every day to the full. Not that
every day was going to be wonderful, necessarily. But you must
make each day as good as it can be.'

'Bravo!' said Poppy. 'I think we can all second that. Duncan
and I certainly try and make sure we do something special each
day. Don't we, darling? Although we live in such a beautiful place
that every day *is* rather special anyway.'

Francis looked round the gathered faces for a reaction;
amazingly, there wasn't so much as a single eye-roll. The level of
politeness was stoic.

'On the other hand,' Liam cut in, 'there can be something quite
refreshing about a day where you do sweet FA.'

'What's that?' asked elegant, straight-backed Angela, who had
been blinking attentively as the discussion proceeded.

'Sweet FA,' said Zoe. 'It's a colloquial expression, meaning,
er, nothing.'

'Meaning *nothing*?' Angela persisted, still puzzled. 'What did
he say?'

'I said,' Liam repeated loudly, 'that it's *nice* to have *some days*
when you do *sweet fuck all.*'

'Oh, sweet fuck all,' said Angela, with a seraphic smile. 'So
sorry. I didn't catch you, Liam. Yes, I agree. I love days like
that.'

Apart from Diana, who remained stony-faced, they all laughed.

It was Stephanie's turn to speak. It was rather nice, she said,
to be in one of those situations where you're given time. 'When
you have a meeting booked, for example, and it's cancelled.
Then you have that rather wonderful feeling of half a free day to
yourself.'

'I agree,' said Mel. 'It's great to do nothing. Just stand and
stare.'

'We all need a duvet day from time to time,' said Belle.

'What the heck's a duvet day when it's at home?' asked Zoe.

'A day when you lie under the duvet and do nothing.'

'That doesn't sound very interesting.'

'Oh, it's lovely. I miss my duvet days if I don't have them regularly. You know what else I miss?' Belle went on. 'Male conversation. I'd like more men in my life.'

This brought laughter, but not from Diana, whose wide forehead was creased with concern. 'Don't you have men in your life, Belle?'

'Not enough of them,' said Belle, 'now Michael's gone.'

'I wonder why that is,' said Diana. 'You're still so attractive, perhaps other women view you as a threat.'

The door pushed open with a creak and they all looked round. But it wasn't a random man, for Belle. It was Roz, carrying a large glass of white wine.

'Mind if I join you?' she asked.

'Of course not,' said Stephanie. 'Take a seat. We're talking about time.'

'Are we?' said Mel. 'I thought we were talking about men.'

'We've rather veered off the main subject,' said Stephanie.

'As we do, constantly,' said Zoe. 'There seems to be no one in this room capable of maintaining even a half-coherent thread.'

'Now Roz is here we can get back to it,' said Stephanie. 'Have you had a nice *time*, Roz – wherever you've been?'

This brought laughter. Really, everyone was having a most agreeable afternoon.

'Yes, a very nice *time*, thank you. I went for a long cycle ride.'

'What did I tell you?' Stephanie said to Francis. 'Francis was worried about you.'

Francis tried not to show his embarrassment. 'Only because we missed you at the dialogue session . . .'

'I'm so sorry about that, Francis. I really wanted to be there. But then I woke up super early this morning and I just had a desire to get out and see more of this glorious countryside. Which I did. And I had a nice lunch in Castiglione dell'Umbria. That's a lively place, isn't it?'

'You got as far as Castiglione?' said Stephanie.

'It's not that far. Fifteen miles or so.'

'I'm impressed.'

Roz did look as though she'd had a good day, Francis thought. She looked well-exercised and her skin was glowing. Whatever heaviness had been bothering her yesterday seemed to have completely lifted.

It was Gerry's turn to give the talk after dinner. It was a PowerPoint – or 'slide show' as the older ones called it – on the subject of Gubbio, the little fortress town they were making a group excursion to the next day. Some, like Diana, had been there before, and joined in with comments and reminiscences as Gerry described the cable car up Mt Ingino to St Ubaldo's Basilica, where the mummified body of the saint lay visible in a gold and glass coffin and there were the most incredible views. The more adventurous could of course walk it, Gerry said, which was more rewarding, but it was a good forty-five minutes, up through the woods, so do be sure to take some water, as it can get very hot. Back down in the town, there were also good views from the main square, Piazza Grande, adjacent to which was the mighty Palazzo dei Consoli, housing, among other things, the Iguvine tablets and a fine collection of Umbrian coins and ceramics. There was probably less amazing art in Gubbio than in some of the other Umbrian cities, but the *Cattedrale* had wonderful stained glass and Gherardi's 'Birth of the Virgin', and there was a fine fourteenth-century fresco by Ottavio Nelli in the little church of Santa Maria Nuova.

Of course, Stephanie chipped in at the end, the excursion was entirely optional. But it seemed as if almost everybody had signed up to it. Only Tony, who had come back from his day out in Perugia with a troubled frown, hadn't committed. 'We leave, promptly please, at nine thirty from the village square,' Stephanie said. 'And we'll get you back by five. And at seven fifteen, as a little extra surprise, I'm delighted to announce we're going to be joined for dinner by Erica St John, who's probably one of our most famous expat artists out here in the Umbria/Toscano *regione*.' She pronounced *regione* in the Italian way, as she liked to do. 'If you don't know her work I can assure you it's great fun, and was a highlight of the British Pavilion at the last Venice Biennale.'

'How exciting!' said Poppy. 'I can't wait to meet her.'

'I'm sure you can't,' said Liam. He turned to Stephanie. 'Conceptual, is she?'

'Gerry?' she called.

'Yes, very much so,' her husband replied.

'She puts human skulls in interesting tableaux,' Stephanie explained. 'And then adds bits of painting to them. And frames. It's all very colourful and interesting.'

'Pretentious crap,' muttered Gerry, with feeling. 'But she does very well with it.'

'Gerry!' cried Stephanie.

FOUR

Francis woke early again but decided not to bother with the dawn this morning. The Gubbio excursion was ahead of him and he needed his rest. He fell back into a fitful sleep, dreaming of African drummers approaching Gubbio across a wide plain, over which ran a naked woman screaming. She was very beautiful, and as she came closer, he realized she was wearing nothing but a fuchsia scarf and it was Sasha. As she beckoned to him, in a provocative manner, he woke up. Christ, what was his subconscious up to? The American was a quarter of a century younger than him. As for the screaming, had that been real? Was it daffy Belle, having another nightmare? Or just in his dream? In his nostrils he could smell the heat of the desert, see the naked Sasha just yards from him. She had wanted him, as women always did in dreams. As he rolled over, unwilling to let go the memory, there was a banging on the door.

'Francis. Are you awake?'

'Yes, come in.'

It was Stephanie, in a scarlet dressing gown. 'So sorry to trouble you, but something awful has happened . . .' Her eyes were wide with shock. 'Gerry wanted you to come.'

'What's wrong?' he replied, getting straight out of bed.

'It's Poppy . . . in the sauna . . . a terrible accident . . .' Stephanie shook her head, unable to say more. 'Come quickly . . . and quietly, please.'

Francis followed her out of the door and along the corridor. Down the main stone stairs to the hall they went, then through the heavy swing door the guests didn't use and down a second flight of steps to the lower level of the villa where the laundry room and storerooms were. On a narrow corridor that opened at the other end into the garden was the little sauna, set to one side of a changing room with pine benches and hooks, with two showers off at one side.

Here they found Gerry, Duncan and Fabio, who was standing over a bag of tools. The glass door to the sauna stood open. The smell coming from inside was of dry heat, stripped pine, lavender and something close to cooked meat. There was another olfactory note in there too, Francis thought, like marzipan. Inside, slumped on the floor, was Poppy. She was face up, but her features were too horrible to contemplate: an unnatural livid crimson, the thin lips of her mouth in a ghastly grimace. Her eyes stared out blankly, the cornflower blue a narrow ring round wide, dark pupils. On the bench was an empty espresso cup, without a saucer.

Francis stood staring at the scene for a good five seconds, barely able to take it in. Then: 'What happened?' he asked.

'It seems the inside handle fell off and she was trapped,' Gerry said. He gestured at the glass door, which was covered with little circular smudges; the marks, Francis realized with quiet horror, of a fist bashing repeatedly against glass.

'Wouldn't someone have heard her?'

'Not down here. With this door shut, and the one to the changing room too. The walls are very thick.'

My dream, Francis thought. The drummers on the plain.

'So who found her?'

'Fabio.' Gerry gestured at the handyman, who nodded grimly.

'I come to clean shower,' he said. 'Normally, like yesterday, she go away at eight. For breakfast. After swim and sauna.'

'And no one else uses the sauna? At this time?'

Fabio shook his head. 'She ask me to turn it on so early. And to uncover the pool also.'

'We always like our guests to have everything they want,' Stephanie said.

'Yes,' said Francis. 'She was telling us yesterday how much she enjoyed her early morning swim.' His eyes reverted to the sauna door. 'So how could a handle fall off? Aren't there safety procedures in a sauna like this?'

He looked from Gerry to Fabio, who shrugged. 'There was nothing . . . broken. It was strong. The handle.'

'It hasn't fallen off before?'

A flicker crossed the handyman's face, but it was only a flicker. 'No,' he said. 'It was strong.'

'Are you sure?'

'Yes, sir.'

'You're going to have to leave all this,' Francis said to Gerry, 'exactly as it is. Have you called an ambulance?'

'An ambulance? But she's . . . dead.'

'You need to call an ambulance, that's normal procedure, I'm sure in Europe too. They have to make sure. And the police as well. You might very well be looking at a crime scene.'

'A crime scene?' Gerry repeated blankly. Stephanie looked appalled.

'How else did this handle fall off?' Francis said.

'What are you suggesting?' Gerry said.

'Nothing, as yet. But you must call the police. To cover your-selves, if nothing else. And they'll be upset if anything is touched. Or moved. Poppy must stay exactly where she is.'

He looked at Duncan, who had been watching silently during all these exchanges.

'Yes,' he said. 'An ambulance and the police.' There was a pause, when it seemed as if the ex-ambassador might be about to impart useful information or experience. But then: 'That all seems to make sense,' he concluded.

'Of course,' said Gerry. 'I'll call them now.'

Francis looked at the handyman and gestured towards the sauna. 'You've switched it off?'

Fabio nodded. 'Yes, sir.'

'Can you lock this outer room as well? For the time being.'

'We have a key somewhere,' Gerry said.

'We never normally lock any of the rooms,' said Stephanie.

'I have key,' said Fabio. 'In the storeroom.'

'At the very least,' said Francis, 'the police will be able to help us with the next stage. I'm not sure how it works out here, if they have a coroner . . .'

'I don't think so,' Duncan said. 'It's a rather different system in Italy. As elsewhere in Europe.' He paused, almost as if he'd said too much. 'I'll be up in my room, if you need me.'

'Please . . . do exactly what . . . I'm so sorry . . .' Gerry was struggling to know what to say.

'You can bring the police up to me when they arrive,' Duncan replied. 'I imagine they will want to talk to me after they've viewed the body.'

He turned abruptly and walked off.

'Good God,' said Gerry.

'The poor man's in shock,' said Francis.

Gerry looked at his watch. 'Half past eight. Christ.' He turned to his wife. 'We're going to have to postpone the Gubbio trip,' he said.

'Although, I suppose,' Francis said, 'you might prefer it if they were all otherwise occupied.'

'No,' Stephanie replied. 'We can't let them wander round a strange city without at least one of us on call. Maybe we should organize some classes here. Francis?'

'Of course. I'd be happy to—'

'Anyway,' said Gerry, cutting him off, 'I'll call the emergency services and then . . . I'll go out and break the news.'

Upstairs in the courtyard, Diana was back in her place in the sun, her bowl of fruit and muesli and yoghourt in front of her, her single croissant waiting with its portion of homemade fig jam beside it on a plate to one side.

'Good morning!' she said cheerfully, as Francis hurried past to the dining room. 'Isn't this just the perfect weather for our little excursion?'

'Yes,' Francis agreed. He should have gone up the back way and straight to his room – what had he been thinking? Now he was stuck. He certainly couldn't break confidence and tell her that there was to be no Gubbio trip today, no visit to the market, no cappuccino on the Piazza Grande, no walk up Mt Ignino or viewing of Gherardi's 'Birth of the Virgin' in the *Cattedrale*, no naughty Aperol spritz *aperitivo*, no antipasto, *primo* or *secondo* . . .

Inside the dining room, he put together his usual homemade ham roll. In the books and movies the sight of sudden traumatic death was supposed to make you throw up, but weirdly the awful scene downstairs had only made him hungry, intensely so.

'You look rather glum-faced,' said Diana, as he reappeared and reluctantly sat down opposite her. 'Aren't you looking forward to today? I love our days out. And Gubbio is one of my favourites, like Perugia and San Sepolcro. I much prefer the little atmospheric places to the famous cities like Florence and Siena, where you sometimes don't feel as if you can breathe for tourists. The last

time we went to Florence it was full of Chinese. Not very Italian,
I didn't think.'

'No,' Francis replied. He didn't feel he could say anything about
Poppy before Gerry did. But Diana was going to hate him when
the announcement was made.

'You'll love it when you get there,' she went on relentlessly.
'And you're young and fit enough, I'd say, to do the walk up the
mountain to the church, what's-it-called, the Basilica of Saint
Someone or Other, I forget.'

'Ubaldo,' said Francis.

'Well done you!' said Diana. 'You must have stayed awake
during Gerry's talk last night. I always find it hard to keep my
eyes open, after our lovely big dinner. And of course I've heard
it all before. I may take the cable car. It is rather an amazing view.
And there's a nice café up there where you can get a latte and a
cake or what have you.'

They were, thankfully, joined by Roz, all set for her trip in
khaki shorts. 'Morning everyone.'

'Good morning,' Diana replied. 'Beat you to it this morning.'
She wagged a triumphant finger.

Mel and Belle appeared, and the discussion of the day out
continued. They, too, were looking forward to a ride on the cable
car, while Roz badly wanted to see the stained glass in the Duomo
before checking out the food shops. She winked at Francis, privileged to be the only one to know about her blog. It was now eight
forty-five and the bus was supposedly leaving at nine thirty. Sooner
or later, Francis thought, they had to be told. He had just got to
his feet to go and get Gerry when their host appeared, pacing
slowly across the courtyard, his hands clasped behind him like
Prince Philip, with Stephanie a yard or so behind him.

'Sorry to interrupt,' he said, 'but I have some very bad news.'

'Don't say you're cancelling the day out,' said Belle jovially.

'That, too, I'm afraid. No, this will come as a terrible shock,
but I'm sorry to say that there's been a most unpleasant accident.
Poppy somehow got herself trapped in the sauna and . . . and . . .
and is . . . now dead,' he concluded abruptly.

'Oh my God!' said Roz, hand to her mouth. 'How?'

'The internal handle fell off the door and it looks very much
as if she was unable to get out.'

'Trapped,' said Belle. 'How hideous.'

Gerry ignored this. 'The police are coming right away,' he said. 'And an ambulance. In the meantime, we've decided that it would be for the best to postpone today's trip to Gubbio.'

'Of course,' said Diana.

'We thought you'd probably rather be here today and just take things quietly. Everything else will be the same. Lunch at the usual time. And we've spoken to Francis and if anyone feels like a distracting writing session that can be arranged.'

Francis looked down at his feet, not wanting to acknowledge what they now all knew – that he had known this horrid news all along. Diana was giving him a look that was close to a glare.

'I'm very sorry,' Gerry continued. 'As I said, we've never experienced anything like this before.'

'A death,' said Belle. 'And not even a natural one.'

'Exactly,' said Gerry.

'Excuse me,' said Francis. He was being a coward, but he really didn't want to be quizzed about what he knew or had known. He turned away and headed across the courtyard to the front door of the villa, then up the stairs to his room at the end.

He lay on the bed, his hands behind his head, looking up at a long crack that snaked across the ceiling. After five minutes or so, there was a light knock on the door. It was Gerry.

'I'm so sorry,' he said. 'That was very inept of me. I put you in an awkward position.'

'Oh, don't worry,' said Francis. 'I'm sure they understand that once I'd promised to keep schtum there wasn't much I could do.'

'But silly of me to implicate you. Not thinking straight at all. I think, on reflection, it would be inappropriate to have any classes today.'

'Yes,' said Francis, relieved.

'Anyway, the cops will be here soon. So we'll see what they say.'

'Horrible,' said Francis.

'I just can't understand how it could have happened. Fabio swears blind the door was in perfect order.'

'If the handle was loose, surely you'd notice that when you went in and shut the door.'

'Maybe not until you'd closed it.'

'Does it self-lock? That would seem unnecessarily dangerous.'

'It wasn't locked,' Gerry said. 'That's the point. But once the interior handle came off, and the latch clicked in, it wasn't able to be moved.'

'It sounds like a major design flaw. Could Duncan sue the company that made it?'

'Let's hope the police have a view. I'm sure it was an accident. With any luck they'll agree and we can get the body off this afternoon.'

'What happens then?' Francis asked. 'Will Duncan fly her home?'

'Presumably. Unless he wants to cremate or bury her here. Which is an option, I suppose.'

'Not the first thing you're going to discuss with him, I imagine.'

'I simply don't know what people usually do.'

Twenty minutes later, lying on his back reading Zoe's memoir, Francis heard the single whoop of a siren. He ran down to find an ambulance had arrived in the courtyard. It was yellow and orange, emblazoned with the word AMBULANZA and below that, MISERICORDIA PERUGIA.

The two ambulance guys, in body suits of fluorescent orange, were already at the front door, being greeted by Gerry. '*Buongiorno*,' he was saying as Francis came down the stairs. Then he led them off to the basement. '*Abbiamo trovato il corpo cosi . . .*' he heard as they headed off.

'You're a dark horse, Francis,' said Diana, as he joined the little group in the courtyard, which now included latecomers Liam and Sasha, who was all dressed up in a floral skirt, floppy hat and fuchsia scarf for the cancelled excursion. 'Sitting there throughout breakfast pretending you didn't know.'

'I promised Gerry I wouldn't say anything. I realized afterwards I shouldn't have come up here at all.'

'Don't be silly,' said Roz. 'It absolutely wasn't your fault. You were in an impossible situation.'

'Poor Poppy,' Zoe said. 'If you knew about it, you presumably saw her, Francis. How did she look?'

'I'd rather not say. Not great.'

'Frazzled, I imagine,' said Liam.

Sasha shuddered. 'Liam, that's so gross!'

'Sorry.'

Belle announced she was going up to the studio to do some painting. 'I hope that's not heartless,' she said. 'I just need to occupy myself somehow.'

'It's not heartless at all,' said Zoe. 'I think I'll go and do a bit of work too.' She looked in Francis's direction. 'I don't suppose you've had a chance . . .'

'To have a look at your memoir? I have it here.'

He waved the manuscript at her in lieu of further comment and dragged a deckchair to a place on the edge of the dappled shade.

'I'm going for a walk,' Sasha announced, while Francis went into the little side room to fix himself a coffee. Roz was already by the Gaggia, frothing milk in the stainless-steel jug.

'D'you want me to do some for you too?' she asked.

'If you don't mind.'

She opened the adjacent tall fridge and added an extra slurp of milk, before returning the jug to the hissing steam wand.

'Don't listen to those silly old women,' she said. 'Honestly. What are they like?'

He said nothing.

'I'm surprised you're not down there in the basement, taking notes.'

'I've seen all I need to. Or want to, quite frankly.'

She leant towards him. 'So . . . what . . . an ambulance crew are here now are they . . . in the sauna . . . checking her over?'

'I believe so.'

'You believe so? I don't suppose it's something that any of us are allowed to see?'

'I really wouldn't if I were you, Roz. It's one of the most horrible sights I've ever witnessed. And that includes a man who died of snakebite.'

Before Francis could elaborate on how ugly that innocuous-sounding death could be, there was another crunch of tyres on the gravel drive. He went to the door to see a snazzy blue and white Alfa Romeo with POLIZIA emblazoned in white on the side nosing slowly down the little slope and pulling up next to the ambulance. Over the front hub, a panther-like head was drawn in a blue line on one of the wide white stripes; underneath this was written Squadra Volante.

Roz's eyes flashed wide. 'The Flying Squad!'

They stood together at the door and watched as the car doors opened and two policemen emerged: the younger, taller, fresh-faced one looked like an Italian Private Pike, with a smart, dark-blue jacket, blue-grey trousers and a flat cap with some fancy golden bird insignia on the front; his older, chubbier, more grizzled companion was in the same uniform, only without a cap, and with two narrow gold stripes on his epaulettes. It was hardly *The Sweeney*, whatever Roz was imagining.

They glanced slowly round the courtyard, nodded perfunctorily at the scattered guests, then made at no great speed for the front door, where Belle was now standing behind a portable easel, doing an oil sketch. To Francis's surprise a burst of rapid-fire Italian followed before Belle led them inside, brushes still in hand.

'She's pretty fluent,' said Roz.

'Enviable,' Francis added. They took their coffees over to the central area where Diana was sitting with Zoe.

'And now the police,' Zoe said. 'Is that normal, Francis?'

'With a death of this kind, yes,' Francis replied. He omitted to mention that it had been his idea to call them.

'So is there going to be an investigation?' Roz asked.

Francis shrugged. 'We shall see. The Italians do things in a somewhat different way from us.'

'Of course they do,' said Diana. 'This is Europe.'

'I've read Michael Dibdin, so I know a little about that,' said Zoe. 'Italian murder mysteries,' she added, to Diana's bemused stare. 'With a Venetian policeman as detective.'

'I never read them,' said Diana. 'Can't see the point. If I want to read about murder I can look in the newspapers. Sorry, Francis.'

'Please, Diana, don't apologize. It's not compulsory to like the crime genre.'

'I love the Donna Leon novels,' said Roz. 'D'you know those? They're also set in Venice. And the detective has a nice wife, who he goes home to every night, and eats delicious food with . . .'

'Oh yes!' said Zoe, enthusiastically. 'I have read one of those. Great fun. What's his detective called?'

'Now you've got me. Bruno something or other, I've got a clear picture of him in my mind.'

'Bruno Tonioli.'

Roz laughed. 'No, that's the guy from *Strictly Come Dancing*—'

'Commissario Guido Brunetti,' Francis said, putting them out of their misery. 'One of the interesting things about those Donna Leon books is that even though all of them are set in Italy she never allowed any of them to be translated into Italian . . .'

'Is that so?' said Zoe.

'Wasn't she Italian herself?' asked Diana.

'No, American,' said Francis.

'Probably worried about being found out,' said Diana.

They were filling in time. Chatting to cover their nerves while they waited and watched to see what was going to happen next. How long would the police stay? Would it be a routine check and then off – after all the drama perhaps just a horrid accident that no one could have foreseen?

Ten minutes later, the ambulance sped off without a body. Five minutes after that Francis looked up to see Gerry beckoning at him from the door of the piano room. He got to his feet as discreetly as possible and headed into the gloom. 'Complications,' Gerry said, as he pushed the glass door to behind them. 'Because it was an "unexpected death" the local police are summoning some bigger cheeses from Perugia. Also the *procuratore*, the public prosecutor.'

'So things are not going to be as straightforward as you'd hoped.'

Gerry shook his head. 'I love this country, but once you get officialdom involved nothing is ever simple. *Fare brutta figura.*'

'What's that mean?'

'It's the opposite of *Fare bella figura.* You know about that?'

'The desire to dress well, look good, make sure presents are nicely wrapped . . .?'

'I'm impressed.'

Francis had always liked the idea of *bella figura*; wished, really, that they had it at home, where most seemed to feel the need to look as nondescript as possible, regardless of what they could afford. Whereas in Italy, even the very poorest turned out for the summer evening *passeggiata* dressed to the nines.

'But I'd never heard of . . .'

'*Brutta figura*,' Gerry finished. 'It's the opposite. Looking bad. They don't like it, so sometimes they go overboard to keep face.'

'So what does this *procuratore* do?' asked Francis.

'Takes charge, I think. It's a bit like France. They have the inquisitorial system out here. The prosecutor gets involved in the case from the beginning.'

Francis's understanding of Continental procedure was sketchy, a mish-mash of half-remembered details from, yes, Dibdin and Leon, not to mention Michele Giuttari and Andrea Camilleri, together with images from the French cop show *Engrenages* (aka *Spiral*), which had the wonderful public prosecutor François Roban ('Monsieur le Juge') out on the road in his suit and tie, leading the scruffy cops in their investigations.

It was Francis who had suggested – indeed insisted on – calling the police, but this was an add-on he hadn't expected. What did it mean? That the police suspected Poppy's death was more than just an accident? Or was it, just as likely, nervous local cops making doubly sure – in a posh house full of foreigners? Gerry didn't know what to think either.

'They're hardly top brass,' he said. 'A *sovrintendente* and an *agente* . . .'

'Sergeant and constable . . .?'

'Exactly. Passing the buck up the chain is the obvious thing to do.'

Five minutes later they heard the sound of tyres on gravel and another Alfa Romeo was nosing slowly down the drive. This one was dark blue, unmarked, with just a blue light on the roof, one that could either be put out or hidden inside.

'*Auto civetta*,' said Gerry, as they stepped outside into the courtyard. 'Literally an "owl car". Unmarked, as used by the Squadra Mobile, the investigative unit. This will be Perugia.'

The front doors of the owl car swung open and a handsome young guy, with quite long dark hair and a trim moustache, in a natty navy blazer, stepped out. From the other door came a good-looking woman in a tight white top, blue jacket and skirt and black boots.

'Sexy lady!' said Roz. 'I do hope she's the *capo*.'

'More police,' said Zoe. 'Whatever happened, they're taking it seriously.'

'I think these two are from headquarters in Perugia,' Francis explained. 'The others are just locals.'

'Covering their arses,' said Liam.

'Do you have to be quite so vulgar,' said Diana, tetchily. '*All* the time.'

Gerry had gone over to greet them, then taken them inside and downstairs.

A few minutes later a van arrived, driven by two policewomen in short-sleeved blue shirts. From the back came two guys and a woman in the international white spaceman suits of the forensics team.

'Now what?' asked Diana.

'Forensics, it looks like,' said Mel.

'Oh my God!' said Zoe. 'This is all a bit more serious.'

'What on earth's going on?' said Liam. 'Do they think one of us has bumped her off?'

He was voicing what everyone was now thinking as they looked round at each other with new concern.

'Don't be ridiculous,' said Diana. 'They can send forensics people for an accident, of course they can.'

Liam raised his eyebrows, but hardly were the words out of Diana's mouth than a second unmarked car was nosing down the drive. From this disgorged two men: one bald as a heavily tanned egg, in a rumpled grey suit; the other in a smart blue blazer, almost identical to the previous police officer, though this guy was older, with thick grey hair. Barely looking round the courtyard, they hurried inside.

'Unless I'm mistaken, that'll be the *procuratore*,' Francis said.

'Who's he when he's at home?' asked Liam.

'The public prosecutor.'

'The public prosecutor?' Zoe echoed. 'But they don't even know . . .'

'It's a different system out here,' said Francis. 'They get them involved right from the start.'

'Right from the start of what?'

'Any investigation.'

'So there is going to be an investigation?'

'Looks like it.'

'Good Christ,' said Liam. 'It's *Murder Under a Tuscan Sun*.'

'For goodness' sakes, Liam,' said Zoe. 'Please keep your more outlandish thoughts to yourself.'

'Hear, hear,' said Diana.

'This is Umbria, in any case,' said Roz.

Liam made the face of a rebuked man who didn't care and there was silence. The three police cars and the blue van gleamed in the sun. Everyone read, or pretended to read, silently. Belle continued with her painting.

'Are you putting the police cars in?' Liam called out, after a bit.

'Of course.'

'Brilliant. You could call it *House Arrest*. Or perhaps *Villa Arrest*.' He gurgled quietly to himself.

Sasha returned, with a bag full of mushrooms she'd found in the woods. These fat-stemmed brown *funghi* were wild *porcini* mushrooms, she told the ladies, rather excitedly, a speciality of the area and the season. She'd also found some rarer ones, called Caesar's mushroom, with an amazing orange-pinky cap, though she wouldn't want to eat them without checking with the cooks as they were very similar in appearance to the deadly poisonous Death Cap, half of one of which could kill you.

'Just what we need at this juncture,' said Liam dryly.

'You seem to know a great deal about mushrooms,' Mel observed.

'We have them in the woods in Oregon, where I come from. And I knew they were big on them over here, so it's quite exciting to have found this lot so easily. They were just there, in this little dell in the woods below the garden.

'I should definitely show them to Benedetta,' said Diana. 'Being a proper Italian, she will know which ones are good to eat.'

A minute later there were Italian and American shrieks in canon from the kitchen. Sasha emerged triumphant.

'They are *porcini*, as I thought. And the other ones they call *ovolo buono*, good eggs. Benedetta's going to make them part of her starter tonight.'

'You sure they're OK, Sasha?' Zoe asked.

'She is, which is the main thing.'

Just after noon a lime green Fiat arrived, containing another middle-aged gentleman in a suit, who carried a square, black briefcase. With him was a much younger woman with bobbed ginger hair.

'Now who's this?' asked Liam.

'I'd say a doctor,' said Francis. 'Maybe a pathologist.'

'Uncle Tom Cobley and all,' said Zoe.

Not long after that, the policewoman and her handsome sidekick and the man Francis had thought was the prosecutor and his companion emerged in a pack and got into their respective cars, before living up to the best Italian clichés and speeding off, sending the gravel flying on the drive.

'Is that it, d'you think?' said Diana.

'Who knows?' said Zoe. 'They certainly seem to be in a hurry.'

'That's just Italians for you,' said Liam. 'You know what shocking drivers they are.'

'That's a bit racist, isn't it?' said Sasha, who was now slumped sideways on a deck chair making a cat's cradle with a skein of red wool.

'It is, darling,' Liam replied. 'Making generalizations about alleged national characteristics is most definitely racist. However, in this case also the truth, as even the shortest trip on an Italian motorway would tell you. Jesus, the bastards are up your arse the entire time, headlamps flashing.'

Sasha laughed. 'Liam, you are just like this totally unreconstructed dinosaur person, d'you know that?'

'Twelve thirty,' said Roz, making a show of looking at her watch. 'I don't know about you, but I'm ready for a drink.'

'Me too,' said Zoe.

As they sat in a rather awkward circle five minutes later, it was Liam who raised a glass. 'Well, folks,' he said, looking quickly round over his shoulder, 'I can't say I particularly warmed to her when she was alive, but nobody could have wished that particular death on her. Broiling to death in a sauna, like some kind of lobster.'

'Please, Liam!' said Diana. 'Do you have to be so very graphic?'

'The least we can do,' the Irishman went on, 'is raise a glass to the poor soul. Let us hope that she has moved on to a better place, surrounded by A-list celebrities and dyed-in-the-wool aristos.'

There was a titter of laughter from Mel and Belle.

'I imagine,' said Diana, 'that Duncan may well join us for lunch, so perhaps we'd better keep our less kind thoughts to ourselves.'

There was the tinkle of a bell. A woman who looked as if she'd just put down the Christ child and walked out of a painting by Piero della Francesca stood at the top of the steps to the dining room in a neat black dress and white apron. She held up a hand glinting with silver rings.

'*Il pranzo é servito!*' she called, exposing perfect white teeth.

'Lunch is served,' said Belle.

'Thank you, Benedetta,' said Diana loudly. 'I'm sure it will be as delicious as ever.'

The beautiful cook smiled graciously as they trooped past in a group, though Francis couldn't help noticing that her shorter, rounder colleague, who hurried past with a basket of fresh rolls, was scowling at her. Perhaps, under that charming surface, the boss was a kitchen tyrant.

The guests queued politely to get plates and cutlery, before helping themselves in turn to the reassuringly familiar spread of cold dishes. Outside, they found places at the long table and did their best to have the same relaxed conversation as they'd had on the days previously. But there was little doubting that a new unease had set in. None of the group were daring to even speculate that the next step up from bizarre and nasty accident was suspicious death.

Stephanie appeared from the front door of the villa and made her way hurriedly past them to the dining room. She emerged two minutes later with a plate piled up with food.

'All right, everyone,' she called, 'I'm just getting a little something for Duncan. I'll be down in a minute with an update.'

FIVE

When Stephanie returned, half an hour later, most of them had finished their lunch and were sitting around with coffees, waiting. She floated towards them across the courtyard in her big red dress and pinged a glass with a spoon as if nothing had changed. Gerry followed behind her and stood to one side. There was no need for anyone to be alarmed, Stephanie told them all, by the strange men in spaceman suits; the police were just being very thorough, as Italian police liked to be.

'But those are forensics people,' said Roz. 'Surely?'

'They are. They're having a thorough look at the sauna, which for the time being, I'm afraid, remains out of bounds.'

'As if anyone would want to go there,' said Zoe.

'And who were the other couple?' Roz asked.

'The doctor and his assistant,' said Gerry. 'Out here, if he deals with a death, they call him the *necroscopo*.'

'The *necr-o-scopo*,' intoned Liam, in a husky Hollywood trailer voice. 'Wasn't that a film?' A *fillum*. 'About a person that can talk to the dead.'

'Thanks, Liam,' Stephanie said, skating over this intervention in her usual bright manner. 'The *necroscopo* has asked for a post-mortem, so once forensics have finished, the body will be taken off to the hospital in Perugia and hopefully that will be that.' Then she and Gerry, she went on, could get to work helping poor Duncan get Poppy repatriated and the rest of them could get back to what they were here for, after all, which was an enjoyable and relaxing time for creative endeavour. 'As you know, Poppy was a very keen writer, with a published book to her name, and I'm sure she would have wanted everyone to enjoy the rest of their stay, as best they can.'

'As best they can,' Liam repeated, Irish irony trickling from his words like treacle. 'So if any of us don't want to stick around, will there be some sort of refund?'

'Now this is rather difficult,' Stephanie said. 'I'm afraid the police are keen that everyone stay. At least for the time being.'

'Can they make us?'

'I'm afraid I think they can. In the circumstances. But hopefully, obviously, it really won't be for very long. And Gerry is hoping to get our trip to Gubbio reorganized for Friday.'

'Oh *good*,' said Diana.

'That's all right then,' said Liam, sarcastically.

After the general briefing, Stephanie called Francis aside. He followed her beckoning finger into the privacy of the library.

'I was just wondering about teaching,' she said. 'I know you and Gerry agreed it would be inappropriate today, but what about tomorrow? I'm a bit concerned we're all going to get bored and restless, stuck here as we are. The police are not only coming back but they want to take statements.'

'That sounds rather serious.'

'I'm sure it's a formality. Hopefully, once they've got the post-mortem done, they won't need them. Between you and me, the *necroscopo* has some crazy idea that Poppy might have been . . . *poisoned*.' Stephanie dropped her voice to a whisper.

'Christ.'

'Gerry and I are hoping that it's just typical Italian dramatics. I mean we're hardly the Borgias here, are we?'

'What on earth made him think that?'

'Something about the expression of the mouth. And her pupils being so wide. And some smell his assistant detected. Almondy, apparently. It all sounds a bit far-fetched to me. But you know what these things are like, especially over here. Once they start to think something then everybody else has to jump on board. I haven't broken it to the group yet, but we've had to hand over everyone's passports.'

'To the police?'

'Yes.'

'So nobody really is going anywhere?'

'Not beyond the border, anyway.'

'They won't like that. Quite a few of them are flying back on Saturday, aren't they?'

'Five of them. And another six are supposed to be arriving for the second week. To stay in the rooms the five are vacating.'

'Problems.'

Stephanie sighed. 'We always have them with our groups. Just not this bad. As I said, we're praying the autopsy will clear all this up. I hope I'm not being a ridiculously *naif* person, but the very idea! That one of our lovely guests would want to poison another. I mean, unless Poppy and Duncan have been off in the woods eating some of those dodgy *funghi* Sasha's been finding, how else would such a thing come about? Let alone why. The worst thing that's ever happened here, in over twenty-five years of us running these courses, was Zoe's asthma attack last year.'

'It does sound most unlikely,' Francis agreed. But it was not what he thought. His previous experience had made him realize that murderous intentions could pop up in the most unlikely places. Money and sex, Donna Leon's Commissario Brunetti had once opined, were the only real motives for murder, but Francis begged to differ. He had seen both revenge and twisted altruism as a motive, quite apart from the follow-up killings that always had to do with being found out and desperately trying to cover up the original crime. With which in mind, he was certainly going to take nothing for granted here. For his own safety he was going to have to pretend to be completely uninterested in whatever events unfolded, even though this talk of poison had quickened his curiosity, for yes, there had been something about Poppy's wide pupils that had worried him too, quite apart from that smell of marzipan. Almondy. Having written seven murder mysteries and read many more he knew what that meant. Cyanide. Which spoke, if it were true, of a planned killing. 'As to the teaching,' he went on, picking up on her original question, 'no, I don't mind doing a few exercises, to keep their minds off things.'

'Thank you, Francis. It would certainly make it easier for us. Gerry's going to do his best to keep the art group busy. If we can somehow maintain some semblance of normality that would be great.'

'People want their money's worth, whatever's happened.'

'Exactly.'

'When are you going to tell them about the passports?'

'Drinky-time, I think. Best temper the shock with a sharpener.'

Francis could feel his internal eyebrows rising, but the face he gave Stephanie was deadpan. She was in shock too, he realized.

He decided to escape to the pool, which was a hundred and

fifty yards or so away from the house, on its own little terrace to one side of the sloping green lawn. It had been built too long ago to be an infinity pool, but it had a quality of that later fashion in that the view was spectacular, out down the valley to the Tuscan ridges and hilltops, the half-hidden rooftops of distant towns and villages, the occasional grand villas with their curving driveways of cypress, and behind it all the magnificently brooding backdrop of mountains and clouds.

For a while he was the only one there, flat out on a lounger with a parasol flapping above him in the light breeze. He was happy to be away from the deliberations that were continuing on the deckchairs in the courtyard, within sight of the police arrivals and departures. Meanwhile, he was cracking on with Zoe's memoir, finding it more interesting than he'd anticipated. Often, on courses like this, his pupils' work was not as worthy of publication as they hoped, and there wasn't an awful lot the teacher could do to right that except point out the most egregious errors or suggest, perhaps, employing a ghost writer or at the very least a saintly editor. But Zoe definitely had something. A crisp, clear style and, more to the point, a story: of the grandparents who had come over from Poland after the pogroms of 1905–6, when sixty had been killed in their home town, where the population was three-quarters Jewish; of rackety immigrant life in Leeds and London; of early memories of front rooms in Hackney, crowded with family and friends, speaking Yiddish; of crusty black rye bread, chopped liver, hard-boiled eggs and onions, smoked salmon, cream cheese, black olives straight from the barrel; of *kosher* and *trayfe,* of *challah* and *chometz,* of *shaygets* and *shiksas* . . .

'Sorry to disturb your quiet idyll.'

He looked up. It was Roz, coming down the steps from the little gate in a navy-blue, one-piece swimsuit.

He smiled. He was glad it was her, rather than one of the scrawny oldies. With her clothes off, she had a surprisingly nice figure, which stirred a frisson of desire in him, even though he knew that nothing would ever happen. While she, foolish woman, pined for her married man.

'No worries,' he replied. 'Just thought I'd get away from the action for a bit.'

'I don't blame you.' She sat sideways on the lounger next to him. Then she rested her hand lightly on his arm. 'Though I'd have thought you'd have wanted to be there. In the thick of it. Being a professional crime writer and all.'

'This is time off for me.'

'Do real writers ever take time off?'

'Ha ha, touché. No, I'm working, even as we speak.' He pointed down at the stack of pages beside him. 'Zoe's memoir. That's the joy of these residential courses: you're a sitting duck for the *magnum opuses*. Or should that be *opi*? So tell me. What are they all saying up there?'

'Well, the forensics people are still there. So that's got some of them thinking that it wasn't just an accident; that something must be going on. What do you think?'

'What I think is I have no idea. Really.'

'Apparently they've confiscated our passports.'

'Who told you that?'

'So they *have*. You'd never make a murderer, Francis. You're far too transparent.'

'You think I did it. Driven crazy by the name-dropping of his most snobbish pupil, the tutor resorted to violent means.'

As they laughed, a tad hysterically, they were joined by Tony in a pair of brightly coloured swimming shorts.

'Nice trunks, Tony,' Roz called.

'What are you two giggling about?' he asked. 'All the conspiracy theorists, up in the courtyard.'

'You've escaped too.'

'Had to. Couldn't concentrate on my book with all those spacemen coming and going. And the speculation. Those old dears are going quietly off the scale. Or noisily off the scale, I should say.'

One by one, they clearly all felt the same. One by one they appeared, clutching books and towels and bathing costumes, till everyone bar Angela, Diana and Duncan was sitting or lounging by the pool. Sasha sighed as she tapped away noisily on her laptop, getting up at frequent intervals to pace up and down the terrace. Then with a splash she was in, breaststroke giving way to crawl and an extravagant backstroke. When she'd finished, Mel and Belle climbed slowly down the metal stepladder, protesting noisily about the temperature, though it was quite warm enough, Francis thought, in the high sixties. Once in, they swam up and down, side by side, gossiping quite unselfconsciously about their life and work in Yorkshire, almost as if there had been no death at all.

Up at the villa, Diana and Angela stayed in the courtyard, reading in deckchairs in a dwindling triangle of sunshine. A second *ambulanza* arrived, with more operatives in fluorescent orange, one male this time and one female. Poppy, now stiff as a giant *grissino*, was carried out in a body bag.

Diana shuddered at the sight. 'Poor dear girl,' she muttered.

'Did she really deserve that?' Angela replied, and went back to her book, Diana Athill's *Somewhere Towards the End*.

The forensics team followed shortly after that. Finally, the local *sovrintendente* and *agente* appeared, climbed silently into their Squadra Volante car, and then they too had swept away up the drive. For the moment, the villa had returned to normal, though Sir Duncan, the new widower, remained firmly upstairs in his room.

Stephanie's announcement about the passports created a ripple of shock, as Francis had known it would. How Roz had found out earlier, he didn't know, but it clearly wasn't general knowledge that they were now properly trapped; in Italy, at any rate, even if not (yet) within the confines of the villa. The pre-dinner drinks session became more animated as people topped up their glasses with wine, and in Liam's case a Martini, made with cold vodka from the American fridge. 'Might as well,' he said, taking a gulp of the clear liquid, 'since we're not going anywhere.' At Roz's request he mixed her the same, then Tony wanted one too.

At dinner there was a special starter, prepared by Benedetta: a risotto made with the wild mushrooms that Sasha had found earlier.

'Hopefully your judgement is sound and we're all going to be OK,' Liam said, as he tucked in greedily, in due course helping himself to seconds.

'It's OK,' said Sasha. 'Benedetta only used the *porcini* ones. She thought the others were fine too but didn't want to risk it.'

'I thought they were supposed to be "good eggs" or something,' Liam said.

'*Ovolo buono*, yes. But the Caesars do look very much like the Death Cap, which they call *ovolo malefico* out here.'

'You're very well informed,' Liam said.

'Benedetta told me the Italian names. But we have all the same mushrooms in Oregon. I love to go foraging at this time of year.'

Angela had discreetly pushed her plate away and laid down her fork.

'Are you not eating your delicious risotto, Angela?' Liam asked.

'On balance, I think not,' the old lady replied. 'But please don't let me put the rest of you off.' She flashed her toothy smile.

'No, please don't be put off,' Sasha reiterated. 'Benedetta's only used *porcini*, which are one hundred per cent harmless and look like no other kind of dangerous mushroom. Really, they're, like, ceps.'

Angela shrugged, but didn't pick up her fork.

'Benedetta knows exactly what she's doing,' Diana told them. 'Doesn't she, Gerry?'

'She does,' he replied.

'In Italian,' Diana went on, 'they say Benedetta has *le mani d'oro* – hands of gold.'

'She certainly has,' Stephanie said, and something in her tone, as well as the way she looked sternly back down at her food, made Francis wonder whether all was entirely well between the villa's owner and her remarkable cook.

Over the *secondo*, an uncontroversial dish involving pork medallions, they found themselves returning inexorably to the subject of the Italian police.

'It is rather unsettling,' Zoe said, 'to feel that we're in their power like that.'

'What's that supposed to mean?' asked Roz.

'It makes me feel anxious, frankly. I mean, we're abroad. They don't speak our language, they don't share our values, anything could happen . . .'

Liam was laughing. 'I don't think they're about to toss you into a rat-infested cell, Zoe.'

'You never know. I wouldn't know how to speak to one and be understood. You know, taken seriously.'

'Whereas in England, your nice middle-class voice would cow them into submission.'

'Don't be impertinent, Liam,' Diana cut in. 'Being a man, you can't possibly understand the anxiety of a woman in a situation like this. Particularly an older woman with limited mobility. They carry guns.'

This sequence of thought made the Irishman bark with laughter.

'It's really not funny,' Diana said.

'I hate to disillusion you, Diana. But those fine British officers you admire also carry guns.'

'Not by and large.'

'Pretty routinely, these days.'

'Our local police in Aldeburgh most certainly do not carry guns.'

At this point Gerry intervened. 'Diana's right,' he said. 'British police are not generally armed, while Italians are. Both the State Police and the Carabinieri.'

'Thank you, Gerry. You may well call me a silly old woman, Liam, but I happen to think there's something rather marvellous about that. It's called policing by consent.'

She glared at him, full of steely righteousness.

'Now come on, Diana. I would never call you a silly old woman. A wonderful old woman, more like.' It was a masterpiece of Irish charm, amusing the others while surprisingly placating Diana, who softened visibly, the thin line of her mouth wavering into an uncertain smile. 'By the way,' he went on. 'D'you know the one part of Britain where the police do routinely carry guns?'

'I thought Gerry had just made it clear—'

'Northern Ireland,' said Liam. 'But I guess that's a different story.'

'So tell me, Gerry,' Belle cut in tactfully. 'What exactly is the difference between the State Police and the Carabinieri?'

Fortunately Gerry was able to explain: how the Carabinieri were a paramilitary organization, with historical roots dating back to before the formation of Italy in the nineteenth century. They were a duplicate police force to the State Police – the Polizia di Stato – complete with a different emergency number. They wore different uniforms and often competed for cases. As if two separate police forces weren't enough, Italy had several others, including the Guardia di Finanza, responsible for crime in the financial sector, and the Polizia Penitenziaria, who managed policing in jails. Then there were other autonomous divisions of the Polizia di Stato: the Polizia Postale, who dealt with the postal service and now also cybercrime; the Polizia Scientifica, who handled forensics; and the Polizia Stradale, the traffic cops. 'Uncouth vindictive bastards; I speak from experience.' This educational analysis had the desired effect of calming the argument down completely.

Up her end of the table, Stephanie was doing her best to keep things on an even keel too. When the time came for the traditional end of dinner *ping*, it was to announce that: 'In the circumstances, we've decided not to show a film tonight. It's been a long day and I think people would rather just retire to their beds. Although do please notice the lovely moon, which is almost full tonight and unusually large and golden. The Italians call it *una luna del raccolto* – a harvest moon.'

Most of them did just stumble away to their rooms, casting long, spooky shadows across the courtyard as they went. But Liam, Roz, Francis and Tony decamped to the battered sofa by the fire in the library and worked their way through another throat-stinging bottle of local grappa.

'You know, the thing that really gets my goat with these grand English folk with their fecken titles,' Liam said, 'is when they lean down towards you and say, "Please just call me Poppy." Why did you accept the fecken handle in the first place then? I have to say I did get considerable pleasure out of calling her Lady Poppy to her face.'

'Like something out of the Wacky Races,' said Tony.

Francis laughed. 'To be fair, Liam, it is Duncan's title. For services to the Foreign Office. It's pretty much automatic if you're an ambassador.'

'Yes,' Roz agreed. 'It is.'

'You know about these things?'

For some reason, she was blushing. 'I am a civil servant . . .'

'A very civil servant,' Liam said. 'I'd employ you.'

He rested his hand on her knee for a moment until Roz reached out, quite politely, and lifted it off. Nothing was said, though Francis was amused to notice Tony bristle slightly. Was he embarrassed by the over-forward behaviour of a man of his age, or was this going to be the next thing? Liam and Tony battling it out for Roz? Had she even told either of them about her married man?

SIX

Diana was first down at breakfast again, out on her own at the long table in the sunshine.

'Life must go on,' she said with a stoic smile. 'I'm always first for breakfast and I'm not going to stop now.'

'I'm sure Poppy would have approved.'

'I'm sure she would. She liked people who had that good old British quality: gung-ho.'

Francis put down the cappuccino he'd just made on the table opposite her, then nipped sideways into the dining room to help himself to what was rapidly becoming his traditional Villa Giulia breakfast: a crusty roll, a curl of butter, a slice or two of ham, a croissant, a spoonful of homemade fig jam, and – greedy pig – a peach. The great thing about hanging out with this lot, he reflected, as he made his way back out into the sunny courtyard again, was that forty-eight didn't seem old, though it increasingly did these days in London.

'It's funny,' Diana went on as Francis took his seat. 'Actually, it's not at all funny. But in all the years I've been coming here, we've never had anything even remotely like this. A death. One year we had a woman who swallowed a wasp and had to be rushed to hospital. Turned out she was perfectly fine, only stung on the inside of her cheek. Then last year, poor Zoe had an asthma attack. We've had other guests who couldn't come at the last moment because they'd been taken ill. And then Belle's dear husband Michael died quite suddenly of cancer. One year he was right as rain, the life and soul of the party, the next he was gone. Of course, that hit me hard, because of my own scare . . .'

'Your own scare?' Francis asked politely.

'Cancer, yes. Five years ago. I had to go through chemo and everything. Hideous. But luckily the Good Lord was merciful and I managed to chase it off.'

'I'm glad to hear it.'

Diana was shaking her head. 'But never an actual death. Here. On the premises.'

'No,' said Francis. 'It is shocking.'

'Accidents apart, we're all getting on, that's the trouble. You wouldn't know this, of course, but quite a few of the regulars haven't come this year. Julian and Esther, for example – they've been coming for years. Not that I particularly mind, because I've always found Julian a difficult man. He rather dominates the writing group when he's here. Terrible stickler for grammar, which can be a bore. And he likes to read extracts from his self-published short stories, rather than do the exercises set by the tutor. Which isn't really the point, is it?'

'No,' Francis agreed. 'It's good to get stuck in with what everyone else is doing.'

'Anyway, poor Julian's got something wrong with his bowels. Can't walk very far at all, apparently. Certainly getting on a plane would be difficult.' She gave him a sad look. 'Old age can be very humiliating. You're lucky you're still young.'

'Not that young.'

'How old are you, if you don't mind me asking?'

'Forty-eight,' he admitted.

'A spring chicken,' she said. 'And you don't even look it.'

'Thank you.'

'Don't take this the wrong way, but I think coloured people like you often have much better skin than us sallow whiteys.'

He laughed, with surprise as much as anything else. He wasn't offended by an old lady's ignorance of the current terminology for people like himself, he just hadn't heard a remark like this for quite a while and it amused him to see where she would take it. 'I'm not sure that's true,' he replied emolliently.

'I think it is. You know, you can get into terrible trouble for saying what you think, these days, but you seem like such a nice young man I'm sure you won't take offence. Of course, I've never been involved with a coloured person myself, but I've often thought that they have much better physiques.'

'Good at sport, that sort of thing.'

'Please don't get me wrong. That's not to say they're not good at other things too. Often very good. Look at Nelson Mandela. An absolutely brilliant man, in my opinion, even though technically he started out life as a terrorist. But when David and I went to Africa on business, which we did quite a lot, sourcing fabrics, I would often look around the local people – blacks, that is, am I still allowed to say that?'

'You are . . .'

'And think: now *that's* what a real man should look like. You know. Muscly, a proper figure of a man. So many men at home these days are so unmanly really. And I'm not talking about gays. I mean normal men.'

'D'you think?' Francis asked, making no comment.

'I do. What's the word they use on the radio? "Metrosexual." God help us! is all I can say. We get quite a few of those types in Aldeburgh. Visiting. In the summer. And the winter, for that matter, these days. I feel sorry for their women sometimes. I mean, what do they have to look up to, with these drips on their arms?'

'I think it's going back the other way now,' Francis said. 'With the younger men. They're all terribly into their physique, spend half their lives in the gym.'

'I'm glad to hear it. Though not the gym, please. That always strikes me as such a terrible waste of time. What's wrong with putting one foot in front of the other and going for a run? In the fresh air. As for all those other machines they have. They'd do better to lift some real weights. Of course, in the old days people didn't need such things. They'd be out in the fields, wielding scythes all day long. Or chopping wood with axes. I'll bet that built up the physique much better than some silly machine.'

'I'm sure it did.'

Diana's attention had switched back to her croissant, which she was now slathering with jam. 'Gooseberry,' she said with a smile. 'I do love the range of jams Stephanie provides. You know they make them all here, in the kitchen, with fruits from the garden.'

'I thought as much, looking at the labels.'

'Stephanie is really very clever, what's she's built up here. And she has one crucial skill, which I'm in total admiration of, not possessing it myself.'

'What's that?'

'Delegation. She never lifts a finger herself to make the jams, for example. But she knows of a man who can. Or rather a woman who can. Lovely Benedetta. Works her fingers to the bone to give us all such delicious treats.'

Francis watched as Diana munched away carefully and then swallowed. Then she gave Francis a long and candid look. 'So what do you think?' she asked.

'About what?'

'Poor Poppy, of course. I mean, you're a crime writer. Do you think there's something suspicious about this horrid accident? Or are the Italian police just making a meal of it because we're foreign?'

They were interrupted by Stephanie, sailing across the courtyard towards them in another colourful frock, this one bright yellow, with a filigree pattern of blue flowers.

'Good morning, good morning!' she called cheerfully. 'Nice to see you both up so bright and early.' She sat down next to them with her cappuccino. 'Oh dear, what a business! I woke up this morning and had a glorious ten seconds of familiar Villa Giulia peace before I remembered.'

'Me too,' said Diana.

'I suppose life must go on.' Stephanie sighed and looked down. 'So this morning the police are coming back to take statements from everyone. I'll make a proper announcement when everyone else has appeared. We're lucky that Gerry managed to dissuade them from their other suggestion: that our entire house party troop into the *commissariato* in Castiglione dell'Umbria and hang around all day there.'

'The *commissariato* is the police station, is it?' Francis asked.

'Yes. In the smaller places. That's for the State Police, the Polizia di Stato, as opposed to their old rivals the Carabinieri.'

'Gerry was telling us all about that last night over dinner,' Diana said. 'It does seem unnecessarily complicated.'

'The Carabinieri are sort of semi-military, like their own little army. Round here, they mostly come from down south. Some of the locals tell jokes about them being stupid, a bit like Irish jokes.'

Diana raised her eyebrows. 'So don't tell me they're about to turn up too,' she said.

'No, I think once the Polizia di Stato have got the case, they hang on to it. Anyway, I'm hoping that once we've got this bit out of the way they'll let us get off and do our excursion to Gubbio.'

'Do we have to ask their permission?' asked Diana.

''Fraid so,' Stephanie replied. And then continued in upbeat mode: 'It'll help take people's minds off things. I'm sure it's what dear Poppy would have wanted.'

'And what about poor Duncan?' asked Diana. 'Is he all right?'

'Still very shocked, as you'd imagine. Luckily his daughter Fiona is flying out from the UK this morning, so he'll have company at least.'

'He's very welcome to join us,' said Diana. 'He doesn't have to stay in his room. He does know that, doesn't he?'

'I'm sure he does, Diana. As I say, he's still in a state of shock.'

The police arrived promptly at ten and set up shop in the library. A long table had been carried in by Fabio and Gerry and upright chairs placed behind it for the officers, with one at the front for the individual witness. The good-looking policewoman was accompanied today by the handsome thirty-something of yesterday, along with the bald fellow in the lived-in grey suit. With them was another young *agente*, in the casual uniform of short-sleeved, dark-blue shirt, white belt and paler blue/grey trousers.

The witnesses gathered next door, in the little side room with the Gaggia machine. They sat around the oblong marble table, nervously sipping coffee and tea and nibbling at biscuits, then going through one by one into the inner room at the invitation of the uniformed officer.

'So what did you tell them?' Tony asked, as Zoe reappeared, a tight little smile on her face.

'What they wanted, I hope. That I was in bed asleep, yesterday morning. That I'd got everything ready for our trip out to Gubbio, then went down for breakfast, all set, only to be told it wasn't happening and poor Poppy had got trapped in the sauna.'

'Was that it?'

'No. They were quite in-depth, I thought. The lady policeman has good English, too, with a rather incongruous Estuary accent. Apparently she has relatives in Essex. Anyway, they wanted to know what I'd got up to the night before, exactly whom I'd sat next to at dinner, whether I'd known Duncan and Poppy before the course, who had been here in other years – goodness, it was twenty questions and some.'

'But you hadn't?' Francis asked.

'Hadn't what?'

'Known Duncan and Poppy before?'

'No,' said Zoe. 'I hadn't.' But there was something in her tone, and the flat, determined smile she gave them both, that made Francis wonder whether she was telling the truth.

All too soon it was Francis's turn. Despite the seven crime novels he'd written, he had only once given a police statement, four years before, during the strange case that had become known in the newspapers as The Festival Murders. In England, on that occasion, there had been just the one detective sergeant, who had taken notes in longhand, compiled a draft and read it back for signature. Now there were two police and a prosecutor. Marta Moretti, the officer in charge, was a *commissario* based in Perugia; her younger colleague, Lorenzi Ricci, an *ispettore* (inspector) from the same police headquarters; the crumple-suited bald one, Leonardo Sabatini was, as Francis had guessed, a *procuratore* or prosecutor, albeit a *sostituto* (assistant). The whole thing felt more like an interview than an attempt to compile a straight statement. Sabatini asked most of the questions, which were translated by Moretti in her funny Essex-Italian accent. Her uncle had a restaurant in Romford, she explained to Francis, and she had been over there to learn English as a teenager.

How had Poppy looked the night before her death? Sabatini wanted to know. Was there anyone in the writing group who obviously disliked her? Had Francis ever met her and Duncan before in the United Kingdom? For how many years had he been teaching? How many courses had he taught? Had anything like this ever happened on one of his courses before? The questions seemed wider and wider of the mark, or of anything that might be required for a single statement, and it took almost forty minutes before Francis's short account of what he'd seen and heard was written out in Italian, then read back to him in English by Moretti and finally signed. He had decided not to tell them about his strange dream, with the African drummers and the distant screaming. Instead he kept things simple. Stephanie, he told them, had woken him and called him down to the sauna, where he had witnessed the horrid scene he described. Nor did he mention the odd early

scream of the day before, allegedly Belle's nightmare. He wasn't
keeping things from them; he just didn't want to be here all day.
He wasn't sure, anyway, about his dream. Had those drummers
been Poppy's fists, hammering on the glass door of the sauna?
Even though his room, Masaccio, was more or less above the sauna,
it seemed hard to believe. The walls of the villa were thick, and
there was a whole floor between them, where the kitchens and scul-
lery area were. Diana, who was resident in Michelangelo next door,
had heard nothing, she'd said. Nor had Zoe, over the corridor in
Caravaggio.

When he finally emerged, the side room was empty. There was
a new distraction. Duncan's daughter Fiona had just arrived, driven
in from Perugia Airport by Fabio. She had been greeted by Gerry
at the front door and then taken straight upstairs to see her father.

Diana already approved, albeit without introduction. Fiona seemed
very nice and approachable, she said, not at all like her mother.

'But she isn't her mother,' Roz said.

'What d'you mean?' Zoe asked.

'Duncan's her father, but Poppy's not her mother. She's a child
from Duncan's first marriage. Poppy never had any children.'

'How on earth d'you know that?' Liam asked.

For a moment Roz looked stumped. Then: 'Duncan told me,'
she said. 'We were having a chat about marriage and kids and
stuff the other night at dinner. He told me then that he and Poppy
had never managed to have children.'

'There's a turn-up for the books,' said Liam. 'So there'd technically be no one to inherit Framley Grange. Except Duncan and the
daughter. Unless it goes to the hated sister.' He looked over towards
Francis and gave him a big Irish wink.

After lunch, Francis took himself off for another walk. Stephanie
hadn't brought up the idea of teaching again, and he wasn't going
to raise it with her, especially as he now felt he'd do anything to
get away from the strange, increasingly stifling atmosphere of the
villa. Did any of them really believe that Poppy had been *murdered*?
By one of them. But then again: what if she had?

This afternoon he went a different way, down the overgrown
track directly below the tennis court and round on to a little twisting
lane, lined on both sides with tall dark cypresses. There was a

sprinkling of village houses here, some with tumbledown outhouses. The grey rendered wall of one was covered with colourful plastic ornaments: ladybirds, butterflies, cockerels, saucepans, spoons, a moon embracing a sun. A real cockerel, meanwhile, crowed behind the netting of a chicken run. As Francis passed, two dogs battered their noses against a fence, barking aggressively. Why was it that foreign dogs seemed scarier than English ones? Up at the villa they had all mocked Zoe and Diana's feelings about foreign policemen, but perhaps that was just a version of the same naturally xenophobic instinct.

The bends in the road widened and the cypresses gave way to shimmering poplars. As Francis came to the bottom of the hill, he could see the big grey sheds of the battery chicken farm. You could smell the pungent shit of the poor fowl, trapped in the gulag, drifting across. Turning left, he took the track along the bottom of the valley, keeping the dried-up bed of the stream to his left. He passed a couple of women, one old, one much younger, picking what looked like small green fruit, unripe plums perhaps. He greeted them – '*Buonasera*' – and asked them in English what they were collecting. They had even less of his language than he had of theirs, so it was in a mime exchange that he discovered they were *noci*, nuts – walnuts, in fact, on closer inspection. They offered him a couple. He cracked one open between the palms of his hands and declared it *delicioso*. Was that the right word? Why was his Italian so terrible? John and Susan Meadowes, his adoptive parents, had sent him to a good school and he'd gone on to uni in York, where he'd been fired up about reading English, 'getting to grips with the whole canon' as his enthusiastic A-level teacher Mr Watson had put it, but now how he wished he'd chosen languages, which would have given him a chance to read the literature of other cultures that he would never have the leisure to study properly again; and pick up, at the same time, a useful language or two. Ah well, he was never one to dwell on the might-have-beens in life. 'I should have done that' was a pointless sentiment.

Further along the valley was the ruined farmhouse and the scrappy bridge, over which came the stony white track that ran down from the football field. A figure was approaching, clacking along briskly in well-worn leather walking boots. It was Tony.

'Oh, hallo,' he said. 'I was just heading over to have a look at that church on the hill. It's such a feature of the landscape I wanted to see it up close.'

'It's all locked up, sadly,' said Francis.

'So many of these places are. Sad really.' They paused where they stood, like two bashful schoolboys. 'You heading that way?' Tony said after a few moments.

Why not? After Duncan, Tony was the most reserved of his writing group and Francis was intrigued by him. Unlike Liam, he wasn't a regular presence in the courtyard either, and came and went in his hire car. What did he do, what had he done, why exactly he was here? 'Sort of counter-intelligence work' had been his taciturn job description, which had made Roz scoff out loud, rather rudely, Francis thought.

It was hardly as if there was nothing to talk about. After a couple of hundred yards of walking in silence together up past the wide field of dead grey sunflowers, they slipped into a conversation about the situation in the villa: what they thought of the police and the almost inquisitorial way they had taken their statements; and then, more tentatively, Poppy's death.

'So what do you think?' Francis asked.

'I have no idea. I didn't even see the body, so what the hell do I know? But the police certainly seem to think there's something untoward. Confiscating passports is a bit more than a formality, isn't it? It's not being treated as a straightforward accident, that's for sure.'

'No.'

'I don't imagine that they're going to come out and tell us outright what their suspicions are. I mean, make a bald announcement that one of us is a murderer and we'd better own up sharpish.'

They walked on in silence up through the olive groves, the crickets humming around them.

'Once they've done their autopsy they'll be on firmer ground,' Tony went on. 'Hopefully, all will be well and they can work out what to do with her. Repatriate her, probably. Although, if they do send her back, and the death is considered unnatural, then an English coroner is obliged to get involved, as they have to investigate any remains that get returned to their district. That always struck me as an odd stipulation, because, surely, if there were suspicious circumstances, the last thing any perpetrator is going to want to do is stir things up by sending the body home for further examination.'

'You seem very well informed,' Francis said.

'My mother died abroad. So I had to sort some of this stuff out then.'

'Here in Italy?'

'No, south of France. Couple of years ago.'

'I'm sorry.'

'No worries at all. The old bird had reached her natural span. One was just grateful, really, that she'd kept her marbles till the end. Unlike so many.'

'Did you send her back?'

'No, in the end we cremated her out there. It seemed easier. We flew the ashes back. Though even with them you have to get special permission. You can't just bung them in your hand luggage.'

'Who's to know?'

'The guys in Security. They see an urn. Or even a plastic Tupperware box, which is what we used. They generally want to know what's inside.'

'And do ashes count as remains? For the coroner?'

'Not if you scatter them p.d.q.,' Tony replied. 'I imagine.' He winked.

They turned on to the little lane that led along the ridge to the chapel. There were high hedges on either side, thick with black-berries. Tony paused to help himself to a couple, and Francis followed suit.

'Only a few days before the devil gets them,' he said, popping one into his mouth.

'Does that apply out here?'

'Do superstitions travel? An intriguing question. To which I'm sorry to say I don't know the answer. There's also the point that it's warmer here, so who knows. We'll have to ask our hosts.'

They walked on in silence.

'I have to say,' Tony said, after a while, 'strictly *entre nous*, very sad and everything, but I did find her—'

'Poppy?'

'Yes. A deeply irritating woman.'

'Off the record, I'd have to agree,' Francis replied.

'Difficult for you, I imagine. You can hardly gossip about your course participants.'

'It would be a tad unprofessional. Even if they are dead.'

Tony laughed. 'What puzzled me about her,' he went on after a moment, 'was how chronically insecure she was. When, as far as I could see, she had everything. The beautiful gaff, the nice husband, even the title. Not that I personally care a monkey's fart about that sort of thing. But there didn't even seem to be a shortage of money, as there sometimes is in those big house situations.'

'I guess that kind of insecurity starts earlier, though, doesn't it?'

'Still trying to impress the general, you mean?'

'The dear old general. Who was the most brilliant young officer in Burma before moving on to sort out Northern Ireland . . .'

'Yes,' Tony said, looking down and away.

Was it too far-fetched to think that Poppy's death could have been some long-planned Republican revenge? With Liam as the discreet, double-bluffing operative? If this thought had also occurred to Tony, he wasn't going to talk about it openly with Francis. Not now, at any rate. Perhaps, Francis thought, he hadn't been joking, and he *was* some sort of counter-intelligence officer (on duty here, even, monitoring Liam?).

'And here's the chapel,' he said with a smile. 'Locked, as you said. What a damn shame.' He walked along to the adjacent house and peered in through the window. 'I wonder who owns this.'

'An English family, probably,' said Francis. 'Or German. Doubtless a holiday home that gets opened up a couple of times a year.'

'I'm not so sure,' said Tony. 'That's a Venetian dresser, if I'm not mistaken. Rosewood. And look at that mirror, hardly the sort of thing the English would bother with.' As Francis followed and looked in again, this time taking in the elaborate, old-fashioned furniture, Tony was already at the second window. 'Come and look at these,' he cried excitedly. 'Renaissance armchairs. Oh my God, look at those backs. No, this is a well-to-do family from Rome or Milan. *Una seconda casa in campagna*, I'd say.'

Before dinner that evening Duncan and Fiona surprised the house party by joining them for drinks. There was hardly a need for

Stephanie to ping her glass, such was the hush as the three of them came into the little side room, but she did it anyway. 'People, people, lovely people,' she cooed. 'Now I just want to say that it's very nice to have Duncan back with us again, despite the very tragic circumstances. All our thoughts and sympathies are with you, Duncan. And can we also extend a very warm welcome to Fiona, Duncan's daughter, who has flown out here from the UK to help her father make arrangements for poor Poppy . . .'

Fiona gave the room a thin, rather nervous smile. She was blonde, skinny, late-thirties, Francis thought, rather careworn, like a mother of young children. You could see the resemblance to Duncan, though if he was the thoughtful bulldog she was the alert spaniel.

'Welcome, Fiona,' said Diana. 'And sorry for your loss.'

'Thank you,' muttered Fiona.

'Thank you, Diana,' said Stephanie, giving her a fond look. 'Now the bad news is,' she continued, 'that the Italian police are continuing to take their time. The sauna remains sealed off and,' she paused for a moment, 'I'm afraid they are still insisting on keeping all our passports. For the time being.'

There was a loud groan from Liam. 'Do they actually suspect us?' he asked.

'Of course not. As I said before, it's merely a formality.'

'A formality that means we can't leave the country,' said Liam. 'I'm supposed to be flying home on Saturday.'

'I'm sure everything will be sorted out by then, Liam.'

'It had better be.'

'But the good news,' Stephanie continued, 'and I think this is most encouraging, is that we're going to be allowed to go on our excursion tomorrow. To Gubbio.'

'Hurrah!' said Diana.

'"Allowed",' repeated Liam, loudly. 'Lucky us.'

'Which is,' Stephanie pressed on, through assorted group shh's and tut-tuts, 'as Gerry explained on Tuesday evening, a wonderfully atmospheric town. With a church on top of a mountain, a cable car to get there, a fine central piazza with fabulous views, and some lovely paintings tucked away in churches and museums. Gerry has maps printed out, which he'll hand out tomorrow morning, or you can get them off him this evening. The coach will be leaving from the village square straight after breakfast at nine thirty. I'm assuming the same people who said they were coming before will be wanting to come again, but if there are any changes to that, we'd be grateful if you'd let us know.'

Like the others, Francis kept an eye on Duncan and Fiona. But he didn't go over, leaving that to more enthusiastically sympathetic spirits like Diana and Zoe. The bell rang and they all trooped through the courtyard and into the dining room. Duncan and Fiona were among the first, heading towards the far end of the long table and sitting opposite each other. People hovered nearby, and then suddenly Diana had dived in next to the bereaved ambassador, while Stephanie had commandeered his other side. Fiona, meanwhile, was deep in conversation with Tony, who had slid in beside her. Francis decided to take his chance and grab the chair on her other side.

On his left, Francis had Belle, who was listening patiently to disgruntled Liam. So he found himself sipping his wine and nodding once again over the table at the redoubtable Angela, who sat straight-backed, maintaining her characteristically brilliant smile. Her hearing wasn't great, so he would have had to yell to engage her. And what could he say, really? *So, did* you *do it, Angela? And if so, what was your motive? Do tell.*

He looked round at the flushed faces troughing into the fig and pecorino salad starter. Liam had been over the top as usual, shouting out like that, but his concern was clearly privately shared. None of them liked this feeling of being imprisoned, even if the food in the jail was still excellent. Was one of them really a murderer? And if so, how safe was everyone else?

With the arrival of the pasta, Tony turned to talk to Roz on his other side and Francis seized his moment with Fiona.

'Hi, I'm Francis. The writing tutor. We haven't really had a chance . . .'

Fiona was flustered and smiley, her long blonde eyelashes fluttering nervously. 'Of course, yes, how nice to meet you. It's all been a bit rushed,' she apologized. 'Poor Daddy's still in shock, really. But there's such a lot to sort out. So many boring details. Registering Poppy's death. Trying to get the death certificate organized. And then we have to decide whether to take her home or let her be buried here. The options aren't exactly appealing. I'm not sure we'd want her in one of those above-ground graves where they're stacked on top of each other in little chambers. Like Japanese love hotels, only for corpses. *Tumulazione*, they're called.'

After a bit of this rapid-fire offloading, Francis managed to get her on to herself and confirmed that Poppy wasn't her actual mother. 'No, stepmother,' she said. 'She met Daddy when things weren't going too well between him and Mummy.'

Francis nodded sympathetically, as was his habit. 'And is she still alive?' he asked. 'Your mother?'

Fiona looked only momentarily taken aback by his inquisitive directness. 'Oh, yes. Very much so. She lives in London with her own new partner. They're much better suited. When Mummy and Daddy were together they were always sniping at each other. For some strange reason.'

'Why strange reason?'

'Because they're both, basically, nice people. Nicer than her, anyway.'

'Poppy?'

'Yes.'

'So were you upset when he went off with her?'

Fiona shrugged, fatalistically. 'Nothing I could do about it. Especially as Poppy did most of the running. Dad's quite lazy, and she just presented herself. In the area all the time.'

'This was in Hampshire or somewhere?'

'Wiltshire. Yes, Daddy was on a four-year stint at the FCO in Whitehall, so we were based down there, near Salisbury. Poppy used to swing by on her horse. And she has this beautiful house.'

'We've heard. Your dad did a talk about it. After supper one evening. The house and the garden.'

'*The Garden That Broke Up A Marriage*.' Fiona laughed. 'You've heard about Poppy's silly book? It was her idea to have Dad in the first place, so if she couldn't deal with him when she'd got him that's her problem. He's a sweetie, if you treat him right.'

'And she didn't?'

'She did for a bit. When she was doing her number on him. Which we all witnessed as teenagers. Back in the day. It was pretty gross to be frank, she can really turn it on when she wants to. But then I think she got bored. With the very life she thought she wanted. The ambassadress. But in reality being posted in strange places abroad for years. She loves . . . loved – God, has she finally fucked off? I can hardly believe it – novelty. Sierra Leone's fine for six months, while she's exploring the beaches and learning some ridiculous dance moves, but then she wants to get back. To her comfort zone. And something else shiny and exciting and new for her to get her greedy mitts on.' She laughed, rather bitterly. 'I'm surprised she didn't make a play for you, Francis.'

'I'm a bit young for her, I think.'

'That wouldn't have stopped her, believe me. Dad's five years her junior. Anyway, you don't just teach, do you? You're a proper writer too, aren't you?'

Francis liked the idea of being a proper writer. 'I guess I am,' he said. 'Funnily enough, crime is my main thing. Though I did use to do celebrity interviews at one point.'

He enlarged on his career for a bit. Then: 'Why did you say "funnily enough"?' Fiona asked. 'Are you one of the ones who think Poppy's death wasn't an accident?'

He gave her a measured look. 'Who are the others?' he asked.

'The police, obviously,' she replied. 'Since they're being so difficult. I'm just glad I'm not in the frame. But they've given poor Daddy an awful roasting.'

'Really?'

'Yes. From all the questions they asked him anyone would think he had something to do with it.'

'I suspect it's the same the world over. The partner is always a suspect.'

'The idea's ridiculous. Daddy wouldn't. I mean. No. Even if they haven't been getting on that well recently.'

'Haven't they?'

'Not really, no. This was supposed to be a make-or-break holiday. To see whether Daddy could make the effort. In Poppy's inimitable words.'

'Make the effort to . . .?'

'Do exactly what she wanted, I think.' Fiona laughed. 'The writing course was part of that. Taking Poppy's bloody writing seriously. Joining in with a project of his own maybe. Becoming like this intellectual couple that she'd decided she wanted them to be now he's fully retired.'

'And he didn't want that?'

'He didn't mind. He's always been very accommodating of her

whims. For no clear reason. But recently he's been a bit more obviously fed up.'

Had she said too much? Whatever, she suddenly dropped the subject and turned the spotlight on him: how old was he? Was he married or single? For how long had that been the case? She had some lovely single friends in her tennis club, if he was interested. Late thirties, early forties, looking for Mr Right. But then perhaps he was spoilt for choice. Successful men of his age often were, in London. She was strangely direct, in a not dissimilar way to him, he thought wryly.

When the *secondo* arrived – grilled chicken legs, crispy, fried, sliced aubergines, proper mash – Fiona turned to Tony again, leaving Francis with Belle. She didn't turn back for the pudding, a creamy *panna cotta* in a ring of sliced strawberries. The interview was clearly over for the moment.

Nobody wanted to stay up for post-prandial grappas tonight. Perhaps they were conserving their energies for the Gubbio excursion in the morning, or perhaps they were all just worn down by the long day of statements and questions and continuing uncertainty as to what was really happening in this big, echoing old house, high on its hill above the remote Umbrian village, the almost-full moon above it, its light gleaming brightly on the villa's two unshuttered windowpanes.

Francis sat on the slope above the drive, on the little bench by the Wendy house, watching the lights in the villa and the bedroom building at the end going off one by one. He had just got to his feet and was about to head back down the steps through the bamboo plantation when he saw the front door open a little and a dark figure appear. It was Gerry. He looked around, then hurried across the courtyard past the writing table under the vine, where he vanished into the inky shadows. Most mysterious. Because this wasn't the walk of the confident villa owner, going about some late-night business in his grounds, nor even the contemplative course leader, heading off for a quiet, pre-sleep stroll. There was only one word for the way he was moving: furtive.

SEVEN

Friday 28 September

As Francis climbed higher, the last tarmacked street of the town gave way to a white gravel track, with a flimsy barrier across it on which was mounted a red and white No Entry sign. For cars, Francis decided. He skirted round it and walked on, all ready to be stopped if need be. But he wasn't. The empty track wound on, making wide curves through the steeply-sloping, tree-covered scrub of the mountain side. There was little sound, except for the light breeze turning the leaves of the trees; down in the long grass, the chirruping hum of crickets; below, the distant sounds of the town: car horns, a shout, the slam of a car door.

After five long turns, Francis came upon a small path heading away through the woods and up to the right. Was this the one Gerry had recommended as the 'nifty short shortcut', when he'd elaborated privately to Francis after his talk about the walk up to St Ubaldo's? He decided to give it a go, left the track and followed the path up towards a creaking sound that was soon revealed as the chairlift. A swathe of trees had been felled here, to accommodate the stubby black pylons that held the cables. High above him, up the steep slope of yellowing long grass, he could see the pulley-wheel station at the top; while far below were the terracotta rooftops of the town. Tall cylindrical open baskets sailed up past him, with no one on board. Then a lone teenaged girl swung into view, coming down. Francis watched her, feeling almost embarrassed he was standing there alone on the hillside, like a voyeur.

'Hi,' he called.

She waved vaguely at him, as if a man standing beneath one of the black pylons was the most natural thing in the world.

He nearly turned back, but out of some odd desire to prove himself to his host, decided to carry on, under the high cables, across the open rocky ground, to find the continuing path on the far side. It was narrower here, less obviously used. Then it threatened to peter out entirely. Francis climbed over a fallen tree, then pushed with difficulty through a brush of vegetation. Was this the path, continuing here, or was that just a stony ledge under this row of trees? Below him, the grey-white scree fell away more steeply. As he stood there, not wanting to turn back now he had come this far, his lower foot started to slip. He toppled over and reached out in a panic, grabbing at loose stones with both hands, but holding nothing, as he slid down the slope with increasing speed. He tried to slow himself with his feet, then when that didn't work, forced his chest and legs down hard into the ground. He was getting filthy, but yes, at last, he was losing momentum. He was slowing. He had come to a halt.

He lay there, spread-eagled, trembling, hardly daring to look down at the town far below. Tentatively, he reached out his right foot to gain purchase on the solid outcrop of rock that had stopped him. Then he followed with his left. He took long breaths, ordering himself to squash his vertigo and not panic. Slowly, he turned his head. Fifteen yards to his left he could see vegetation clinging to the slope quite satisfactorily. The band of rock he was on cut through the scree and reached over to that. He just needed to stay calm to get there.

Carefully, foot following foot, he inched his way across. How had he allowed this to happen? he wondered. There he'd been, worrying about some probably highly unlikely murderer in the group at Villa Giulia, who might – preposterous – have intentions in his direction. Meanwhile, a stupid misjudgement and he'd almost tumbled to his death himself. Or if not death, at the very least a broken leg. It was a long way down – and it only got steeper.

He made it. Got to a position where his arms were wrapped round a tree. He got his breath back and regained his equilibrium. From here, it was easier. The hillside was thick with undergrowth. And he could hear, not far off, the creaking of the funicular again.

He made his way back to the treeless strip. Was this where he'd crossed it before? No. He was further down. Wasn't he? On the other side of the open ground the woods were denser. Who cared? At least that would stop him falling again.

He looked up at the baskets of the cable car, passing relentlessly up and down. A couple were sailing up: a chubby guy in a white baseball cap taking pictures of the view while the skinny woman in his life looked out the other way. Then, coming down, another couple. Good God, it was Tony and Roz, locked in an embrace. They were snogging. Though Tony, Francis saw, was also looking round at the other cars, perhaps nervous that he might be seen by someone from the Villa Giulia group on the way up.

Neither of them had seen Francis, standing underneath his little tree. He let them get completely out of view before he moved, then hurried across and dived into the woods on the far side. It was as it had looked, hard going, with several fallen trees to climb over. Finally he stumbled on to a narrow footpath. Was it the one he'd been on earlier? It wasn't. But it led, quite quickly, out on to the main track. Inexplicably, he was higher up than he'd been before.

He was drenched with sweat, he realized; though now, in the heat, it made for a pleasant chill on his skin. He took several deep breaths and a swig of water from his bottle and kept going, on up the track, passing a young woman with headphones and a set expression striding purposefully down.

Tony and Roz, who would have thought it? That explained Tony's odd bristling last night, when Liam was getting over-familiar with Roz. It also explained why Roz had scoffed when Tony had said he was in counter-intelligence. If he wasn't, she would be the one to know, if not to mock. So was he also her married man? Or had she started something new to annoy the absent married man, make him jealous or get him to make his mind up? Perhaps Mel had been right, and Roz had been out with Tony on the day he was absent and she had vanished, the day before Poppy died. At any rate, the snog put paid to one idea Francis had been considering: that Sir Duncan might be Roz's married man.

Or did it?

There was certainly plenty to think about as he paced on. Five more turns and there it was, ahead of him, the Basilica of Saint Ubaldo. Chunkier than he'd imagined for a hilltop church, with a fine square bell tower on the right and steep steps up to an imposing frontage in pale ochre stone.

Just before the steps, on the right, there was a café with a sunny terrace behind, from which there was a terrific view. Not just of the patchwork of terracotta squares of tiled rooftops far below, but out beyond the green parkland around the Roman amphitheatre to the flat brown plain stretching away to distant wooded hills.

'Francis!'

It was a trio of ladies from the villa: Diana, Zoe and Mel. They were all looking a little guilty, holding double-scoop ice creams in waffle cones. 'Caught us at it!' said Mel with a laugh. 'Belle's still being dutiful in the church, if you're going up there.' They had done St Ubaldo and now they were having a little treat. Had they too seen Tony and Roz together? Francis wondered. Surely not in the compromising position he had.

Francis had arranged to meet Gerry and Stephanie for lunch at one o'clock, so after a nose round the Basilica, and a look at the dark-skinned St Ubaldo, in red skull cap and cream clerical robes, asleep in a huge glass case on top of a marble plinth, he made his way back down the baking stony track to the narrow streets of the little town and thence to the wide oblong of gleaming terracotta tiles that was the Piazza Grande.

Stephanie was at first her usual upbeat self, showing off the jacket she'd bought for peanuts in the market. 'But what happened to you?' she asked Francis, spotting the white dust on his T-shirt and jeans. He told them of his adventure on the hillside but didn't mention what he'd seen on the cable car.

'Sounds like you took the side path too early,' said Gerry, looking concerned. 'I'm so sorry. I should have drawn you a map. The shortcut's about halfway up, pretty clear when you see it.'

Francis shrugged. 'Oh well, I survived.'

As the *bruschetta* arrived, and their glasses of wine were refilled by the saturnine waiter, who looked, in his dark-brown waistcoat and purple shirt, as if he belonged to an Italian offshoot of the Addams family, Stephanie switched abruptly to confessional mode. She obviously didn't want to involve Francis, but she had to admit that she and Gerry were worried by the antics of the police. What were they up to? And if they didn't return the passports tonight, there would be serious inconvenience. For the four who were supposed to be travelling back tomorrow, quite apart from the scheduled new arrivals. What were she and Gerry supposed to do? Put them off? Or should they let them come, then accommodate them in one of the two *pensioni* in the village. It was an unprecedented and frankly impossible situation. But the *commissario*, Marta Moretti, she of the helmet of black hair and the long, painted fingernails, was very forceful. There was no getting around her.

'We shouldn't be here in Gubbio at all,' Stephanie said. 'But then again, it was all getting a bit stir crazy up at the villa. I do think everyone needed a day out. And some of them look forward to it so much. Diana, bless her, would die if she didn't get at least one excursion. And I know Roz is looking for ideas for her blog.'

'So you know about that?'

'We haven't said anything to her,' Gerry said, with a sly smile, 'but we're hoping for a nice write-up.'

'There is one other thing,' Stephanie continued, 'which I'd rather you kept under your hat until we get back. The police are searching the villa.'

'While we're out?'

'Yes, I know, quite a thing, but they've promised not to disrupt anything. It will just be a cursory look.'

'And nobody else knows this?'

'The police didn't want anyone to know. It would spoil the point of it, they said.'

'That'll put the cat among the pigeons.'

Stephanie shrugged. 'The Moretti woman insisted it was routine. But what do you think, Francis?' she asked, leaning forward, chin cupped in her palms.

'About . . . the search?'

'That too, but about the whole situation. Poor Poppy's death possibly not being an accident. Can we believe that? Or is Commissario Marta just off on some mad track of her own?'

'It was the *necroscopo* who wanted the post-mortem, wasn't it? What do you think, Gerry?'

'The *necroscopo* authorized by the prosecutor,' he replied. 'You wouldn't imagine they'd want to waste their time if there was really nothing to go on.'

'You don't think it's just because we're expats?' Stephanie said. 'In the nice villa. And all that.'

'I don't,' Gerry said. 'There's some novelty here, certainly. But you don't pursue an investigation like this just for novelty. Once we have the post-mortem result things will be clearer.'

'And when's that?' asked Francis.

'We've been promised tonight,' Stephanie said.

'We shall just have to keep our fingers crossed,' said Gerry, making the gesture.

'Dear Gerry,' said Stephanie, copying him. 'Always so optimistic.'

Out of politeness, Francis joined in. The three of them sat with crossed fingers for five seconds.

'You mentioned poison?' Francis said.

'Yes.'

'What I don't understand is this. If you went to the trouble of poisoning someone, why would you then bother to trap them in the sauna?'

'To make doubly sure,' said Gerry, with a grim smile.

'But the use of poison, which is traceable, would rather negate the death-by-sauna plan, which isn't.'

'Unless our murderer thought the sauna would act as a cover. And nobody would be looking for anything else. Meanwhile making quite sure Poppy died.'

'Good point,' Francis said. 'But if it really is foul play,' he went on, dropping his voice as Signor Addams brought their plates of pasta, 'it does make you wonder who might be responsible. I mean, who on earth would want to murder Poppy?'

This question brought nervous laughter.

'Quite,' Stephanie agreed. 'But seriously . . .'

'It's terribly clichéd, I suppose,' Francis said, 'but there is that beautiful house. We know from his talk that Duncan loves it with a passion. And the garden.'

'Which Poppy has also written about,' said Stephanie.

'*The Garden that Led to Murder*,' said Gerry. 'But if you're really suggesting that Duncan was involved, you have to ask: why on earth would he come all the way out here to do it?'

'It's a good question,' Francis agreed. 'Maybe you think you'd be less of a suspect, away from home. Or perhaps there's something about the Italian legal system which makes it less likely that you'd get caught.'

'Really? Such as?'

'I have no idea. But a diplomat might know about such things.'

'Are you seriously suggesting,' asked Stephanie, 'that our lovely Sir Duncan is a murderer?'

'I'm just throwing out ideas.'

'As crime writers do,' said Gerry.

'As crime writers do,' Francis repeated thoughtfully. 'But if Poppy's death is discovered to be unnatural, Stephanie, we have to face the fact that someone's done it. And it's hardly likely to be one of the folk in the village.'

They were a surprisingly merry party heading back in the bus that afternoon, laden down with purchases: clothes and shoes and leather goods from the market, the pretty little painted tiles of 'typical occupations' – *ciabattino, medico, contadino, soldato, sacerdote* – that people had all found in the same backstreet shop. Diana was delighted with a belt she had bought from a dear little man at the leather goods stall, in the Italian colours of red, white and green. Roz was thrilled with the photos she'd got, not just of *tipico* food, but of the *porte dei morti*, the 'doors of the dead', which were oval openings to the right of the main front doors in some of the central streets, where corpses had once, it was said, been carried out. Getting away and seeing the beautiful town and its artefacts, with the accompaniment of a couple of cappuccinos, a panini or a meal in a *ristorante*, had taken everyone's mind off the situation at the villa. But as the coach grew closer to home, crossing the bridge over the dried-up river in Civitella, then making its way across the plain of vibrant green tobacco and sombre grey-brown sunflower fields to wind up the steep hill to Pianetto, the mood grew sombre.

As the party drew up by the fountain in the village square, Stephanie asked for their attention. The announcement she then made, about the police's search of the villa, didn't go down well.

'Nothing personal, Stephanie, we're all too fond of you for that,' Diana said. 'But I really do think you could have told us.'

'You *should* have told us,' Zoe agreed. 'Heaven knows what they've done in there.'

They all piled out and marched at remarkable speed through the wrought-iron gates and down the gravel drive. To see . . . nothing. The cops had been and gone.

There was another shock at dinnertime. Doubly so, because whatever search of the villa the police had done had been surprisingly low key, and the initial anger had rapidly subsided. As far as Diana could see, they hadn't even touched her lipsticks, which was one of the things she'd been worried about. 'It just feels so personal,' she said. 'Strangers rooting through your washbag.'

Now, as the puddings were finished and the waitresses came round with orders for tea and coffee, Stephanie got to her feet and pinged a glass. She had a bit of bad news, she announced. 'I'm afraid that the police are not, unfortunately, prepared to release any passports as yet. And tomorrow, Procuratore Sabatini has asked permission to reinterview everyone.'

For two seconds the room was silenced. Then the protests began. What? Why? What were they thinking? The five who had been planning to fly back the next day – Liam, Zoe, Roz, Tony, Angela – were now seriously inconvenienced. Liam was going to miss his connecting flight back to Derry and was just grateful he had decent travel insurance. 'The whole thing is a mighty pain in the arse. I've got classes to teach next week. Do they not understand that some of us have proper jobs to go to?'

Roz also had important work to get back to. She was hoping this farce wouldn't continue much longer, otherwise her team was going to be running around like a headless chicken.

Zoe was going to be missing a golden wedding. 'It's heart-breaking. I've known Gay and Ronnie since I was twenty-one. I was at the party where they first met. In Pimlico, in the Sixties. I really should be there.'

Angela been looking forward to a ninetieth birthday party. 'On the other hand,' she said, eyes twinkling, 'I can hardly complain about being stuck out here. It's ten degrees warmer than it is in London at the moment.'

Tony was the only one not complaining; if he had something he should have been getting back to, he wasn't – apparently – fussed. Perhaps he was a patient sort; perhaps he was happy to have more time with Roz; perhaps his work was here anyway.

'And what about the people coming for the second week?' asked Zoe.

'We've had to put them off,' Gerry said.

'The thing I don't understand,' Diana said, 'is why anyone would ever want to come here for *less* than two weeks. Once you've landed in paradise, why would you want to rush off?'

'Because you've got other, slightly more important things to do, maybe,' said Roz, barely concealing her irritation.

'What could be more important than being out here, having a nice time, being creative, surrounded by lovely friends?' said Diana. 'I can tell you this, Roz: when you're lying on your deathbed, you're not going to be thinking about all the office meetings you missed.'

'I'm not so sure about that.'

'More fool you, if you are. You may be a very loyal employee, and good for you, but you can be jolly sure your company isn't going to care two hoots about you when you've gone. They never do. Gold watch, possibly, if you've done a very long stint, but nothing more than that. If you've been given a legitimate chance to bunk off, I should enjoy it.'

Roz's laughter was scornful. 'I work for the Civil Service,' she said. 'I don't think they've ever handed out gold watches.'

'Well, there you are,' said Diana. 'The government. They could hardly be less grateful. Look how long they give the poor prime minister when they've finished with him. Or her. Bundled out the back in a furniture van that very afternoon.'

'Civil Service pensions are very generous, Diana. Not that I'm doing it for the pension. But if you're doing a reasonably responsible job, you do have a certain loyalty to your team.'

'It's like people who leave a party before it's over,' Diana went on, obliviously. 'All that effort the hosts go to, to make things nice. All the distances people travel to get there. All the effort with dresses and make-up and putting scent on and washing themselves that the guests put in. And then some people turn round, almost before they've put their nose through the door, and want to go home. My ex, David, was like that. He'd take one look around. And if there wasn't anyone in the room he thought might be useful to him, he'd want to be off. "I hate small talk," he'd say. But as far as I'm concerned, what is small talk anyway? It's talk. It doesn't have to be small. As long as you're interested in other people, you can make it as big as you like. That's what I always used to tell him.'

'No wonder he left you,' said Roz.

There was a short, shocked pause, during which Liam's loud chuckle could clearly be heard.

'Now that is just rude,' said Diana.

'Excuse me,' said Roz, getting to her feet. 'I must be getting to bed.'

'I really don't think that was called for,' Diana said, into the silence that followed her exit.

'It wasn't,' said Tony. 'But she's probably under a lot of stress, if she needs to get back to her job and she can't.'

So what was going on between them, Francis wondered, that Tony hadn't immediately made an excuse to go after his secret paramour? Too obvious perhaps; better this measured public sympathy.

'I was only trying to cheer her up,' Diana said.

Liam was still laughing. 'Ah, come on, Diana,' he said. 'No need to get your knickers in a twist. It's good to have a bit of conflict from time to time. Otherwise what are you left with?'

Diana didn't reply. As Liam said the word 'knickers' her mouth dropped open, but for a change, no words came out.

They were saved from themselves by Sasha, who announced that she was going to do her party trick, which was to provide on-the-spot character analyses. Her friends in Oregon had told her she was a bit psychic, she said with a giggle. With a little jocular encouragement, Liam went first.

'So you're a man of a certain age,' Sasha began, to laughter from the group.

'And what age is that?'

'I don't know, forty-something . . .'

'Keep talking,' said Liam. 'I like this analysis.'

'Maybe fifty-something.'

'Now I'm not so sure.'

He had probably been married in his younger years, Sasha said, or at least in a serious monogamous relationship. But something had gone wrong with that, maybe because Liam was the kind of guy who always needed new stimuli, new adventures, and he found the idea of staying with one person exclusively a bit boring.

'How am I doing?' she asked.

'You tell me,' said Liam.

'It's very personal,' said Zoe.

'I don't mind,' said Liam. 'Who's to say she's right? Go on, then.'

Perhaps there had also been a desire, Sasha continued, no, more than that, a longing, to have children, but that had never happened.

And that had quietly eaten away at that relationship. Francis wasn't the only one of the group to surreptitiously check Liam out as the young American said this. The Irishman's eyes were fixed on Sasha. His demeanour had softened as he listened; he certainly wasn't disagreeing or objecting. Then again, he did have an obvious soft spot for her.

Since the ending of that long and significant relationship, she went on, Liam had been involved with quite a few women but none of them had really stuck. He had been like a butterfly, flitting from plant to plant, enjoying himself maybe but never deeply satisfied. Meanwhile, on the career side of things, he had been very ambitious about one thing.

'Yes?' said Liam. 'What's that?'

'Something serious. To you, at any rate. Maybe it's the poetry. You've always wanted to achieve some kind of greatness, and perhaps that's there, but there's also something in you that stops it. It's like you're your own worst enemy. There's some lack of confidence about your own abilities.'

Liam was nodding now, in a way that said, *Maybe you've got a point.*

'There's something else there, too,' Sasha said. 'Some other big passion. It runs very deep.' She cocked her head like a puppy as she looked at him. 'Maybe that's what messed up the long relationship.'

'Who knows,' muttered Liam.

'Maybe it's, like, political or something. D'you know what, I think it takes you over at times, it's almost more important than the other thing you're ambitious about. Maybe it even is the thing that stops you in the thing you're ambitious about.' She was nodding excitely. 'Am I right?'

Liam was looking rattled. He laughed a little too loudly. 'Not bad, Sasha, not bad at all. I'm not saying anything. Maybe you should do somebody else now.'

There was a pause, while they all looked at each other.

'OK, then,' said Diana. 'Do me. I'm quite intrigued to know what you make of an old lady like me.'

Sasha turned and studied her, almost as if she'd never noticed her before.

EIGHT

Francis lay in bed for quite a while the next morning. The sun was bright on the curtains but he wasn't inclined to move. He didn't have to – his first teaching week was formally over. This Saturday had originally been scheduled blank. A day for some people to go home and for others to arrive. For those who were booked for the second week, it was, as Stephanie had put it in the first briefing, in her airy, upbeat way, a day 'to relax, to read, to think, to paint, to walk, to wonder'. She was right about that last: there was plenty of wondering going on now.

Francis had ended up drinking too much red wine, and then when the older ones had gone to bed, he and Liam and Sasha had repaired to drink grappa on the sofa in the side room. 'I'm not saying you got me one hundred per cent right,' Liam was telling the young American, 'but there were some pretty intriguing insights there, given that I hardly know you. Actually, I really don't understand how you did that. I'm quite respectful of your talent, if it is a talent, you witch.' He cackled with laughter. 'As for Diana . . .'

Sasha had reduced Diana to silence; almost, it seemed, to tears. The small group left around her at the long dining table had watched in quiet amazement as that confident, challenge-all, Sphinx-like exterior had crumpled in the face of Sasha's apparently innocent analysis. Sasha was so young and breezy, you had to think it *was* innocent; but maybe, Francis thought, she was a darker spirit than he'd at first judged under that bright, kooky manner.

She had started by telling Diana that she was a very passionate woman. That had gone down well. 'I *am* a passionate woman,' Diana acknowledged. 'I'm glad someone's noticed. I'm also – I hope – a kind and friendly woman.'

'I'm glad someone's noticed *that*,' Liam chipped in.

Diana's life, Sasha had continued, had held two significant relationships which had absorbed that passion. The first had been a close family relationship, a father perhaps, or a brother. The second had been an adult love, a husband or a long-term boyfriend. With these two comments you could see Diana, initially sceptical, engage. Like most of the others in the party by now, Francis knew about the adult love, but not about the significant family relationship, if there had been one.

Both relationships had gone badly, Sasha said bluntly. The first had always been bad, the second had started out well but had ended in some sort of betrayal. 'A betrayal you took very harshly.'

Diana's face was now a picture: of a woman who was sufficiently self-obsessed to want to know more from this seer but didn't necessarily want her life laid out bare in public.

Francis noticed her wine glass was empty. He leaned over and refilled it with the red she had been drinking.

'Thank you,' she said, throwing him a grateful glance. She took an uncharacteristically big gulp, then fronted up to Sasha again.

'Go on,' she said, nodding.

'Do you want me to? I feel as if I might be intruding.'

'I'm interested in your take,' Diana said. 'On things you have no reason to know anything about. And like Liam, I'm certainly not going to reveal, in any case, whether there is one iota of truth in what you're saying.'

'OK,' Sasha replied. 'What I do see, though, in both these relationships you've had, is a very strong positive energy coming from you. It's like you're not the kind of person who lets things get in your way. You try and make things work, whatever. Am I right?'

'You are right,' said Diana. 'I see that as a good thing.'

'And so, when someone lets you down, you feel it much more powerfully, like, personally maybe. You're like, *I'm not having that.*'

'No.'

'So you fight it. And if and when you fail to win, you get angry. Very angry, in fact.'

Diana shrugged and smiled thinly. 'Carry on.'

'You don't let go. You try to change things. But if you fail, you don't forget. I'm guessing that you're the sort of person who holds grudges. Not about the little things, but about the big things.'

'Well . . .' Diana was on the ropes. As an officially nice person, she certainly wasn't going to admit to being a grudge-holder. But Sasha was good at this. 'Maybe grudge is the wrong word,' she went on. 'Maybe you're the sort of person who believes more in fairness. In justice for wrongdoing.'

They were all agog now, watching Diana's reactions as they flitted across her face, like cloud-shadows over a statue.

'I do of course believe in fairness,' said Diana. 'And in justice. As I'm sure most worthwhile people do.'

'Of course,' said Sasha. 'Though here's another thing. About you. I think . . .'

'Go on . . .'

'Ultimately, if something is meant to be, you are wise enough to accept that.'

'I am.'

And so Sasha had progressed, with a mixture of flattery and apparent insight that had the effect of getting Diana to admit to more and more about her life. It was like watching therapy in action. You could see that for all her stated belief in people holding themselves together, keeping their self-control and dignity, Diana was longing to talk about these issues. Even with this little audience, perhaps particularly with this little audience, she couldn't stop herself. She was soon back on to David, the man she had spent twenty-five years with, living and working, and yes, his terrible betrayal. 'With a woman I never even met,' she said. Then how, after the affair was over, even though she, Diana, had still been single, and had still, yes, loved him, she couldn't take him back. Because the trust had gone.

These were the repetitions of an old gramophone record, Francis realized, hearing the story again. The ancient vinyl of her pain, to be replayed over and over until even she was bored with the story and eventually it was just scratches and hiss.

At this point, when you could see that Diana's big blue eyes were glistening, and she was tired and tipsy from the wine, Sasha had skilfully backed off, to focus on her first significant relationship, the close family one.

'You're talking about my father,' said Diana. 'There's hardly any point in trying to conceal that now.' She looked at the attentive little group around her. 'I suppose we're all going to get to know each other better now, trapped as we are. Yes,' she sighed deeply, but it was almost a relieved sigh, 'he was the other significant man in my life. Significant by being absent, most of the time. And even when present, not really there. In the sense of wanting to spend any time at all with his young only daughter, who admired him and wanted to be his friend so very much.'

'What was he?' asked Liam. 'In the line of work?'

'He was an artist,' said Diana. 'A painter of oils, landscapes, very much like Cezanne in a way. The Scottish Cezanne, some critic once said, and that stuck. At least in his mind. I don't personally think he had quite the same level of talent, but he was very competent, and he certainly had the necessary self-belief.'

'Strange that he didn't want to spend time with you,' said Sasha. 'You'd think, being artistic and all that, he'd be, like, sensitive . . .'

Diana let out an uncharacteristic squawk of laughter. 'He was sensitive all right. To himself. Cross him or upset him in any way, shape or form, and he'd fly off the handle. But no, not very sensitive to his daughter. Or his wife, for that matter.'

'And was she good to you, Diana?' asked Belle. 'Your mother?'

'Oh yes. In her way. But I was always only second fiddle to Daddy, the great artist, even if he did treat her appallingly. Shooting off whenever he wanted, having affairs, drinking too much, gambling – oh yes, all that too.'

'But she stuck around?' asked Belle.

'Oh yes. She stuck around. Like glue. Women did in those days. They were bred to be there for their men, however badly their men behaved.' She turned towards Sasha. 'This was in the days before feminism, dear, when it was rather a different world.'

'I've read about this,' Sasha replied, and it was hard to tell how much irony lay under her powerful surface sincerity.

Diana had spoken some more about her father, but then, suddenly, there had come a cut-off point; as if she'd sobered up and realized she didn't want everyone knowing everything about her. Francis suspected there was another aspect to the story, deeper and darker. Abuse, even? But she'd pulled back, the shutters had come down, and that was that; at least as a public discourse. She and Sasha sat talking together for some while, and it seemed as if the older woman's antipathy for the younger might finally have dissipated.

Fuelled up on booze, as they all were, there had then of course been a call for Sasha to 'do' someone else. She was reluctant. She didn't like to overdo it, she said. Or get boring.

'You're not boring, dear,' said Zoe. 'This is the most fun I've had in ages. If you don't want to do one of us, why don't you do Francis? He's always a bit of a mystery man. He teaches us and gets us to write lots of pieces about ourselves and our personal lives, but we never ever find out about him.'

'I'm fine, honestly,' Francis had said. 'Anyway, there's nothing much to say.'

'You're a single man in your forties,' said Zoe. 'Of course there is.'

'There probably is,' Sasha agreed. 'But I don't want to upset my relationship with my excellent tutor.'

'Creep,' Zoe said cheerfully.

It was nine thirty now, Francis realized. Time to haul himself from the gloom of the curtained bedroom and get going. He needed a shower and then one of those double-shot coffees from the mighty Gaggia; accompanied, hopefully, by a nice ham roll, if there were any left. The police were coming for more questions, and he wanted to be on form; not to get *involved*, not this time, but to satisfy his own curiosity about the hare they were now undoubtedly chasing.

The unmarked 'owl car' of the Squadra Mobile was already parked in the courtyard when he got downstairs. The usual suspects were littered around the courtyard on deckchairs, reading casually, though it was a defiant sort of casualness.

'Ah, Francis,' said Diana, cheerfully, as if last night's revelations had been nothing but a forgotten bad dream. 'There you are. You've missed breakfast, I'm afraid.'

'Police already here, I see.'

'Yes, they're busy doing the staff at the moment.'

'Fabio . . .?'

'He's off for the weekend. But yes, Benedetta and all the cooks and waitresses. They're being very thorough.'

Breakfast had indeed been cleared away from the dining hall, but there was still a collection of pastries on display under one of those wire mesh domes that keep flies off food. Francis made himself a frothy-topped coffee and took that and an apricot-jam-filled *bombolone*

out to one of the deckchairs in the courtyard. There was a choice of
sitting near Diana or Tony or Fiona.

He chose Fiona.

'Good morning,' he said politely.

'Morning,' she replied, not looking up from her book. He decided
it would be tactful to leave her to it. He took out Zoe's memoir,
found his place and started reading.

'How was Gubbio?' Fiona asked after a couple of minutes.

'Alarming,' he replied. 'I nearly fell off the mountain at one
point.'

'Really? There's a mountain?'

'More of a very steep hill that rises up above the town and has
a church on top. No, I left the main track up and took a shortcut
on a little footpath Gerry had told me about. But I must have got
the wrong one, as it led me to a near vertical slope which I slid
down for a good twenty yards before being stopped by a rocky
outcrop. Anyway, no damage done, apart from scratched wrists
and knees.'

'But you've recovered?'

'I was fine once I'd got back to the main track again. Shaken,
but intact.'

'And what's the rest of the place like?'

'Charming. You know, classic Italian town. Up high with narrow
old streets. An amazing central piazza, with a great expanse of
shiny terracotta tiles. Museum, cathedral. Not a lot of great art,
strangely, but I didn't really have time for that anyway.'

'I'm sorry we had to miss it.'

This was just politeness, because of course she and her father
wouldn't have had time for sightseeing. 'So how's it all going?'
he asked.

'Slowly. As you'd imagine in Italy. Lots of strange stipulations.
Twenty-four hours must pass from the time of death before the
body can be prepared for burial or repatriation. That sort of thing.
We've got most of the logistics sorted now, I'm glad to say.'

'I thought there was a post-mortem happening.'

'It's happened. Yesterday. Not that they release the body in a
hurry. We're hoping to get that back early next week.'

'Any results?'

'Not that they've shared with us.'

'I'm sure they will. And then?'

'Daddy thinks it best to cremate her here. We can take the ashes back and have a memorial service at home. Otherwise there's a lot of trouble and expense getting the body preserved or embalmed or whatever – before it's flown back. It's all very boring, really. As are the other details, like registering the death, which we've now discovered we're not able to do until the post-mortem's all done and dusted, as we need the pathologist's certificate to register. We had a fruitless trip to the Palazzo Comunale in Castiglione yesterday to discover that even though the death certificate won't indicate the cause of death, they still need the first doctor's certificate showing what the cause of death was to get the death certificate. Et cetera et cetera, on it goes. You even have to cancel the deceased's passport – did you know that?'

'I didn't.'

'Just in case she decides to shoot off on holiday somewhere. And you can't do that until you've got a copy of the death certificate.'

'Catch 22.'

'You can't even take the ashes back home until you've got a consular certificate giving you permission. As well as the death certificate. Anyway, we had a nice Negroni in the main square afterwards. That's one thing the Italians can do.'

'Yes,' Francis agreed. 'So they're not interviewing you, anyway?'

'I think they are.'

'Really?'

'They definitely want to talk to Daddy again, and me too, was what that female rottweiler in boots said. Once they've finished the staff.'

'And what are you going to tell them, since you weren't here?'

'I don't know. Background stuff, I suppose. Whether Daddy ever had murderous thoughts towards Poppy.' She laughed. 'Which I fear he did, given the way she was. Seriously, though, what I don't quite get is this: if someone really wanted to bump off Poppy, surely they'd do it back at home. Also, this is a set of entirely random guests who are here to do civilized things, as far as I can see, like write and paint. I mean, unless someone's found out that Poppy was coming on this course, and deliberately booked on to it too, why would anything bad even be likely. It's the level of preparation required I can't quite get my head around.'

'Only of course if someone really does want to kill someone that much, careful preparation is exactly what they do.'

'It all seems a bit far-fetched to me.'

Sasha was upon them, cartwheeling across the gravel in a pair of magenta sweatpants and a baggy white T-shirt that read TO YOURSELF in orange letters. This morning, for once, she was without the fuchsia scarf.

'Good morning, folks!' she cried. 'Another beautiful day in paradise.'

Was this supposed to be ironic? Francis wondered.

'Doesn't that hurt your hands, doing that?' Fiona asked.

'I'm quite used to it. If you do it all the time, like I do, your palms get toughened.' She spun on her heel and circled off towards the drive. The back of her T-shirt read BE KIND, Francis saw.

Fiona was on her feet. 'Looks like the tranquillity has gone. Anyway, I'd better go and get Daddy ready for his police interview.'

'Mind if I slump here?' said Sasha, returning.

'Feel free,' Francis said.

'Not disturbing you or anything, am I?'

'Not particularly.'

'Can I ask you a question?'

'Please do.'

'About writing – is that annoying for you?'

'No,' said Francis, 'it's light relief after all this talk of death.'

'OK. So when you're writing your characters in one of your detective novels, are they always based on people you know?'

Francis smiled. He loved the old chestnuts. Next she would be asking him whether he used a pen or a word processor, or whether all chapters should be the same length. 'It's a funny thing about characters,' he replied. 'In my experience, anyway. They often start based on somebody I know, or at least have met. But then, quite quickly, they morph into something entirely different.'

'So would it be terrible to take something that a real person had told you in real life and put it straight into the mouth of one of your characters?'

'I wouldn't say so. Writers keep their eyes and ears open and incorporate interesting quirks of people they come across into their work all the time. You never know, Sasha, I might end up putting you into something one day.'

She gave him a quizzical look back. 'But am I interesting enough?' she said. She accompanied this with a theatrical gesture; lying back, like a fainting Victorian lady, with her palm across her brow. 'So if there was,' she went on, sitting up again, 'like, something someone told you, almost in confidence, is it OK just to take that and use it, d'you think? Is it ethical?'

'I'm not sure ethical necessarily comes into those sorts of decisions about writing.'

'Doesn't it? I thought the whole point of writing was about being ethical.'

'There may well be an ethical purpose behind the whole work, and yet the writer might be quite ruthless in practice, in getting what he or she wants and needs.'

'The end justifies the means kind of thing.'

'Exactly.'

'So I *could* borrow something that somebody said . . .'

He was wondering what she was so burningly interested in. Something from last night? Liam's story? Diana's? Or was it something – someone – else entirely?

'Who are we talking about?' he asked.

'I'd rather not say. Anyway, not necessarily anyone here. Just the principle, I suppose. It keeps coming up.'

'It will do. What can I say? Different writers do different things. Have you read any Rachel Cusk?'

'No, should I?'

'She doesn't have many scruples about using real-life models. You might find her work encouraging. I suppose the bottom line here is: who would ever know? I mean, where do you live? In Oregon, I think you said.'

'Portland, Oregon, yes.'

'Quite a long way away from here. I doubt the person in question is ever likely to see what you write.'

'Unless my book becomes an international bestseller and they go, "Hey, wasn't that that crazy chick we met on that writing course in Tuscany?".'

Francis laughed. 'Umbria,' he corrected. Then: 'That's a risk only you can decide on.' They sat in silence for a few moments. 'For someone allegedly crazy, Sasha,' he went on, 'I was quite impressed with your efforts last night.'

'Were you?' She looked at him coyly, eyes wide, finger on her lips.

'Is it something you often do?' he asked.

'Only when I'm drunk.' She laughed; that loud, self-regarding laugh that peppered her talk about herself.

'For someone who was drunk it was pretty perceptive.'

'It's not rocket science, Francis. For example' – she lowered her voice – 'if you're talking about a single person of a certain age, you can usually suppose that they've probably had at least one major relationship in their lives. Either satisfactory or unsatisfactory. You only have to prod them a little to get them going. And almost everyone has a complex thing going with their parents, not to mention some ambition they wish they'd achieved . . .'

'I still think that's all quite perceptive. For a young woman of, what, twenty-three.'

'Twenty-four. Please don't patronize me.'

'Sorry. I was trying to compliment you.' He paused for a moment. 'So would it be patronizing to ask if you've had your one major relationship yet?'

'Depends what you mean by major. I've not been married.'

'And your parents?'

'Divorced. When I was little. They're both quite cool, but not people you'd look up to particularly.'

'So what was your dad's burning ambition then?'

'To be Jimmy Page.'

Francis laughed. 'I guess he didn't pull that off then.'

'In a limited circle he did. He's reasonably well-known in the jazz clubs of Portland. Catfish Lou's, places like that.'

'Sasha White-Moloney!' It was the young policeman, stumbling on the surname, calling from the front door.

'I think that might be you,' said Francis.

'Okey-dokey.' She got to her feet and smoothed her hair. 'Coming. *Arrivi! Pronto!* Is that it?'

'*Pronto*'s what they say out here when they answer the phone,' said Zoe, from her deckchair. 'Ridiculous girl.'

'Wow,' Sasha said, when she emerged, twenty minutes later. 'They're getting quite forensic in there. Ping ping ping, question after question.'

'Such as?' Francis asked.

'Why did I choose this course? Did I really find it on the Internet? What other courses did I consider? Who paid for me to come out here? Had I ever met or known any of the people on the course before? As if.'

'They really do suspect foul play,' Francis said, 'by the sounds of it.'

'"Foul play",' said Sasha with a laugh. 'That's such a strange expression. What does it mean? Murder, I guess.'

'It comes from Shakespeare,' Francis said. 'Hamlet blamed his father's death on "some foul play".'

'Is that right?'

'Diana MacDonald!' It was the young policeman again, calling from the front door. Diana rose slowly from her deckchair. 'Off I go,' she muttered, looking round at them with an almost proud smile. She proceeded over the gravel like a tall ship under sail.

Francis was the last to be called. It was almost lunchtime when he made his way into the gloom of the library, where he found Marta Moretti, the *procuratore sostituto*, Leonardo Sabatini and the older policeman who had accompanied him that first morning of Poppy's death. This grey-haired figure was almost classically handsome, with film star cheekbones and chin, only let down by a large nose. His thoughtful brown eyes, too, were set a little too close together for him to be invited to appear on the front of the Saga catalogue, or its Italian equivalent. Marta introduced him as Vice Questore Ceccarelli, from the police headquarters – or *questura* – in Perugia. A *questore* from the *questura* – he was clearly a big cheese.

'Mr Meadowes,' Marta began, riffling through her notes. 'May I call you Francis?'

'Please do.'

'Last time we spoke you confirmed you were here as a writing tutor of some experience. And that you were also a writer – in fact, a crime writer. You didn't tell us, though, that you had some experience as a detective.'

She looked at him, a neatly trimmed eyebrow raised.

Francis shrugged. 'Well . . .'

'One of the others has "grassed you up", I'm afraid. To use one of my favourite English expressions.' She turned to her colleagues and muttered a couple of words in Italian. *Spia*, it sounded like, and then *tradito*. Ceccarelli nodded. 'It seems you solved a murder case yourself,' Marta continued, 'at an English festival.'

'I helped,' said Francis. 'A little. The police also did their bit.'

'I'm sure you must say that,' Marta said. 'At least to us. Our informer tells us, though, that this case was quite famous. You were in the news, I think.'

'For a very short while.'

'Not that short,' said Marta. 'I Googled you.'

It was funny how things were, Francis thought. People always talked about his role in the murders at the Mold-on-Wold literary festival four years back, 'The Festival Murders' as the press had dubbed them. But finding the person responsible hadn't been difficult. He was prouder, personally, of what he'd achieved on a cruise along the coast of West Africa, three years later; though what had happened on the *Golden Adventurer* had barely been reported. A small news item about a woman who had fallen overboard, suspected suicide, and that was that. Cruise lines liked to keep their secrets and there was no campaigning investigative newspaper for the high seas.

'So I was wondering,' Moretti went on, 'perhaps you might have some ideas about the situation here since you know all the participants of the courses better than we do. And have their trust. What are they saying? What are you thinking? If I may ask.'

'Nobody knows what to think,' Francis replied, truthfully. 'Mainly because nobody knows for sure what Poppy died from. We know there's been a post-mortem, but we don't know if that's concluded,' he fibbed, 'or what any results might be. And so, as you'd imagine, there's just speculation. Some think – or thought anyway – that you guys were only taking an interest because we were a bunch of foreigners staying in a nice villa.'

Marta looked round at Ceccarelli and did a quick translation. 'I am glad they think we have so much time,' he said to Francis in a thick accent.

'I personally assumed something serious must be up,' Francis replied. 'Especially when you confiscated the passports. That put the wind up them, certainly.'

'*Spaventati*,' glossed Marta to Ceccarelli, who nodded and replied quickly in Italian.

'*Sí*,' said Marta. 'We have to do that,' she went on to Francis, 'if we have any reasonable suspicion.'

'That's what they thought,' he replied. 'But it unsettled them. As did the search. Some of them are suspicious of a foreign police force. They don't understand how you operate. They don't, to be absolutely frank with you, quite trust you. Gerry had to explain the difference between the Polizia di Stato and the Carabinieri the other night. At least one of them is worried that you're routinely armed.'

Marta looked round at Ceccarelli, who repeated 'Carabinieri' and raised his eyebrows. 'So they think we are about to shoot them?' she said with a smile.

'Not really. But they are old, some of them, set in their ways. They would feel more comfortable with police who spoke their language. You understand.'

'Of course, it's natural. Perhaps we should put on those nice English helmets, like the big gherkins, make them feel at home.'

As Francis chuckled politely, Marta translated her joke to Ceccarelli, who laughed too. 'Perhaps you should,' Francis said. 'And then,' he went on, 'Stephanie told me, in strict confidence, that the *necroscopo* had some idea Poppy might have been poisoned.'

This had the desired result.

'*Avvelenata?*' asked Ceccarelli.

'*Sí*,' Marta replied quickly. And then to Francis. 'You say "strict confidence". So the others haven't heard this?'

'No. I don't think so. Stephanie didn't believe it. "My guests aren't the Borgias," she said to me.'

Moretti translated, but there was no laughter from Ceccarelli this time.

'So have you had the result of the autopsy?' Francis asked.

Marta turned to Sabatini and Ceccarelli and they had a short three-way consultation, which Francis got the gist of but couldn't properly follow.

Finally Marta turned back with a smile. 'We have. We would insist, obviously, that you keep this to yourself. But yes, she was poisoned. It was cyanide, which as I'm sure you know, acts almost immediately.'

Even though he'd asked for it, he was surprised the police were sharing such sensitive information with him. Whoever had revealed his detective past must have bigged him up quite considerably. Unless of course they had some other motive? Getting him on side against the others?

'Cyanide,' he repeated slowly. Despite what Stephanie had told him, and his other developing suspicions, he was shocked. There was now no longer any pretending that this wasn't murder, and cyanide spoke of a level of preparation that put any thoughts of accident or opportunism to one side. Where had the murderer – for yes, that's who he or she was – got it from? It was hardly something you'd risk bringing through airport security. Although you wouldn't need a lot. He couldn't remember how much was fatal, but it was well below the 100 mg limit for liquids in hand luggage, let alone unchecked hold luggage. It could easily be hidden in a nail varnish bottle or similar. This explained the reason for the surprise search of the villa; though surely if you were organized enough to bring cyanide on the plane, you wouldn't be leaving it lying around your room.

'We don't think it would be helpful to share this with the others,' Moretti went on. 'It might create some kind of a panic. You all still have to live together. Meanwhile, Francis, if you find you have any new information or suspicions, we would ask you to help us.'

'Of course.' He was flattered if puzzled that they seemed to have ruled him out as a suspect himself. God help him, though, it might not be wise to be too closely identified with the police, especially as he was still sleeping in an unlocked room.

'And what about Stephanie and Gerry?' he asked. 'Do they know all this?'

'Yes, we have told the hosts.'

They too, it seemed, were not under suspicion. But they weren't off Francis's own personal list. 'And how does this work with being trapped in the sauna?' he went on. 'You think she was poisoned before she went in?'

'She must have been,' said Moretti. 'The killer, perhaps, hoped that the broken sauna would be a distraction. That we wouldn't be looking for any other cause of death.'

'Yes,' said Francis.

'As to the rest of the case,' Marta asked, 'is there anything else you want to share with us now?'

'I'm no clearer than you are, I'm afraid.'

Moretti sat looking at him, almost as if she didn't believe him.

'I'm not protecting anyone, if that's what you think.'

'We don't think that. However . . .' She looked over at Ceccarelli again, as if asking permission.

'Do you know about this big house that Sir Duncan owns?' she asked. 'In the English countryside. Framley Place.'

'Grange,' Francis corrected her.

She nodded. 'Apparently he gave a talk about it to you all the other evening.'

'He did. A PowerPoint presentation, with slides.'

'One of your fellow guests said he was very proud of it. And in particular the beautiful garden.'

'He was. He is.'

'But as I understand it from his daughter, and also now from him, Framley Place, Framley Grange was a property owned by Poppy. Inherited from her father.'

'That's right, yes.'

Maybe, Ms Moretti elaborated, Duncan loved the house but not his wife any more. If he divorced her he would lose it. Maybe there was even another woman involved. It was possible, Francis agreed; although he had to say that Duncan had appeared to get on fine with his wife, when she was alive.

'If he was planning to kill her,' Moretti said, 'he would hardly allow himself to be arguing with her, would he? In front of the other guests.'

'This is true,' Francis agreed; he didn't share what Fiona had told him about them not getting on well recently. That was for her to tell them, if she wanted to.

There were more suspects and theories to be considered. Francis gave his honest input to each, though none of them convinced him or, he realized, them. By the time they let him go, twenty minutes later, he had a strong suspicion that the police were as much in the dark as he was. Unless, that is, they had decided to construct an elaborate double bluff. Moretti handed him her card, with an invitation to call her if anything occurred to him or anything else interesting came to light.

'So you're not letting them go any time soon?' he asked, as he took leave of them.

'This woman was poisoned,' Moretti replied bluntly. 'They are all suspects in a clear case of murder. All I can hope is that this pressure cooker will make one of them crack.'

NINE

T he scream that rang through the villa the following morning was louder and more sustained than the one that Belle had claimed as a nightmare four mornings before. Francis knew immediately that something terrible had happened. He threw down the remaining pages of Zoe's memoir, sprang from his chair and ran down the corridor. The last door on the left was swinging open. Botticelli. Sasha's room. It was one of the best in the villa, with two tall windows looking down over the valley.

Sasha lay central on the king-sized bed, her fuchsia scarf beside her. But she was no longer going to leap in with a quirky intervention or remark. Nor was she going to surprise them with a searching character analysis, nor cartwheel across the bedroom or do a handstand by the writing table. Though her mane of frizzy hair was just the same, her big brown eyes stared lifelessly up at the ceiling, bloodshot and no longer beautiful. The golden-brown skin of her neck was marked with a smudged, encircling line of red, no stronger than a pale blush. All around were scattered those pinky-orange mushrooms she had found in the woods, some whole, some broken in two, some with bite-sized pieces taken out of them, as if she had sampled them and these were not the harmless Caesar's mushroom she had thought, the *ovolo buono,* but the deadly lookalike, the *ovolo malefico,* aka the Death Cap.

'Jesus Christ!' said Francis.

It must have been Stephanie who had screamed. The look she gave him now was one of blank horror. At her side, still holding her hand, was Gerry; silent and appalled.

'Sasha,' muttered Stephanie, shaking her head backwards and forwards, bewildered. 'I just knocked on her door. I was going to ask her if she wanted to organize some sort of exercise class.'

'We must phone the police,' said Gerry.

Outside, on the windowsill, a bird chirruped incongruously.

The scream had brought others to the door. Tony, Roz, Zoe.

'Oh my God!' said Zoe.

'What's going on?' It was Liam, striding in past the others. 'Mary, Mother of God, what is this?' As everyone else stayed where they stood, he walked over to the bed. 'It's like a stage set,' he said. 'She hasn't touched these mushrooms, has she?' He looked round. He was right. That was the word for it. Staged. If she had eaten a poisonous mushroom, it wouldn't have acted that quickly. Or cleanly. Francis needed to do his research, but he was fairly sure there would have been gastro-intestinal disorder first. You didn't just eat a toad-stool and die, like the victim of some bad fairy in a children's story – or cyanide for that matter. 'What is this?' Liam went on, bending towards her neck. 'Looks more like strangulation.'

'No!' Francis heard himself cry. 'Don't touch her. We need to be very careful here. We need to back out, all of us, and leave this situation exactly as it is. The police need to see this, absolutely as it is.'

'You're right, Francis,' Tony said. 'This is a crime scene. We must all go. Now.'

Liam turned. For a moment Francis thought, from the lost expression on his face, that he was about to put up an objection, be difficult in some eccentric way. But: 'You're right,' he said. 'We must go. R – I – feckin P, Sasha.' He looked round at the others, and it was almost a look of accusation. 'What is goin' on?'

He shook his head, turned and walked out between them.

'I can't believe it,' said Zoe.

'Right,' said Gerry, sighing deeply. 'I'll phone the emergency services. And then I'll let everyone else know what's happened. I think for the time being this room should be locked. Don't you, Francis?'

'Definitely.'

'We never use keys here,' said Stephanie, in a thin voice. She looked like a ghost.

'And then I think we should all meet downstairs,' Gerry said. 'By the coffee machine. In, shall we say, forty minutes. Ten thirty, more or less.'

They all backed out, murmuring 'yes' and 'OK' as they went. Francis was relieved that Gerry had taken charge. Somebody had to.

*   *   *

There wasn't a lot to say, as they sat round the oblong marble table, quietly sipping the coffees they had lined up to make, picking at the two plates of almond biscotti the kitchen staff had thoughtfully put out for them. An ironic choice of snack, given the means of death for at least one of the victims. But what about the other? They had all seen Sasha the night before, at supper, when they had chewed over the more detailed police interviews they had all been subjected to, until someone – Liam perhaps – had suggested they change the feckin' subject and an altogether jokier mood had set in. Sasha had been a part of that. She had her kooky side but was nothing if not fun.

Now it was hardly possible to believe that she lay upstairs, dead – strangled, it definitely looked like to Francis. Though why would a murderer who had poisoned one victim strangle another? And, unless surprised, why would a murderer leave what looked like the weapon, the fuchsia scarf, right next to their victim? He, Stephanie, Gerry, Liam, Tony, Roz and Zoe had seen the dreadful scene. The others – Diana, Duncan, Fiona, and the art crowd, Belle, Mel and Angela – had not. Nor had the villa staff, who were now going about their business without their usual smiles. Eyes down, they had good reason to believe they were cooking for a murderer.

There was no escaping this thought for any of them as they talked over this latest shock. This was it. Unless some crazed villager or vagrant from the forest with a hatred for literary and artistic-minded Brits had sneaked in and done these two killings, it was one of them, seated round this very table. None of these elegantly turned-out people present looked guilty of two murders, but then again, looked at in a different way, they all did. A self-consciousness that nobody was talking about had undeniably crept in, Francis thought. They were all looking at each other surreptitiously and thinking: could it be him, could it be her? And if so, why?

'We find ourselves in a very strange situation,' Gerry said, cutting into the nervous mutterings around the table. 'One that is unprecedented in my experience—'

'I'm sure in all of our experience,' Zoe interrupted; her hands, Francis noticed, were fidgeting madly.

'But here we are,' Gerry continued. 'In a few minutes the police will be back again, and they will have their procedures. But we, somehow, are going to have to sit this out.' He looked slowly round the group. 'Until this morning, there was a part of me that didn't quite believe what the police were telling me, that poor Poppy had been murdered. Part of me was thinking that we were suddenly going to be told that Poppy had indeed just been the victim of a horrid accident and you were all free to go, and Stephanie and I were free to reclaim our lovely home as the safe space it has always been, in all the years we've lived here. But now—'

Even as he spoke, there was a familiar screeching of brakes and the cops were upon them: an owl car containing Moretti, Ceccarelli, Sabatini and Ricci. Hardly had they crunched to a halt on the gravel than an unmarked van sped in behind them. This disgorged the team of three forensics, the Polizia Scientifica, who emerged one by one in their white spaceman suits.

Gerry abandoned his little speech to go and greet the police and the *procuratore.* Not one of the officers looked in to acknowledge the guests gathered in the side room, they all headed straight upstairs with Gerry to view the corpse. Stephanie followed, murmuring an apology as she went. The green Fiat came racing down the slope.

'The *necroscopo,*' said Liam, who was standing by the window. 'Running a little late, I'd say.' It was the same doctor as before, with the same ginger-haired assistant and the same neat black case. They slammed their tinny car doors in virtual unison, marched over the gravel and through the front door. Two minutes later, as if not to be outdone, an *ambulanza* arrived – MISERICORDIA PERUGIA – with two new emergency personnel, albeit in the same lurid orange outfits.

'Here we all are,' said Liam. 'Two down, eleven to go.' He was counting round the room on his fingers as he spoke. 'Thirteen if you count Gerry and Stephanie. Unlucky thirteen.'

'For goodness' sake, Liam!' said Zoe. 'You take things too far sometimes.'

'I was just stating a fact.'

'Fifteen if you count Fabio and Benedetta,' said Mel.

'More if you include the rest of the cooks and waitresses,' said Belle.

'I hardly think any of those women in the kitchen is responsible,' said Diana. 'Or nice handsome Fabio, for that matter.'

'Is he nice?' said Mel. 'He always looks a bit spooky to me. Hangdog, if you know what I mean. Never says anything to anyone.'

'Why should he?' Diana replied. 'He does his job, is perfectly polite if you speak to him properly. I certainly don't find him "spooky". Honestly. Anyway, he's off for the weekend.

'But he lives in the village,' said Belle.

'I'm not sure this is very constructive talk,' said Duncan, after a moment.

There was silence; they all respected the widowed ambassador.

'What will happen to her?' said Belle eventually.

'Sasha?' said Roz.

'Yes.'

'Francis?' Roz asked, looking in his direction.

'I imagine her next of kin will be informed. Perhaps, like Fiona did for Poppy, they will fly out here to come and take her home. Or at least to sort out the arrangements to bury her here.'

'May I ask,' said Diana, 'what's happened to poor Poppy? Did they ever explain why they needed an autopsy?'

Francis looked over at Duncan and Fiona. This wasn't his call.

'They did,' said Fiona.

'And?' Diana persisted.

Fiona looked round at her father, who shrugged; they might as well know now, his silent features seemed to say.

'They reckon she was poisoned,' Fiona said, which brought a series of theatrical gasps from around the table.

'Christ!' cried Zoe.

'Poisoned,' asked Diana, quite matter-of-factly. 'What with?'

'Cyanide,' said Fiona.

'That doesn't exactly grow on trees,' said Zoe.

'Or in the woods either,' added Liam.

Having enjoyed his black joke, was the Irishman, Francis wondered, now about to point out the starkly obvious: that it was almost certainly someone around this very table who had sourced and brought with them this innocent-looking white powder, which can be fatal in amounts as tiny as five per cent of a teaspoonful and causes death within a few minutes?

But at that moment the shocked silence was broken by the whoop of a siren and the sound of a departing vehicle.

Liam was immediately up by the window. 'Misericordia Perugia,' he said. 'Off already. And without a body.'

Before anyone could comment on the significance of this there was a knock on the kitchen door.

'Come in,' Fiona called.

The young policeman appeared round the corner. He nodded in Francis's direction.

'Mr Meadowes. Commissario Moretti would like for you to come upstairs, sir, if you please.'

Francis was relieved to go. The atmosphere in the side room was one of a weird awkwardness. Somebody was putting on a fine show of normality. Nobody was above suspicion. He followed the young policeman out and into the gloomy hallway where three white-suited Polizia Scientifica sat waiting on chairs. Then on up the familiar, well-worn stone stairs. In the room called Botticelli, sunlight now streamed through the windows on to the bed where Sasha still lay, looking almost as if she had passed out after one of her wilder cartwheels. The *necroscopo* was right beside her, his hand stretched out to the pulse at her wrist; his pretty assistant was next to him; on the left, the three policemen stood awkwardly beside the *procuratore*. Gerry and Stephanie were over by the window.

'Thank you for joining us, Mr Meadowes,' said Moretti.

'Not a problem.'

'This is a very sad circumstance.'

'It certainly is.'

'So young . . . and beautiful . . . and full of life.'

'She was.'

'No,' said the doctor, laying Sasha's golden-brown arm back down on the white sheets of the bed. '*Niente.*' He looked over at Francis. '*Non mi aspettavo nulla di diverso.*'

'Not that he expected anything different,' Moretti translated. 'Is it fair to say,' she went on, looking over at Francis, 'that we are now definitely looking at a murderer from among one of the guests downstairs in the kitchen?'

Stephanie was looking at Francis too, as if he might suddenly be able to put things right, come up with some theory that ruled out her beloved course members. But there wasn't one.

'Who knows?' he replied. 'But it doesn't look like an outside job, does it?' Moretti turned to the *procuratore*, glossing this in Italian. Then she went on: 'We really don't want a situation where this murderer, whoever they are, is bumping off any more of your residential course members, do we?'

'Certainly not,' said Gerry.

'Now we must leave Dottore Rosati to his examination,' Moretti said. 'And after that, the Scientifica are waiting. Meanwhile, I'm afraid we must talk to the guests again. Not for long, since we spoke to them in detail yesterday, but just to see if they have any updated information. Francis, would you be able to join us in the library? Perhaps your presence there will make them happier to open up.'

So Francis, for the first time in his life, found himself sitting in on a police interview. Besides Commissario Moretti and Prosecutor Sabatini, there was dashing Inspector Lorenzo Ricci and nearly handsome Vice Questore Ceccarelli. It was almost odd, the way Moretti was so keen to elicit Francis's help. In the two previous investigations he'd been involved with his problem had been the opposite. Now, as he sat watching his housemates troop in one by one and sit down in the comfortable brown leather armchair that Moretti had placed between her and the other officers, he wondered whether the *commissario* had misjudged the situation, whether his presence was inhibiting. After all, Francis was one of the gang.

Moretti's technique was nothing if not direct.

'So,' she asked Diana, when the few questions about what she'd been doing this morning, whether she'd heard the scream, how she had reacted, were over. 'Do you have any idea who might be responsible for this double murder?'

Diana looked across at Francis.

'That's what you think it is, do you?' she said. 'Double murder.'

'Yes, Signora.'

Diana nodded. 'I do have a couple of suspicions, but I'm not sure . . .'

'You're not sure?' Moretti echoed.

'Whether I should say.' She nodded at Francis. 'Nothing personal, but you are staying here with us, Francis.' She turned

back to Moretti. 'When you've gone back to Perugia we do all
have to live together. I have no idea what people repeat in private,
especially when they've had a few drinks.'

'Diana,' said Francis. 'Honestly, I am the soul of discretion.'

'*La discrezione in persona*,' Francis heard Moretti murmur to
the others. A look of concern passed over the features of the young
ispettore – Ricci.

'So you say,' the Scotswoman replied.

'I can leave, if you prefer,' Francis said.

Diana regarded him thoughtfully. 'I'll trust you,' she said. 'But
don't let me down.' She looked over at the others. 'Now I do have
the very greatest of personal respect for Sir Duncan,' she said.
'He's such a considerate and gentle man, just the sort of man I'd
go for myself, if I were a bit younger. But one has to say, he does
love his garden.'

'His garden at, er . . . Framley Place?' said Moretti, looking
down at her notes.

'Framley Grange, yes. He gave us a lecture about it on Monday.
It's quite beautiful. And you have to think, if he wasn't getting on
too well with Poppy, which he wasn't—'

'Wasn't he?' asked Moretti.

'I thought not. Didn't you, Francis?'

Had Fiona been speaking to her, he wondered, or had she noticed
something he hadn't? 'I thought they were fine,' he replied, 'from
what I saw.'

'I disagree,' Diana said firmly. 'So imagine he was thinking
that he didn't want to stay with Poppy, that he wanted to go for
some sort of separation or maybe even divorce, then he would
also have been thinking that he would lose all that, the house and
the garden, because as we know it belongs to her. And I speak as
one who once owned a beautiful house and garden myself, which
I had to very reluctantly say goodbye to when my divorce came
through.'

Here we go again, thought Francis. Summon the violins. Though
as he'd understood it, Diana had actioned the divorce, not her ex.

'So why d'you think Sir Duncan wanted to leave her in any
case?' Moretti asked.

'The question I was always asking, when I saw them together,'
said Diana, 'was why he'd ever wanted to be with her in the first

place. I mean, she was no great looker, she was tiresomely snobbish, and quite stupid to boot. I just imagined it must be the Demon S.'

'The Demon S?' asked Moretti; the other officers looked similarly puzzled.

'Sex,' said Diana, baldly. 'One can only think she must have been extremely adventurous in the bedroom to get him to put up with the rest of the package.'

Ricci looked over at Ceccarelli and they both stifled a laugh.

'I'm not trying to be funny,' said Diana.

The detectives composed themselves.

'It's often the case, in my experience, that this is the explanation for the unlikeliest couples. So,' she went on, 'if that side of things had waned, and he had suddenly seen what he was left with, like Titania in *Midsummer Night's Dream*, he had a problem.'

'Like Titania,' Ceccarelli queried. 'In midsummer . . . *mi dispiace, non capisco.*'

'In *Midsummer Night's Dream*,' said Diana. 'It's a play. By Shakespeare. Our great English playwright. The Queen of the Fairies, Titania, takes a love potion and falls in love with a donkey, and then it wears off and she sees what she is embracing – a donkey.'

'Ah yes,' said Moretti, 'I remember this.'

Ceccarelli nodded thoughtfully. He clearly didn't.

'Especially,' Diana went on, determinedly, 'if there's another woman involved.'

'You think there's . . . another woman?' Marta asked. 'Seriously?'

'You never know, do you,' said Diana. 'But there generally is. Men are very lazy, in my experience. They often say that they just want to be free, or they're sick of the *status quo* or whatever. But almost always they've lined something else up. Women are different.'

'Are they?' asked Francis, glancing discreetly at the Italian men present; there was no visible protest on their faces at this outrageous generalization; perhaps they agreed with her.

'I'm afraid so,' Diana continued. 'I'm not saying, necessarily, that there was, or is' – she raised her eyebrows – 'a mistress, just that it's a possibility. I also have my suspicions about his daughter. Bear in mind she's his daughter, not hers. She might never have liked her stepmother. And if Poppy's gone and Duncan gets the house, then unless there's some special arrangement in place, it will eventually pass to her. So maybe she's involved. Maybe she's a friend of the mistress. Maybe she even introduced the mistress to her father.'

She sat back with a 'put all that in your pipe and smoke it' look on her face.

'This is all very interesting,' Moretti said. 'But it's speculation, no? You didn't like Poppy, and you do like her husband. But you have no evidence for any of this.'

'I don't need evidence,' Diana replied. 'I can see it in his face. That he's relieved. Oh yes, he looks sad, and concerned, of course he has to play that part. But underneath you can see, he's delighted – excited even – that she's gone.'

Moretti made a note and looked round at her colleagues.

Diana's other possible suspect was Liam. 'I mean who is he, what's he doing here, that's what I'd like to know. He's a very strange man, by anyone's standards. He says he likes drugs. But there are no drugs here, unless he's taking them privately. He says he's a poet, but this is a prose writing course, not a poetry course, it never has been. He's a relatively young man – why does he want to spend a week with a lot of much older people? He lives in Londonderry, in Northern Ireland – that's quite a long way away. Don't they have creative writing courses there? You would imagine, being Irish, that the place was stuffed with them. So either he hasn't done his research properly or he's got some other agenda.

'Poppy's father was a general,' she went on. 'Who served in Northern Ireland. During the Troubles, in the 1970s, you know what they were?'

'Your colonial war with the Irish,' said Moretti.

'It was never colonial,' Diana replied tersely, 'as the inhabitants of Northern Ireland, the majority of them, want to be part of our United Kingdom. Still do, to this day. This is what foreigners never understand. But you're right, it was a war, though we always tried to gloss over that fact. Now, say Poppy's beloved papa was in charge of some operation that had resulted in the death of one of Liam's family, or colleagues' – she raised a suggestive eyebrow – 'Liam might well be acting in revenge. Years later. You know, or perhaps you don't, what long memories the Irish have. A few years is nothing to them. You sit with them in some bar and they'll tell you about stuff that happened in the seventeenth century, as if it were yesterday. So . . .'

She smiled, tightly, and looked meaningfully at them.

'I thought it was we Italians who went in for vendetta,' Ceccarelli said.

'Oh no, the Irish are much worse, believe me. I was married to one.'

'You think Liam might have killed her?' Moretti asked.

'You asked me for my suspicions,' Diana replied. 'I'm giving them to you.'

'And what about Sasha?'

'She obviously saw something. Or knew something. She was a bright little piece, Francis knows that. The other evening she did a character analysis of a couple of us, didn't she, Francis?'

'She did.'

'Myself and Liam. It was surprisingly clever. Where she got her information from I don't know, but underneath that silly show-off manner of hers, she was a sharp cookie. Maybe she somehow revealed to Liam that she knew what he'd been up to.' Diana nodded significantly. 'So yes, I think she found something out. Something compromising. So she had to go.'

'That's what you really think?'

'It's a possibility, isn't it? She was far too young to have enemies in the normal way of things.'

Luckily, Liam came after Diana in the running order. He had 'of course' heard the scream this morning, why wouldn't he have? It had shattered the neighbourhood. And he'd run straight out of his room and along to Sasha's. Was the room called Botticelli? Francis had seen him there. He had been as shocked as the rest of them.

'Why did you choose this course out here?' Moretti asked him.

'This course? Out here?' Liam looked taken aback for a moment, but only a moment. 'Have you ever been to Derry? Where I come from. In Ireland.'

'No,' Marta replied.

'It's a beautiful spot. Steeped in history, as they say. I love living there. You're right on the border, so you can get out to

Donegal within the hour, up to Malin Head for a bit of fishing should you wish. But it rains a fair amount. Particularly in July and August. So I fancied a bit of sunshine before I went back to work. And I love Italy. Always have done, ever since I came out to Rome after uni in my early twenties.'

'And what were you doing in Rome?' Moretti asked.

'Teaching English as a foreign language. I went on from there to Perugia for a while.'

'To Perugia.' Moretti nodded. 'This is our *questura*, headquarters, Ceccarelli's home town. How long were you there?'

'For a year or so. Hung around the Università per Stranieri. I loved it there.'

Ceccarelli nodded approvingly.

'So you have a little Italian?' Marta went on.

'*Un poco.*' He smiled. 'I can get by. *So solo mettermi a sedere e ordinare da mangiare.*'

This brought a smile to the Italians. 'He can order a meal,' Moretti explained to Francis.

'*E cosa piú importante, ordinare da bere.*'

She laughed, in the way that foreigners do at quaint English humorists. 'And, more importantly, a beer,' she glossed to Francis. 'OK, so we will continue the interview in Italian. *È sicuro di volerlo fare?Non vuole che Francis capisca?*'

'*Come preferisce lei.*'

'OK. I think for the benefit of Mr Meadowes, we'll stick with English. So what are you doing now, Mr O'Donoghue, for work?'

'I teach. Like Francis here. Only to a younger crowd.'

'And what are you teaching?'

'Creative writing and Irish studies. At Ulster University. Magee campus. We have quite a reputation for our little course.'

'Creative writing. So why, if I may ask, are you out here, on a creative writing course, if you already teach creative writing?'

'A good question,' said Liam. 'I'll be honest with you. I'm sorry, Francis, I should have levelled with you before. I'm doing a little survey. Of other creative writing courses. Seeing what other people do, and how they do it.'

'With the idea of using some of the techniques you discover yourself,' Moretti asked. 'Stealing ideas, even?'

It had been on the tip of Francis's tongue to put the same

question, but he had decided that unless he badly wanted an answer to something that came up, he was going to let Moretti conduct the interview. She had invited him to sit in on a police enquiry in progress, which was, to a crime writer like him, acutely interesting. He had read police interviews in books; he had watched them, endlessly, on TV ('For the benefit of the tape, I am showing the suspect Exhibit 34b, a bloodstained handkerchief', etc.), but he had never been privy to the real thing, and certainly not to the real Italian thing. It was a luxury to be given this opportunity and he wasn't going to screw it up.

'Something like that,' Liam replied. 'Though I wouldn't say stealing ideas. It's more like a comparative study. Seeing how other teachers tackle the same problems. Show not tell, ding-dong dialogue, that sort of thing. Francis here knows what I'm talking about.'

'And are you impressed by his teaching skills?' asked Moretti.

'I am,' Liam replied.

There was a pause, while the Irishman looked round at them in anticipation. *Do you really believe me?* his eyes seemed to say.

'OK, thank you,' said Moretti. 'Do you have any further questions, Francis?'

'No,' Francis replied. There was part of him that would have liked to quiz Liam about Northern Ireland, how much he'd been involved, whether he'd ever directly crossed swords with the British Army, exactly what he'd known about the activities of Poppy's papa – but it wasn't the right time to do that now.

'Do we believe him?' asked Moretti, when Liam had gone. The four Italians had a consultation in their own language, which Francis could make neither head nor tail of, though he recognized a few words. Then she turned to him. 'Francis? What do you make of this untidy Irishman? Is he really out here to study creative writing courses? Is it at all likely he was acting in revenge for some long-ago action of Poppy's father, as Diana seems to think?'

Francis shrugged. 'One thing I've learned is that anything's possible. But Liam's not top of my list of suspects. You have to think: if he is the murderer, a) how did he know that Poppy was going to be out here on this course, at this time? And b) even if his surveillance of her movements was so good that he did know all about her holiday arrangements, why did he want to do it here in any case?'

'Exactly what we were saying,' said Marta, nodding at her colleagues. 'Why here? Why not at home in the UK?'

'For a murderer who had planned very carefully, there might be advantages of taking your victim out of their home environment. I mean, it's probably easier to get to them when they're away from their own space and their usual routines. There's also less danger of any casual witnesses. Locals who know Poppy, for example, witnessing something they're not supposed to witness. But to counter that, to decide to murder someone on a residential course like this, which you're also part of, would require a steady nerve, I'd say. Because there's no running away afterwards, is there? You've got to stay and sit it out.'

'These are good points,' Marta said. She looked at her colleagues.

From the sour expression on Lorenzo Ricci's face, it was clear he could do with some persuading.

'The only thing I can think,' Francis went on, notwithstanding, 'is that whoever killed Poppy assumed that they would get away with it. The whole sauna thing. They didn't think the *necroscopo* was going to be suspicious and demand an autopsy.'

'Even if they were using a traceable poison like cyanide?' said Moretti.

'Cyanide is interesting,' said Francis. He knew quite a bit about it, having used the poison for one of the murders in his third George Braithwaite mystery, *All Souls Day*. Because of the rapidity of its action it was the preferred suicide agent of the Third Reich; also, famously, the poison of choice, diluted in Kool-Aid, for the mass suicide of the nine hundred plus members of the Jonestown community in Guyana in 1978, and the substance that the Bosnian Croatian general, Slobodan Praljak, drank publicly at the International Criminal Tribunal in November 2017 when his guilty verdict was returned.

'It has a very short half-life,' he explained now, 'so if blood samples aren't obtained quickly, it becomes untraceable. If you left a body for even a day or two a toxicology test wouldn't find an elevated concentration of the poison in the blood.'

Moretti turned to the egg-bald prosecutor. 'Leonardo?'

The *procuratore* shrugged and said something in Italian which sounded very much like, 'How would I know, I'm only the freaking prosecutor.' At any rate it ended with the word *'procuratore'* and made the others laugh.

'I think you're probably the expert here, Francis,' Moretti said, then something else in Italian. *You see, I told you it would be a good idea to have him along*, was Francis's best guess, as it brought nods from the older two and a studiedly blank expression from Ricci.

'The other relevant point,' Francis went on, 'perhaps a little controversial, is that if our murderer was a bit of a gambler, which maybe he – or she – was, then maybe they thought they were more likely to get away with murder out here than back at home. I'm not criticizing your system of justice, but you don't have coroners in Italy, do you? As I understand it there's no official death investigation agency.'

'This is true,' said Moretti. 'But we have the prosecutor.' She nodded towards Sabatini. 'And the USL, the local public health structure, to which the *necroscopo* is obliged to make report.'

'But the decision on whether to have an autopsy,' Francis continued, 'remains with the *necroscopo*. And as I understand it from the little look I had online, the *necroscopo* doesn't have to recommend an autopsy in the case of suspicious or violent death. As they do at home. In some of these cases there is no autopsy.'

Moretti looked over at Sabatini, and a rapid Italian interchange ensued. 'Usually,' Sabatini said, frowning, 'it is the police, or myself, who will make that decision. About autopsy. Though yes, in this case, it was the *necroscopo* who first requested this. Maybe a different doctor would have a different opinion. But this one, he had a fixed opinion, based on some things he found at the death scene . . .'

'I see,' said Francis. 'And once he, the *necroscopo*, has asked for a post-mortem, are you bound to go along with it?'

'Bound?' asked Sabatini, puzzled.

'Obliged,' said Marta. *'In tal caso, sei obbligato a ordinare l'autopsia?'*

Sabatini turned back towards Francis. 'We arrive. We listen to him. He tells us what he thinks. We decide.'

'I see,' said Francis. 'So he was convincing . . . about . . . whatever it was he saw – or found – at the death scene.'

Sabatini turned again to Moretti, who translated again. *Convincente.*

'Yes,' said Sabatini. 'He was . . . *convincente.*'

'What did he see that so convinced him?'

Sabatini looked over at Moretti, who nodded. 'There was a widening of the eyes, the central part, what do you say, Marta?'

'The pupil.'

'The pupil, yes.' He smiled. 'Like in a school.'

Francis smiled back. 'Exactly. Same word, different meaning.'

'Also a particular smell,' Sabatini went on, 'associated with cyanide. The smell of *mandorle.*'

'Almond nuts,' said Moretti.

Francis nodded.

'Also, some *ipostasi, lividezza . . .*' He looked over at Marta.

'The bright colour of the skin, after death,' she explained.

'Lividity,' said Francis. That was another classic symptom of cyanide poisoning.

'Li-vi-di-ty,' Sabatini repeated, with a smile. 'The same word. Almost.'

'Though if she'd been in the sauna for some time,' said Ceccarelli, 'she would be a bright colour . . . *in ogni caso.*'

There was a short silence, broken by Moretti. 'So, Francis. All that apart, you're serious in thinking that our murderer might think he would have a better chance to get away with a murder here than back at home?'

'If Poppy's death was planned,' he replied, 'as it surely was, then being out here, in this place, on this course, was part of the plan. So I would be interested in trying to understand why that was.'

He looked round at the prosecutor and the policemen. Sabatini and Moretti were nodding; Ricci was looking away, a scowl on his face, as if trying not to listen. Or was he offended by Francis's aspersions on Italian justice? This was, Francis was aware, a sensitive area with the Perugian police, after the trial, conviction, acquittal, retrial and eventual re-acquittal of Amanda Knox and Raffaele Sollecito for the murder in that city of fellow student Meredith Kercher, an eight-year saga which had seen both the police and the legal system come under sustained criticism from foreign, and particularly US, media.

'Also,' Francis went on, 'you have to think that this does rather cut down on the suspects. Because whoever got Poppy out here to kill her had to be in a position to suggest that she came, if you follow me. On this course, to this villa. I mean, take Diana, for example, who has been coming here for over twenty years. Say she had Poppy in her sights, and had planned to murder her here, for whatever reason. Even if she'd known her before, in some other part of her life, which is perfectly possible, how would she have persuaded her to come out here now to do this particular course?'

Marta was nodding. Now she spoke in rapid-fire Italian again to Sabatini and her fellow detectives. There was another little confab, the gist of which Francis struggled to follow, even when he could hear the names of the guests in the mix.

'These are two very good points, Francis,' said Moretti. 'Particularly this second one. So if we go through our suspects thinking about this, who are we left with? Sir Duncan, Poppy's husband. Fiona, his daughter. And that's about it.'

'*La famiglia. Come sempre*,' said Sabatini.

TEN

Seated in the central armchair, surrounded by inquisitive Italian investigators, Sir Duncan seemed sad, but also resigned and poised. Francis couldn't help but ask himself how this elegant, thoughtful man could have ever got involved with a nightmare like Poppy. Perhaps Diana was right, and it was all down to 'the Demon S' (though the thought of Poppy cavorting in that mode, let alone with the corpulent Sir Duncan, made Francis feel slightly ill).

'Thank you for talking to us,' said Moretti. 'Especially at this time of grief for you and your daughter.'

'Of course,' Duncan replied, 'you must do your interviews with everyone. I can't be treated any differently.'

'Thank you for your understanding,' said Moretti. She was a bit over the top, Francis thought, but then again she had the experience – perhaps the kid glove approach was the best way to treat grieving relatives who were still in the frame.

'So how is your investigation going?' asked Duncan.

Marta smiled back. 'Slowly. We are still trying to establish some motive. As to why anyone here would want to . . . would want to . . .'

'Murder my wife,' Duncan concluded, putting the *commissario* out of her misery.

'Exactly.'

'And you feel certain that it is someone here – at the villa – rather than from outside?'

'Yes,' said Marta. 'We do.'

Duncan nodded thoughtfully. 'I just thought you would want to keep all options open at this stage.'

'An outsider seems like an unlikely option,' Marta continued. 'This villa is so remote. There are perhaps a hundred people living in the nearby village, Pianetto. They are mostly small families. Many of them are old.'

'A couple of the cooks live in the village, I understand,' Duncan replied.

'Again, you come up against motive. What would be the reason for one of these rural women to murder a foreign visitor? Who they might be cooking meals for, but otherwise have no relationship with at all. So may I ask, on a different matter,' Marta went on, 'did you tell your friends at home that you were coming out here for this week?'

Duncan looked puzzled at this question.

'Of course,' he replied. 'Those that we saw.'

'And anyone else? Do you perhaps have people working for you – at home?'

'We have a cleaning woman who comes in three times a week and a gardener who's in most days. Why is this relevant?'

'Because we need to know who knew you were coming on this course, to this place, Villa Giulia.'

'Quite a few people, I imagine. Poppy was very active in the village, and also, being the person she is – was – in the local town, not to mention her activities further afield. She might have told any one of those what we were planning. In fact, knowing her, I'd make that "might" a "would".'

The policewoman nodded. 'So this village is called . . .?'

'Framley.'

'And is how large?'

'I don't know exactly. Perhaps five, six hundred souls.'

'Souls?'

'People,' Francis chipped in.

Moretti nodded. 'You say she was active?' she went on. 'In what way was she active?'

Duncan smiled round at Francis. 'Francis here would know what I'm talking about. I don't know how it works out here, but in an English village like ours, people do stuff. There's a church, which Poppy was very much part of—'

'So she was religious?'

'Not madly religious. Just involved. Again, it's a rather English thing. You can be involved in church activities without being religious.'

'This is the Church of England?' Sabatini asked, and was there just a touch of contempt in his question?

'Yes. There's also the WI, the Women's Institute—'

'This is another church?' Ricci chipped in.

Duncan laughed, and looked over at Francis to share the joke. Marta was smiling, but not going to embarrass her colleague. 'No,' he replied, 'it's not a church, although perhaps it is in a way. It's a club, for women.'

'In the village?' Ricci asked.

'And elsewhere. With the greatest respect, I think we're in danger of getting bogged down in cross-cultural confusion here. This organization I'm talking about, the Women's Institute, known as the WI, is quite famous at home. It's like a club for women across the UK – perhaps I should say some women, middle-aged maybe, with time to spare. Poppy was involved with them. She was involved, as I say, with the church. She was involved with the local modern dance club. She was involved with amateur theatricals in our local town. And then she was also active in other groups and societies elsewhere, some of which meant meetings in London. So to answer your question, she might have told anyone from any of those groups that she was planning to come out to Umbria to do a creative writing course.'

Marta nodded. 'I understand. She was a busy lady who talked to many people.'

Duncan nodded. 'Yes. It was no big secret that we were coming out here.'

Francis was intrigued, watching this exchange, and the sequence of questions that followed, to see how unflappable Duncan was. Not that Moretti was aggressive, but she was sticking to the point that a murder on a residential course in a foreign country did rather cast suspicion on the people the victim knew best. Duncan conceded this, conceded also that this put him and Fiona more in the frame than the others, yet acted as if nothing could in fact be less likely than that he, or his daughter, would want to murder his wife.

'When did you book it?' Francis chipped in. 'The course?'

'Over a year ago. We were originally going to come last year, but then Poppy couldn't do it. She had her Grade One saxophone exam so we had to pull out.'

'*Sassofono?*' said Moretti, miming playing the instrument. 'Your wife was learning the *sassofono*? In her sixties?'

Duncan smiled. 'Seventies. She was seventy-one. She never stopped,' he said. 'Also, she has this theory – had this theory – that learning new things was a defence against dementia. "I'm keeping the grey cells lively," she used to say.'

There was silence. For a few moments they were left with the memory of Poppy and the slow tick of the clock on the mantelpiece. From the other room came the sound of Liam laughing. Infectiously, as he did.

'So what made you want to come here?' Francis asked. 'Was it your idea or Poppy's?'

He smiled. 'Poppy's. She was always on at me to write my memoirs. My reply was usually that though I had enjoyed writing dispatches, and speeches and so on, as you do as a diplomat,' he looked round at the police, 'which is what I was, that that was it. I wouldn't know how to tackle the larger challenge of a book. Quite apart from not wanting to expose myself personally in that way, as you have to do, I think, to be any good. So, Poppy being what she is – was – booked us both on to this course.'

'Did she find it on the Internet? Like Sasha. Or what?'

'She heard about it from Zoe.'

'From Zoe?' Francis sat forward, as did the others.

'Yes, they were on a similar course together in London. At the *Guardian*. A life-writing masterclass or some such thing. Poppy loved doing courses. She met Zoe there and then in due course Zoe recommended this. It ticked all Poppy's boxes. Learning stuff, but in nice surroundings, with agreeable people, and good food.'

'I see,' said Marta. 'So Zoe knew you were coming.'

'Of course. Didn't she say?'

'She claimed not to have met you before.'

'That's true. I did only meet her here. But she'd met Poppy, as I say. Just for a weekend, on this course.'

Significant glances were exchanged. 'OK,' Marta went on, 'before we finish, you have told us that you love this beautiful house you share – shared, I'm so sorry – with your wife?'

'I have – and I do.'

There was a short silence as Moretti sat back. It was almost as if she were deciding how to proceed. Then: 'Let me make up a little story,' she said. 'A man like yourself, who has been successful in his career, has reached retirement and now has no financial worries, is nonetheless tired of his wife. The couple argue, they misunderstand each other, there is no passion left. Perhaps, even, this man has met another woman, who makes him happy. She makes him laugh, she is sexy, she returns him to his younger self. Usually, this kind of situation ends in divorce. But in this case the wife owns a beautiful house. Which the man loves. If he divorces her he gets his new woman, but not the house. And so he starts to think of other possibilities. Initially, such possibilities seem absurd, stupid. But then, talking it all over with his lover, they come up with an idea that could work. On a holiday abroad, the now hated wife could be safely removed. Once she is dead and buried, ideally in the foreign country, away from the eyes of friends, neighbours and the English coroner, the house passes to the man. Now he has everything he wants.'

Duncan's expression as Marta spoke was beyond impassive; it was impossible to read at all. Even his blue-grey eyes, with the yellow-grey *arcus senilis* ring around the cornea, offered only mild, slightly bored disapproval. Perhaps this was the diplomatic training, that however deeply you felt, your face never gave you away. When she'd finished, he looked round at this posse of foreign police and sighed.

'It's a perfectly believable story,' he said. 'I particularly like the description of this man rejuvenated by this new woman, which is something I understand all too well. Some years ago, I was in such a marriage myself. One which had, sadly, degenerated into rancour. To say the passion was gone was to put it mildly. For several years my wife and I slept in separate rooms. We went through the motions publicly, we had to, for my job, but privately our only physical engagement was when we tried to strangle one another. And then I met a woman who freed me from all that. Running against the cliché, she wasn't the famous "younger model". She was a bit older than myself and my first wife. But though she was highly extrovert, no doubting that, she was also very kind and loving. At least to me, and that's what mattered. I think you know who that was.'

'Poppy,' said Marta, stating the obvious. Diana's intuitions had been spot on, Francis thought.

'Poppy,' Duncan repeated. He looked over at Francis. 'I'm not insensitive. I know all too well she wasn't to everyone's tastes. She could be a bit full-on at times. But underneath all that she was a very sweet person. Perhaps sweeter than some other women who might tick all the conventional boxes in terms of how they present themselves.

'Your little story was interesting,' he went on, looking directly at Marta, 'because if one had believed it, one might almost have thought it could provide a motive for murder. Murder is not just a horrible, intensely selfish crime, but a difficult one to pull off successfully, so not often indulged in cold blood in the real world. Most murders are hot-blooded, stupid mistakes. A step too far in a violent relationship, a fight that gets out of hand. If you were trying to make such a scenario fit the case of my wife's death, you would be doing me the compliment of saying that I was a sophisticated and level-headed operator. Cool as a homicidal cucumber. The only problem being that this supposition doesn't fit the facts. Even though I was married to Poppy, Framley Grange doesn't pass to me after her death. Because of his desire to keep the place in the family, come what may, her father's will dictates that it passes to her sister, Araminta – Minty, as she's known.'

If Francis were the gasping type, he would have gasped. Having been the prime suspect, Duncan was now – surely – off the hook. As was his daughter, previously Prime Suspect No. 2. The inheritance motive had passed firmly to someone who wasn't even in the country, let alone the villa. Unless, of course, Duncan was bluffing.

'I see,' said Marta. 'If you will excuse us for a moment.' She turned to her colleagues and there was another rapid Italian pow-wow. Did Marta know whether Duncan spoke the language? With his own rudimentary smattering, Francis certainly felt at a disadvantage, trying to pick up the gist of this fast-flowing exchange but recognizing only a few words, most of which were names. Duncan, Fiona, Ara-*minta*. Did *ragazza* mean 'children'? Or just 'girl'?

'Thank you for telling us this,' Marta said, turning back to Duncan. 'May I ask: does this mean that you will no longer be living at Framley Grange?'

Duncan looked down and then slowly up again. 'I fear that it does.'

'Does your sister-in-law – Araminta – have family?'

'She does. Two daughters and a son. And two of them have

children of their own. It's a bit of a dynasty. I expect they will make very good use of that lovely place.'

'And when she dies?'

'It goes to her children. Poppy never having had any.'

'Is there a husband?'

'Minty's, do you mean?'

'Yes.'

'No. Not any more. He was a lot older. Passed on a few years ago. Poor fellow was in rather good shape but had a sudden stroke.'

'So may I ask: is she on her own? Or are there other men in her life?'

Duncan stalled. It looked as if he really didn't want to answer this question. 'This is very personal,' he replied. 'About someone who isn't even here to defend herself.'

'But necessary. Even if she isn't here, this sister now has a motive.'

Duncan shrugged, but seemed to accept her point. 'There are various men, I believe, but Poppy wasn't always put in the picture. Having lost her much older husband, she prefers younger ones these days.'

Like her sister, Francis thought. 'And how old is she now?' he chipped in. 'Minty?'

'There were two years between her and Poppy. So sixty-nine, now. Yes.'

Marta looked down at her notes. 'And will you be visiting Framley Grange now,' she asked, 'on a regular basis, d'you think?'

'No.'

In the silence that followed Francis realized that Marta Moretti was not just an experienced but an impressive inquisitor. This was an excellent question and she didn't press home with the obvious follow-up but waited patiently, albeit that the little white eraser at the end of the sharpened blue pencil she held in her right hand was drumming silently against the base of the thumb of her left. 'As Francis here could tell you,' Duncan continued, 'because this came out in one of our writing sessions, there wasn't a lot of love lost between Poppy and her sister.'

'They didn't like each other?' asked Sabatini.

'I'm afraid not.'

'Has this always been true?'

'Certainly as long as I've known Poppy.'

'So you are not friends with this Minty?'

'I've never met her.'

Now the gasps were real. Even Francis could feel an involuntary intake of breath.

'She didn't even come to your wedding?'

'No. Poppy didn't want her there.'

'And yet you know about her children, and her grandchildren?'

'Of course. Although they didn't speak, they kept close tabs on each other.'

Marta nodded, and spoke briefly to her colleagues. Francis guessed she was glossing the 'kept close tabs' expression.

'But you may have to meet her now?'

'I may. On the other hand, there is a great deal that lawyers can achieve.'

'*Gli avvocati possono fare molto*,' Marta translated, to nods from her colleagues.

'Perhaps she will come to the funeral,' Francis said. 'People often act in strange ways when their relatives have died.'

'Indeed,' agreed Sir Duncan, but didn't add to it. Francis liked his style. He was old school, dry, to the point. You could almost sense the tone of his diplomatic dispatches in the way he answered these questions, at what was, surely, underneath his composed surface, an emotional and difficult time.

Shortly after that, he was dismissed. Marta asked him to tell his daughter that she would be the next one they would like to interview. Not immediately, though. They would call for her in a few minutes.

When the ambassador had departed, Francis asked if he should leave too. He felt sure that hard-boiled Marta was perfectly capable of telling him when his presence was no longer required, but then again, he wanted to keep relations with her and her colleagues as cordial as possible. He couldn't imagine an English DCI inviting an amateur like him to be part of the investigation process, however helpful he was being, so he was trying not to take anything for granted.

But no, if he was happy to stay, Moretti insisted, that would be useful. There was another brisk Italian confab, which seemed to bring approval for this position, though Francis, watching their faces carefully, wasn't sure if this was a unanimous decision. Lorenzo Ricci was casting meaningful looks in his direction, though if he did have an objection to Francis's presence, it was overruled by both Sabatini and Moretti. Then the four of them veered off into a more general discussion. Francis sat patiently, trying to follow what was going on. It was interesting that Sabatini, having remained silent throughout the interview with Duncan, was now taking a dominant part in the conversation. There was something he wanted Moretti to do, though what that was was infuriatingly beyond Francis's understanding.

When they'd finished, Moretti turned back to Francis. So what did he think? she asked. About this sudden revelation of Sir Duncan's?

'Which one?'

'Both. But mainly, I think, that he doesn't get the beautiful house.'

'Or so he says.'

'You don't think it's true?'

'We only have his word for it,' Francis said. 'It will be interesting to see what his daughter says.'

'But if it isn't true, we would soon know, because he would be staying on at the house.'

'Are you going to check up on him? From out here? In six months' time? I'm not – and I live in the same country. So maybe he thinks that if he can get away with this story for now, it will put you off suspecting it's him, and then once you're investigating someone else, or have given up on the case, it will be too late.'

Commissario Moretti laughed, then spoke in Italian to her colleagues. 'That would be a crazy risk,' she said to Francis. 'Would he really think we would investigate some innocent on no evidence?'

'I'm not saying it's not true. It probably is. It's a bold claim to make and, as he well knows, a game changer. He'd hardly murder his wife so as to have to leave the house he loves, would he?'

'No.'

'Even if he hated her,' Sabatini added.

'I don't think he did,' Francis said. 'That little defence of her struck me as sincere.'

'Me too,' said Marta. 'We are going to have to look elsewhere for our culprit.' She called to the uniformed young policeman standing silent by the door. *'Giacomo, puoi chiamare la Signorina Fiona per favore?'*

Duncan must have spoken to her, Francis thought, because Fiona looked self-assured to the point of smugness. Once again Moretti was super-courteous, apologizing for having to do such an interview in this time of grief.

Fiona nodded respectfully in return, though she gave Francis a sneaky look which seemed to say, *You know the score.*

Preliminaries over, Moretti got stuck in. It was perhaps a stupid question, she said, but she had to ask it: had Fiona ever met any of the other guests on the course; did she have anything in common with any of them, however remote?

'No, I'm sorry to say, they are all strangers to me.'

'Don't be sorry, please. This only makes it easier for us.' Marta explained what Sir Duncan had told them about Framley Grange. 'It will be a little sad for you, I think, to have to leave this beautiful place.'

'It will. Though sadder for Daddy than for me. It wasn't a home for me, or even a home from home. Francis knows, and it's no secret, that I never got on that brilliantly with Poppy.'

Moretti nodded.

'You preferred your own mother?' Francis asked.

'I did. I do.' Fiona smiled broadly, as if relieved that her mother was still alive.

'So on the odd weekend away from London, you would be more likely to stay with her than with your father?'

'I stayed with both of them. Don't get me wrong, Framley was lovely in the summer. I often went there. But I didn't go there to hang out with Poppy.'

'Understood,' said Francis, looking over at Marta to hand the conversational baton back. She nodded and gave him a slightly guarded smile. Next to her, Lorenzo Ricci pursed his lips; he clearly wasn't happy with Francis's intrusion, even though, Francis thought, I'm being as helpful as I can here, just trying to remind them that Poppy was Fiona's stepmother and what that might mean.

'Thank you, Francis,' Moretti said. She turned back to Fiona. 'And yet, you were the one to fly out immediately once you'd heard of her death?'

'Of course. I'm here to support my father. He loved her, whatever we all thought.'

'Sorry to interrupt again,' said Francis, 'but when we spoke before, you pointed out that you were Duncan's only child, so—'

'We know this,' said Ricci impatiently.

'I'm sorry,' said Francis. 'But I think that perhaps explains why Fiona was so quick to come out here. It would be fair to say that there was no one else to support your father, was there?'

'No.'

'Your mother would hardly be wanting to come out here, now.'

Fiona laughed, as if at a private joke. 'As I told you, she has another partner. I'm afraid she gave up on Daddy a long time ago.'

'She's not a fan of Poppy's either?'

'To put it mildly, she hates her. Blames her for breaking up the marriage. Which she pretty much did, I have to say.'

Had Francis been alone with her he might have continued. Instead, not wanting to annoy the others more than he already clearly had, he nodded at Moretti, as if to say, *Nothing more from me.* Sabatini now took the floor, with a string of questions that didn't add much to the picture, in Francis's humble – and obviously unspoken, especially with Ricci glowering away in the background – opinion. What did Fiona do for a living? She was a solicitor, she replied. Where did she practise? In London. Was she married herself? No. Did she have a boyfriend? Yes. What was his name? Nick. Did he live in London too? Yes. How long had they been together? Five years. What did he do? He was a television producer. Did he have much money? Yes, he was quite successful and made a good living. Were they planning to get married? At this point, Fiona balked, quite understandably in Francis's opinion. Had he been the judge in a court hearing he would have ruled such a question inadmissible. Even more personal than those that had preceded it, and surely irrelevant. Where was this going? Was Sabatini still holding on to the idea that Fiona might somehow be involved in Poppy's death, when it was now obvious that she had nothing to gain whatsoever? Not Framley, nor even any money.

'You don't need to answer that question if you don't want to,' said Moretti, butting in.

'It's fine,' said Fiona, looking over at Francis. 'It's really no skin off my nose.'

'*Non è un problema per me*,' Moretti glossed.

'Nick hasn't asked me,' Fiona continued, 'and even if he had, I'm not sure I'd be that bothered. We're perfectly happy as we are.'

'So you live together?' asked Sabatini.

At this, Fiona looked at Francis, as if to say, *Do I have to answer this?* Francis was sorely tempted to interrupt but, clocking both Sabatini and Ricci's faces, decided it would be wisest not to, if he wanted to stay in the room. He shrugged, smiled and nodded discreetly.

'Not technically,' Fiona replied, with a smile. 'Nick has a flat of his own. But he spends most nights at mine.'

'Thank you,' said Sabatini with a strange finality, almost as if this answer had solved some tricky problem for him. '*Per me, va bene*,' he added to Moretti.

'Anyone else have any questions?' Moretti asked.

Now it was Ricci's turn. As she must know, he told Fiona, until her father had explained that the beautiful house, Framley Grange, would pass direct to his sister, they had had some suspicions of both Duncan and her. Now, it would be fair to say – he looked round his colleagues rather grandly – that those suspicions had 'been erased'. But did she have any suspicions herself? Coming out here to this place, meeting this collection of strangers. Was there any one of them that she thought might have been responsible for this foul deed, this double murder?

Fiona looked taken aback. 'That's hard for me to say. I've only been out here for three days. Most of that time I've been with my father, trying to sort things out. Making arrangements for Poppy's funeral. I hardly know these people.'

'Is there no one person who stands out to you?' Ricci insisted. 'As someone who would be capable of this?'

Fiona shook her head. 'Really, I'm the wrong person to ask.'

They had reached, it seemed, the end of the road with Fiona, and shortly after that she was dismissed and they broke for coffee.

Moretti led the other three into the little side room where they
lined up by the Gaggia machine and made themselves cappuccinos.
When they then sat down at the marble table to drink them, Francis
left them to it. He didn't want to impose.

He took his own coffee outside to the courtyard where, incongruously, the sun still shone. The sky was blue and it was a perfect
late September day: soft, mild and warm enough, yet not too warm.
Sitting there with his frothy cappuccino cooling between the palms
of his hands, it was hard to believe that he had landed in the
middle of another murder inquiry. Who would they interview next?
And what would be the line of questioning now? He was going
to take a back seat, he decided. Resist asking any more questions
himself. Surely the intriguing thing for him was to observe how
the police and the prosecutor worked together. If he got involved,
he was changing that dynamic. But then again, it was frustrating
when they asked the wrong questions; when they followed up on
some line of attack that was clearly going to lead them nowhere,
as Sabatini had with Fiona. Why had he been so interested in her
home circumstances? With the revelation about Framley, she was
off the hook. Even if his questions had revealed that she was penni-
less, that was still not going to help with a motive now. As it
happened, she was clearly fine. Well off enough even without her
TV producer boyfriend.

His reverie was interrupted by Marta Moretti, standing over his
deck chair with her coffee. 'Francis, may I have a word?'

'Of course.' He jumped to his feet and stood facing her.

'Thank you so much for your help in there.' This sounded
ominous.

'Not a problem. It's good of you to include me. I hope some
of my questions were helpful?'

'They were. I definitely found them useful.'

'Who do you plan to get in next?'

She smiled, her charming film star smile, totally disarming. 'We
have a little list. The thing is, I hope you don't mind, but the others
feel that it would be best if we keep it just us from now on.'

'I see.'

'Please don't take this the wrong way, Francis. It's a question
of protocol as much as anything else. Because you are going to
be staying here with everyone, and everyone is basically a suspect,

we don't want to put you in a position where you have to keep difficult secrets. Or where you're put under any pressure from the others to say what went on in this or that interview.'

Surely you would have considered this earlier, Commissario, was what he thought. But: 'Obviously I'd be totally discreet,' was what he said.

'I appreciate that. I'm personally certain that you would. And will be, about the people we've just seen, Sir Duncan and his daughter, in particular.'

'Of course. My lips are sealed.'

'*I* know that. Anyway, that's the decision Sabatini has made. I'll let you know if we need you again. Many thanks.'

She turned, quite brusquely, and went back inside. Francis was not convinced by her explanation. He found himself wondering which exactly of his interventions had caused the problem. Or perhaps it was just Ricci's all-too-obvious antipathy.

Ah well, what had he told himself? He didn't want to get involved. Let the police solve it. It was their problem, their legal system.

He returned to his deckchair and closed his eyes.

ELEVEN

The interviews continued for the rest of the morning. One by one the guests were called in, to re-emerge with their take on what they had been put through. The police had been terribly intrusive, Zoe told Francis, particularly that younger one with the 'tache. 'I really don't see how my private life is relevant to this situation. Some of the questions they were asking! About things that happened years ago.

'And they're fixated on this idea that I recommended Villa Giulia to Poppy. I did, yes, but the idea that I knew her at all well is ridiculous. We were on a course together. It was a stimulating weekend and we circulated emails at the end of it. When Stephanie asked us last year to be kind enough to tell anyone who might be interested about Villa Giulia, I sent the details round the group. I wanted to help Stephanie.' She dropped her voice to a whisper, though there was really no need, given the circumstances. 'Sod's law, of all the lovely people on that weekend, I got the one I couldn't stand. To be honest, I was feeling a bit embarrassed she'd come. She was so ghastly, wasn't she? If people had known I'd recommended her, they might have thought I liked her.'

'But you did tell us that you'd never met them before, didn't you?' Francis said.

'I didn't say "met", Francis, I said "known". There is a difference. Apart from noticing her as an embarrassing presence across the room, on one weekend in King's Cross, no, I hadn't known her.' She shrugged. 'Anyway, I thought you were going to be in there with them.'

'No. As you can see, I've left them to it.'

'Did they kick you out?'

She didn't mince her words, this one, did she? 'They did,' he replied with a smile.

'I rather thought they might have done. Fair enough. It's their investigation. Doubtless they wanted something from you and once they'd got it you were redundant. Used and abused.' She chuckled. 'As we all are.'

Zoe nodded towards her memoir, which was stacked up in his lap.

'How are you getting on?' she asked.

He had reached the point where she was in her early twenties, going to London parties, being taken out by various young men, very much part of a Jewish circle but flirting with the idea of stepping outside it, particularly with this one man, a talented composer, who was *goy*, but very attractive to her. Their love affair was well-described, and the aftermath also, when he left her abruptly for a younger woman. Now quite gripped, Francis had the mischievous thought that if the police wanted to know about Zoe's past, they could do worse than read her memoir.

'I'm enjoying it. But I'd like to finish it before I say any more.'

'Of course.' She gave him a satisfied little smile. 'But I'm glad you're enjoying. I've had quite a life, haven't I?'

'You have.'

Tony was taciturn when he eventually emerged from the interview room.

'How was it?' called Roz.

'They've certainly upped their game,' he replied. He was holding a glass of white wine, Francis noted, which he now took a hearty gulp from. It was twelve forty-five, almost lunchtime, so a drink was understandable. But it was the first time Francis had seen the counter-intelligence officer (if that's what he really was, or had been) look in any way rattled.

Lunch was served as usual – '*Il pranzo!*' called the lovely Benedetta – on the dot of one p.m., but in the library the interviews continued. Roz had been summoned in after Tony and emerged wiping her brow theatrically. 'I see what you mean,' she said to Tony. 'Hardcore. And that young one . . .'

'Ricci,' said Francis.

'Is that what he's called?' asked Tony.

'Was bordering on the offensive. *Ve haf ways of making you talk*,' she said in a German accent.

'Now you're making me nervous,' said Belle, with a laugh.

'Oh, I'm sure they'll be gentle with you,' said Roz. There was an unspoken thought here which rippled silently down the table: if one of them sitting here in the sunshine was a murderer and had locked Poppy in the sauna before strangling poor Sasha, it wasn't either of the arty pair from Yorkshire. Not that Francis himself would ever rule anybody out. What had happened at Mold-on-Wold and then subsequently aboard the *Golden Adventurer* in West Africa had taught him that the least likely people can turn out to be the culprit. But even with that experience he wasn't putting the Yorkshire ladies very high on his list of suspects.

'Belle Thompson,' came the voice of the young policeman, as if on cue.

'Wish me luck,' she said, smiling nervously as she put down her knife and fork with a clatter and headed off inside.

When he'd finished his lunch and washed it down with a short sweet espresso from the Gaggia, Francis decided to absent himself from the unravelling psychodrama. He nipped upstairs to his room, switched on his laptop, then made his way to the cast-iron bench halfway down the stairs where you could get the best Wi-Fi signal. Even here, it wasn't great, but it was enough. He did a search for Framley Grange, and within a minute or two had got Poppy and Minty's maiden name: Pugh-Smith. Uncommon in every sense – perfect. Then it was on to the *gov.uk* website to look for wills. If Poppy had had Framley for 'about twenty years', that probably put General Pugh-Smith's death in the late 1990s. He tried 1998. *No results with the name PUGH-SMITH and the year of death 1998,* the website read. There was nothing in 1997. Or 1996. 1995 required him to switch to a previous record system.

But then – bingo!

PUGH-SMITH GEORGE WILLIAM FREDERICK OF FRAMLEY GRANGE FRAMLEY SALISBURY DIED 19 JUNE 1995 PROBATE WINCHESTER 27 OCTOBER £538477 9552425977K

He paid over his ten pounds and bought himself a copy of the will. He wouldn't get to see it for ten working days, but hey ho, you never knew. At least he had checked up on the surname and had the probate figure. £538,477. A tidy enough sum, but not a fortune, even in 1995. Did that include the house, or had the general done some clever work and handed it over to his elder daughter well before his death? Thus avoiding inheritance tax, a hefty forty per cent above the threshold, which with a place that size might even have involved selling it.

Francis had some thinking to do, but as it was a fine afternoon, it was thinking he would rather do under the shade of a parasol than in the gloomy shadows of his bedroom. He picked up his swimming trunks, went and got himself a brightly coloured towel from the neat pile on the chest in the basement, then walked down the corridor past the now locked and sealed changing room and sauna, marked off with red and white police tape, and headed out into the sunshine, across the sloping lawn to the pool.

Even though he had decided not to get involved in this case, he needed to get his thoughts down on paper, otherwise he'd go quietly crazy. Not that he thought he personally was in any kind of danger. But who knew? Sasha had probably had that idea too. One thing was for sure. They might not traditionally use keys at the Villa Giulia, but he was going to lock his door tonight.

He sat up on the lounger and pulled notebook and pen out of his jeans pocket. OK, so first off:

VICTIMS:

Poppy – deeply irritating second wife of retired ambassador Sir Duncan. At 71, a few years older than him. Champion name-dropper and know-it-all. Actual clinical narcissist? In any case, always had to have done better than anyone else present. At everything. Also a fantasist. Did she really have a plane? Was she really a personal friend of Jilly Cooper/Billy Connolly/Princess Anne, etc.? Nonetheless, her book about her garden had been published. Key point: she was the owner of Framley Grange, a house so lovely that a person would kill to live there/own it. But would they really? Necroscopo thinks she was poisoned. Is it possible that was a misdiagnosis? Seemed so to start with, but not now. Though having worked out the sauna-accident scenario, why would any murderer implicate him/herself by adding a poison element? Unless they thought sauna-accident would be a cover for poison. Also, presumably, it takes ages to die in a sauna.

Sasha – delightful, talented not to say beautiful young American. From Portland, Oregon, a place where apparently it rains a lot and there's something of a hippy vibe. Found the course on the Internet and clearly knew none of the people on it before coming – why would she? Found lying blamelessly on her bed surrounded by poisonous mushrooms. That looked staged. If it was an attempt to make a murder look like something else it was a poor one. If she had been poisoned by funghi it wouldn't have been such a clean or rapid death. So . . . strangled? Poisoned with the same cyanide as Poppy? Key point: what had she seen/worked out about Poppy's death that meant a murderer had to silence her?

Francis paused for a moment and looked out across the valley. Above the distant mountains, the rays of the sun shone down in clear lines from the bank of cloud – God's fingers. He closed his eyes for a moment and lay there, flat out, listening to the silence; nothing but the wind whistling through the pampas grass that stood behind the rolled-up blue plastic pool cover at the end of the paving surround. Then he sat forward again and started a new category:

SUSPECTS:

Sir Duncan – Poppy's husband, with strong motive (Framley Grange) that turned out not to be a motive. But we only have his word for this. Then again, the general's will is available to check; the Italian police might be able to expedite speedier viewing than the ten days wait for member of the public like me? Poppy's will is not available publicly for months, until well after probate, but if general had left Framley to Minty, surely she couldn't overrule that? So if Duncan was telling the truth, then his main motive is gone, indeed reversed as he now (apparently) has to leave house he loves. Could there be another motive? Another woman? Money? Perhaps Sir D is broke and Poppy held the purse strings. For all their prestige and trappings while in office, ambassadors are not paid vast amounts. Nor was he ever in a top posting. Of all suspects he certainly had best access. Indeed, if it wasn't him, how did the murderer manage to poison P in the first place? Since she would have spent the night with D. Then again: espresso cup in sauna.

Liam – possible historical motive in that P's dad was general in Northern Ireland in 70s Troubles and L's father, by his own account, was involved with IRA. L also? But not clear why he would choose to take revenge on general's daughter 50 yrs later. Nor why here, on this course. And how would he have known she was coming here? On the other hand, stated motive that he's here to check out creative writing courses seems flimsy. Once here, though, access to victim easy, especially if he's a trained operative, like his dad.

Tony – involved in counter-terrorism previously (?). This might give him experience perhaps of killing, even if no clear/ obvious motive. But is it true? Roz scoffed when he mentioned it. Anyway, how would he have known that P was coming to VG at this time? Could he be employed by someone else? Minty even? Otherwise seems like dark horse with no partic-ular reason to be on this course. Key worry: why was he snogging Roz? Is this something new they want to keep quiet, or does this predate the week, in which case what does it mean? Is he her married man? If so, why would they both be here and keeping their affair secret? Also: what about his interest/expertise in Italian antique furniture?

Roz – has confessed to affair with married man. Initially thought that might be Duncan, but that now seems unlikely. Is Tony MM? Or has she started something new to annoy absent MM/get him to make his mind up? Perhaps she's just highly-sexed – she was certainly quite touchy-feely at the pool. Or is the whole MM thing just the fantasy of a lonely middle-aged woman?

Fiona – would have had to be working with someone else to have killed Poppy, as she wasn't in the country when murder

took place. And though she made it v. clear she has no love
lost for stepmother, that's hardly a motive for murder. Nor
does it seem she's that bothered about her dad losing Framley.
Not in line to inherit anything from P.

Minty – another possible absentee murderer, with excellent
motive. Could she be committing her crime remotely, with
help from hired killer (Tony? Liam?). Even though they don't
get on or even speak, she would likely have known P & D
were coming to the villa at this time (?).

Mindful of his previous experience, and the lesson never to rule
anyone out, he jotted down some less likely candidates:

Diana – doyenne of the holiday/oral archivist. Clearly disliked
P, but that's hardly a motive for murder. Ditto Sasha, although
she seemed to warm to her suddenly after the 'analysis'.
Intensely loyal to Steph and Gerry, their course and the
holiday. A regular, so might know all about sauna and its
possible deficiencies. But how/why would she have known
P & D were even coming at this time? Unless Zoe told her.

Zoe – also disliked P, but again, this is hardly a motive for
murder. However: why did she deny knowing P & D? Was
that really just embarrassment because P was so 'ghastly'.
Did she feel that her recommendation of VG was accidental,
so didn't count? Or was she lying to cover up the fact that,
yes, she was luring her out to murder her? But why? What's
her motive, if she really had only met her briefly on a memoir
writing course. Her writing wasn't that bad, surely. And there's
no mention of P in the memoir itself. On the other hand,
having recommended VG to P, she presumably knew P & D
were coming out at this time.

Mel and Belle – no obvious connection to P, or S – or even
antipathy. Unlikely to know that P & D were even coming.
However, they have an interior dec business in Knaresborough,
and for a short while P supposedly had one in Harrogate.
Was that another fantasy? Exaggeration? Or significant?

Angela – ditto as above. A regular. But seems as blameless
as her lovely white smile. Not strong enough to strangle Sasha
surely, unless a sedative was used first.

Stephanie and Gerry – like Duncan and Fiona, would of
course have known Poppy was coming out at this time. But
is it good business practice to murder participants of your
courses? Regulars, obv. Two concerns: 1) what the hell was
G up to the other evening, in the moonlight? It surely wasn't
my imagination that there was something odd about the way
he was behaving? 2) G would know more about sauna and
its dodgy door than anyone, except possibly . . .

Fabio – rather a strange man, despite the smile that Diana
likes. But he was in charge of maintaining the sauna, and
also switching it on first thing. Which he did, ironically, so
that Poppy could use it before breakfast. Any murderer would
have had to go into sauna after F had switched it on, unless
F had somehow failed to see the broken handle, which he
said he didn't. He definitely had the opportunity. But no
obvious motive. Unless someone – Minty? – was paying him.
Was also not working in the villa on the morning Sasha was
murdered.

Benedetta – beautiful cook with golden hands. Stephanie was
a bit off about her, which is odd, considering she efficiently
delivers such delicious nosh. Also that short round one clearly
didn't like her. Kitchen politics – or something more? But
zero obvious motive for Poppy.

Other local cooks and waitresses – ditto re. motive.

So there it all was, in black and white, as clear as the heavy slabs
of umber mud in the ploughed fields around the villa. With so few
likely suspects it was tempting to imagine there might have been
outside involvement. But that left the problem of access. Unless
you thought an outsider had paid Fabio or one of the cooks.
How likely was that? Not very. But then again, a cook or a wait-
ress could easily add cyanide to a plate of food. No, that was a

ridiculous supposition. Imagine if the chosen operative had got the wrong plate! In any case, Poppy must have taken the poison shortly before she died. The most likely idea was that someone added it to that espresso. Surely Moretti et al will have had that analysed.

'Making notes on the case?' It was Liam, infuriating as ever. He had appeared silently, and was now hovering nearby.

'No, no,' blustered Francis. 'Just catching up on some general stuff.'

'I'll believe you,' the Irishman replied. 'Though thousands wouldn't.' He laughed. 'It's one heck of a puzzle, isn't it?'

'Is one way of putting it.'

Liam had tossed a towel, some green bathing shorts and a book on to the lounger two along from Francis. Now he stooped to pick up the towel. He wrapped it round his midriff and started to wriggle, rather clumsily, out of his jeans. 'I mean, in my view,' he went on, 'there's no point looking for outsiders. With the best will in the world, how would they have got to her? Poppy, that is. And then again to Sasha, four days later. They'd have to be staying in the locality to get both. Unless they've bribed Fabio or something. And I don't really see him as the type to be a hired assassin, speaking as one who's known a few assassins in my time. Do you? Really?'

'Not really, no.'

'It's one of us. That's the horrid truth. *Smile and smile and be a villain.*' Liam tugged his trunks up surprisingly hairy legs, pulled his shirt over his head, and stood back on the paving stones. His chest matched his legs, hair thick and dark over a well-toned physique. He was in better shape than you'd expect an Irish creative writing lecturer to be.

'So how long did you last in there?' he asked. 'With the *polizei*? I saw you were with them for Sir Duncan and his daughter. And then that was it, was it? Did you upset the Dark Lady in some way? Or one of her sidekicks?'

Francis said nothing.

'Your private affair, is it? Interesting, how those who dish it out can't necessarily take it. With the greatest respect, Francis, you're hardly backwards in coming forward with questions, are you? I understand. You're being loyal to your *compagni* in the force. Perhaps they didn't kick you out. Perhaps they sent you down to lurk at the pool and pick up the wayward opinions of people not in the inquisition chamber.'

'I'm sure you understand, Liam, why I have to be discreet.'

'Don't worry. I was just trying it on. Wasn't really expecting you to spill the beans. Even if you have any beans to spill. Right, let's try this lovely water.' Liam walked over to the edge and dipped in a toe. 'Oddly, despite the hot sun, a bit cooler than yesterday. It must be the cold nights.'

He walked round to the deep end, put his arms up and executed a neat swallow dive.

'Ah, that's more like it,' he cried, surfacing. 'Just what the brain needs. You should come in, Francis. Might help those thought processes of yours.'

He swam breaststroke down towards the shallow end, then flipped over in a neat somersault and powered back up the other end in an energetic crawl. Another flip and he was back to the breaststroke, motoring gently up the pool with a happy smile playing around his lips. Was this really the face of a vengeful IRA operative who had recently committed two murders?

'Ah, this is where you boys have escaped to . . .'

It was Belle, with her friend Mel in tow, carrying towels and bags.

'Finished with you, have they?' called Liam.

'I'd say that was about it,' Mel replied with a laugh. 'They're finished with us, all right.'

'More full-on than the first time, was it?' asked Liam.

'Certainly was. Anybody would think we had something to hide.'

'Perhaps you do.'

This jovial remark was met with silence. The attempt to keep things light was clearly wearing thin. Mel gave her friend a dark look, and they walked silently down to take loungers on the far side of the pool.

'They've even called Gerry and Stephanie in,' Belle said.

'The police?' asked Liam.

'Yup, the Italiano fuzziwuzz.'

'Weren't they interviewed before?'

'I don't think so.'

'Francis?'

Francis looked up, perhaps a little too obviously, given that he'd been taking in the whole scene anyway.

'I'd assumed the police were chatting to them,' he said. 'About the situation. Informally.'

'It didn't look very informal to me. They were both *summoned* in,' said Belle.

'Suspects like the rest of us,' called Liam.

'Shall we leave this subject now,' said Mel. 'Just enjoy some quiet time by the pool in the sun. I'm sure we'll be returning to it all later.'

'I'm afraid we will,' said Liam.

Apart from the sighing of the breeze in the pampas grass, there was silence. Liam continued doing his lengths. The two Yorkshire ladies sorted themselves out, put up their parasols, worked out how to get the head rests at the right angle to read.

'That's it,' Mel said eventually. 'Comfortable at last.'

'You've got to be comfortable,' said Belle.

'You have, pet, you have.'

'Bit more of a breeze than yesterday.'

'There is, isn't there.'

They rattled off into a d'you-remember-that-time reminiscence about a day out in Scarborough that Francis could only half hear, not that he was bothered. All it told him was that they were very old friends, who pre-dated their relationships with their husbands, by the sounds of it. Belle's Michael, now that he had passed, was on a pedestal that Mel's Brian, aka The Toggle, had yet to attain, if he ever did. Still, laughed Belle, they were never going to go home now, were they, so the poor Toggle was going to have to make do. To be fair to her, Mel was worried. The Toggle's meals, cooked and frozen and labelled by time and day in the freezer, were going to run out today, Sunday, and what would the poor man do then? He couldn't boil an egg, let alone manage anything more substantial. He could warm up a fisherman's pie from Waitrose, surely, said Belle. Mel doubted it. He wouldn't even know where to find a fisherman's pie, let alone what the right oven temperature was when he got it home.

'You're maligning him.'

'I'm not. You should have seen what he did with a carton of Covent Garden soup.'

'Ah, so this is where you all are.' It was Tony, in a stylish white towelling dressing gown; another refugee from the villa. He strolled down to take a lounger on the men's side. 'Breaking news,' he said. 'Sasha's mother is joining us tomorrow.'

'Oh my God!' said Mel.

'From America?' asked Belle.

'I imagine so,' said Tony.

'Just the mother?' asked Francis.

'Apparently so,' said Tony.

'The plot thickens,' said Liam.

An hour before dinner, Francis thought he would go for a walk. Out through the village, down into the valley by the ruined farm buildings, along the track by the walnut trees, then back up the twisty road past the smallholdings at the bottom of the village and into the villa garden. The sun was low, and it was that time that cameramen call 'the golden hour', when the landscape glows in a screensaver fantasy.

But when he got to the mighty wrought-iron gates at the top of the drive, he found them locked. A young policeman in uniform was on the other side.

'Excuse me,' Francis called. 'May I get through. I'm going for a—'

But he got no further. The *agente* was shaking his head. '*Non si esce, Signore. La villa è chiusa.*'

'What are you saying?'

'No exit, *Signore*,' he said. 'The villa is closed.' Close-*ed*.

'But I'm staying here. I'm just going out for a short walk before dinner.'

The *agente* continued to shake his head. 'I am sorry, *Signore*. This is my order. To keep gate closed. Nobody can exit. *La villa è chiusa.*'

'Whose orders are these?' Francis asked. The policeman said nothing. 'Whose – orders – are these?' Francis repeated.

The policeman understood. 'This is the order of Commissario Moretti,' he said, slowly. '*Mi dispiace.* I am sorry, *Signore*.'

Francis wasn't taking no for an answer. He turned round and headed back down the drive, then, looking round to see he wasn't observed by Plod, or perhaps Ploddo, cut down across the lawn, past the tennis court, and on to the little path that led out, past the tiled potting shed, into the village at the bottom of the property. The way he had intended to come in by at the end.

He was astonished to see another policeman, pacing up and down. In for a penny, in for a pound, he said to himself. But this hard-faced character was even less helpful than his colleague. The villa was, most indisputably, *chiusa*.

As he walked unhappily back up the pathway towards the house, it occurred to Francis that he could make a dash for it across the newly ploughed field that ran below the sloping lawns. But there was a deep, muddy ditch to cross to get to it, and the rows of freshly turned clay on the other side didn't look as if they would be easy to negotiate.

He decided to leave it. He would speak to Gerry tonight, and Moretti tomorrow. Security was one thing, but preventing the residents from going for a walk was clearly ridiculous. The police had their passports; what did they think this doddery lot were going to do? Run away and hide in the Casentinesi Forest?

The wind had got up. There was now a chilly, north-easterly breeze, bringing air down from the mountains. Shutters in the old building rattled and banged. Upstairs, Francis reached out of his window to close his. It made his room dark, but it stopped the clatter.

They were a strange, uneasy house party that evening. The police posse had departed, telling none of them anything. Tales of what had been asked in this interview or that had been exchanged, one to one, here and there. But none of the gossip was general.

They all turned out for drinks at seven fifteen. But despite some false bonhomie from Mel and Belle, it was an awkward, muted affair. Sir Duncan and Fiona had also tried to go for a walk and been turned back. Everyone agreed that it was outrageous that they were penned in like this. Gerry had been briefed on this decision by Moretti. He had 'of course' protested. 'But to no avail, I'm afraid. The prosecutor insists.'

'We're basically living in the Big Brother house now,' said Liam. But no one laughed. It was too close to the truth for comfort. Granted there were no cameras, but everyone was, discreetly or not so discreetly, watching everyone else.

Duncan, Fiona, Roz, Liam, Diana, Zoe, Tony, Mel, Belle, Angela, Gerry, Stephanie. All currently on the pasta course, tonight a delicious *spaghetti alla puttanesca*: anchovies, olives, capers, chillis, in a rich garlicky sauce clearly made with fresh tomatoes. Forks rose and fell. Glasses of white or ruby red wine were sipped at or gulped. Conversation was made. One to one, one to two, spreading out into chat among three or four. There was even laughter.

'You didn't. I don't believe it . . .'

'It was a long time ago . . .'

'We had no idea then, of course . . .'

'I've never been one for that sort of thing . . .'

But none of them could escape the fact that one of those pairs of hands, now toying elegantly or not so elegantly with the long strands of crimson-coated pasta, had barely twelve hours before taken a scarf and twisted it round the soft-skinned, young neck of poor Sasha.

This thought stayed with Francis as he strolled through the grounds again before he went up to bed in Masaccio. The moon was no longer full, but still big and round, casting its eerie light down the long valley. As he turned from his favourite vantage point by the tennis court, where the shadows of the wire netting made a pattern of parallelograms on the mown grass, and walked back up towards the villa, he saw the figure of a man coming out through the stone arch from the walled garden, then hurrying down the gravel footpath to the potting shed at the bottom. It was Gerry, looking round nervously as he walked. As Francis watched, the door of the outhouse swung open. There was a flash of familiar white teeth in the moonlight, then an elegant hand, rings glinting silver, had pulled him in. He could only imagine what Benedetta's lovely features might look like, close up, in the shadows.

TWELVE

Mrs Barbara White-Moloney arrived by taxi from Bologna Airport in the middle of the afternoon. Having been informed by the police of her daughter's death, she had gone straight to the airport and got on the first flight out of Portland to Northern Italy. Now here she was, a surprisingly small, neat, skinny woman in her forties with long dark hair emerging from the back of the taxi and looking round the ochre-pink courtyard with wide eyes, like someone caught in a bad dream.

'Villa Giulia?' she asked Diana, who was sitting reading on the upright bench just outside the front door. The wind of the night had dropped, and the sun shone again from a clear blue sky.

'Yes, this is Villa Giulia. You must be . . .' Even Diana was temporarily lost for words.

'Barbara White-Moloney. Sasha's mother,' she replied.

'Of course, yes.' Diana looked at her wide-eyed, like a fan meeting a celebrity, and Francis, watching from a deck chair at the side of the courtyard, felt nervous on her behalf as he wondered how she would handle this awkward situation.

Diana shook her head slowly from side to side, then took Barbara's hands between hers. 'We're all so shocked,' she said. 'Sasha was . . . was . . . such a lovely, talented young woman.'

Barbara White-Moloney stood rooted to the gravel. 'Thank you,' she said.

Fortunately the taxi driver provided a distraction. He had unloaded a big black shell suitcase from the boot and a smaller leather carrying bag. Now he stood to one side on the gravel, waiting for payment.

'Excuse me,' Barbara said to Diana. She went to him, took out her wallet and handed over the requisite notes.

When she turned back, Diana was waiting for her. 'Come on in, I'll call for Gerry or Stephanie. Our hosts,' she explained. 'I'd expect you'd like a coffee or tea after your journey. Or perhaps something stronger.'

'Actually a cup of coffee would be great.'

'We have our own machine,' Francis heard Diana say as she led Barbara into the side room. Shortly after that Gerry scurried out through the front door to claim the shell suitcase. Were they going to put her in Botticello? Francis wondered. Or was that still a crime scene? He had been tempted to leap to his feet and get involved, but then again he wasn't the host here, and presumably the poor woman didn't want to be swamped with either sympathy or welcome at this stage.

Half an hour after she'd arrived, she was off again in Gerry's car. He, at least, was allowed to leave the premises. They'd gone to Castiglione dell'Umbria, Stephanie explained, to identify Sasha. If the police were involved with this procedure, they didn't keep Barbara, because she was back well in time for dinner. Not that Francis thought that any of them would see her at the formal meal. She would, he imagined, be more likely to have a sandwich in her room, especially after her long flight. But no, here she was, dressed up in a smart black polo neck jersey and skirt and looking remarkably poised. Perhaps she was still in shock, acting on automatic. Perhaps it was easier, being in company, than sitting alone in your room with your thoughts. As Stephanie brought her into the side room where the regular gang were already standing drinking, she smiled politely, if a little guardedly, as she was introduced to each in turn. Was she thinking, *One of you killed my daughter, so I'd like to get a good look at you all individually*? If she was, it didn't show.

Stephanie stayed beside her, though, and when the bell rang and they all went through for dinner, she placed Barbara between herself and Duncan, with Gerry and Fiona opposite.

Then: 'Francis,' his hostess called. 'Do come and sit with us.'

He apologized to Zoe, whom he'd been standing next to prior to sitting down, and moved on up to sit on the other side of Fiona.

Nothing was said about Sasha initially. Duncan was the model of old-world courtesy, asking Barbara about her flight, which had been, she told them, with KLM, thirteen hours, with a two-hour wait at Schiphol. Then there was more polite chat about Portland, Oregon, where Barbara lived, and Sasha had lived and studied too.

The mention of her daughter brought respectful silence from the little group. None of them was obviously going to ask Barbara more than she wanted to volunteer. None of them even approached the question they all clearly wanted the answer to: was there a Mr White-Moloney? If so, was he likely to be joining her?

When he thought about it the next morning, Francis couldn't quite remember how they had got on to the subject of Poppy, and then, from there, inevitably, on to the murder enquiry. But once they had, the stilted chit-chat was replaced with something altogether more urgent. Duncan and Fiona were explaining about the various options available to them, flying Poppy's body home as against getting it buried out here, outlining other stuff that had to be done: the death certificate, the cancelling of the passport and so on.

Barbara nodded and listened but asked no questions. She was flying Sasha home, she said eventually, when whatever formalities that needed to be done in this country had been done. She wanted her relatives and friends to be able to say goodbye to her.

Duncan and Fiona didn't comment; Poppy wasn't going home, Francis knew that.

'So how are the police getting on?' Barbara asked. 'With the enquiry?' *Enk-wherry*. 'Do they have any idea at all what's happened here?'

'You haven't met them yet?' Fiona queried.

'No.'

'I thought they might have been present at . . . when . . .'

'I went to see Sasha? No. It's not necessary here, apparently. I just had to hand in her passport.'

Again, Francis was surprised by her composure. You might have expected, in the circumstances, that she would be close to breaking down, but her speech barely faltered. He was surprised too that neither Gerry nor Stephanie seemed to have briefed her on the police activity. Perhaps they had, and what she wanted now was Duncan and Fiona's take on things. OK, so that was probably the story, because Gerry wasn't commenting and neither was Stephanie as Fiona launched in, quite urgently, with her perspective: that, as far as she could see, the police had *no idea* what was going on. They were totally at sea; they had put her and more importantly her father through unnecessarily intense, borderline offensive, questioning.

'That would be standard, though, wouldn't it?' said Barbara. 'Aren't close relatives always in the frame?'

'Fair enough if they were actually here at the time of . . . of . . . of . . .' Fiona stuttered. 'The death,' she managed finally. 'But I was in London when my stepmother died. And your daughter was a total stranger to me. What on earth was my motive supposed to be?'

There was a pause. Barbara didn't answer this bizarrely tactless question. Instead, she looked sideways at Stephanie.

'Francis,' said Stephanie, picking up the embarrassment baton, 'what's your view? In addition to being a brilliant teacher,' she explained to Barbara, 'Francis is also a crime writer of considerable distinction.'

'I'm not sure about that . . .' Francis demurred.

'Looks like you've come to the right place,' said Barbara.

'I'm certainly learning something,' he replied. 'I don't know how things are in the US, but the system out here is very different to what we have at home in the UK.' He explained about the lack of a coroner and how the *procuratore* worked closely with the police, before moving on to describe Marta and her team.

Sadly Barbara hadn't seen either *Spiral* or *The Killing*, so comparisons to Chief Inspector Laure Berthaud and Detective Inspector Sarah Lund didn't work. As for police procedure in the US, Barbara wasn't an expert, she said. But she thought they did have coroners, in some states anyway. 'I know we do in Portland, because there's a fine old house that's the County Coroner's Office, which I often drive past.'

The truth was, Francis went on, that none of them knew what the police and the *procuratore* might do next. They had interviewed everybody three times but didn't appear to be close to solving the case.

'I guess it feels a little odd,' Barbara said, 'being far away from home, in the hands of a strange authority. Or rather, a strange set of authorities.'

'Exactly,' Fiona agreed. 'I'd never have thought I'd say that I would have preferred my stepmother to die at home. But it would have been, if not easier, a bit more comforting, if that's the right word.'

When the *secondo* was over, Barbara suddenly made her

apologies and went up to bed. It had been lovely, she said, to have something to eat and drink, but it had been a long day and she needed her sleep. Stephanie offered to walk her up to her room, but she told her not to be silly, she could easily find her way, it was just across the courtyard.

'What a very charming woman,' Duncan said after she'd left.

'To be so together,' said Gerry, 'after flying out from America overnight and then viewing the body of your dead daughter, all in one day. Remarkable.'

'She's clearly in shock,' said Stephanie. 'She's at the stage where things are all a bit of a dream and you're just coping, if you know what I mean.'

'I do know what you mean,' Duncan said. 'I'm still there myself.'

'I didn't mean . . .'

'No, you're right. Things do still feel a bit unreal. Don't you think, Fiona?'

'Not particularly,' his daughter replied crisply. 'It all feels pretty real to me. My main concern is what are they going to do now?'

'The police?' asked Gerry.

'Yes. How long are we going to be trapped here in this, excuse my French, effing villa? I mean, do you think they have any kind of answers at all? Are they moving forward? Or are they just floundering? Have they said anything to you, Gerry?'

'No.' He looked round at Stephanie. 'They consulted us, at the start, and then when they've needed something, but as to what they're thinking, they've kept their cards very close to their chests.'

'Francis?' asked Fiona. 'What about you?'

'They're not sharing much with me, that's for sure.'

'But you were there, sitting in, for a while. What was all that about?'

'Search me. They had me in. I watched a couple of interviews. Then they kicked me out.'

'Mine,' said Duncan. 'I was glad you were there. To witness Ms Moretti's climbdown.'

'Climbdown?' asked Stephanie, with wide eyes.

'Moretti was pushing it a bit with her questions. At one point she virtually accused me of murdering my wife. She had no evidence. Just, as it happens, an erroneous understanding of Poppy's father's will. I wasn't impressed. Were you, Francis?'

Francis shrugged. 'I'm afraid, until you told us about Minty inheriting Framley, we were all rather thinking the same thing.'

'Jumping to hurried conclusions. And how does poor Sasha fit in?'

'The most likely scenario would be that she saw or found out something that incriminates the murderer. There's no other obvious link.'

Duncan was drumming his fingers impatiently on the table. 'They basically have nothing to go on. Whoever fiddled with the sauna door was careful to leave no fingerprints.'

That was an interesting observation, Francis thought. 'How do we know someone fiddled with the sauna door?' he asked.

'They must have done,' Duncan replied brusquely. 'How else was poor Poppy trapped in there? The police have explained that the inside handle fell off. Was that an accident? It seems a little convenient, don't you think?'

'I thought she was poisoned.'

'That's what I mean. It seems a little convenient that the door handle fell off shortly after she was poisoned.' He paused. 'A particularly nasty element of her death was that with the poison in her system she couldn't get out to get help. Prints of her fists were on the glass door. But as far as I can see from everything they've said to me, every question they've asked me, the police have as little idea as anyone else who was responsible for this monstrous form of murder. Tantamount to torture, in my opinion. Can you imagine.'

Perhaps the ambassador had drunk too much red wine, but this was the first time Francis had seen him lose his composure and reveal some passion about his wife's death. Either he was a very good actor, playing a deeply devious game of misdirection, or he really had had nothing to do with it.

The others went to their rooms after supper. All except Roz, who joined Francis for a grappa on the sofa in the library. With the fire lit in the heavy, cast-iron stove, the room had a cosy, autumnal feel, the orange light flickering on the rows of books on the shelves.

'Can't quite bring myself to go to bed at nine fifteen,' Roz said.

'No,' Francis agreed. Everyone needs time off from their lover, he thought, then wondered if perhaps the pair had fallen out in some way.

'So come on then,' she said, 'how was she? Sasha's mum? What's the story? We were all trying to make her out down the suspects' end of the table.'

'The suspects' end,' Francis repeated, chuckling.

'That's what we are, isn't it? Hosts and victims in one group, suspects in another.'

'Is that what you feel like?'

'I do. Personally. Don't know about the others.'

'Does your distinction work anyway? Because Duncan and Fiona are surely prime suspects.'

'Are they?' Roz gave him a knowing look. 'I thought they were off the hook now.'

'How d'you mean?'

'In that he isn't going to inherit the big house.' She pronounced it, for some reason, with a mock-cockney accent, *the big arse*. 'So his motive's rather gone up in smoke.' She gave him a twinkly, amused look. 'Wouldn't you say?'

'How d'you know that?'

'Fiona told me. She said she was sick of people looking at them as if they were a pair of murderers.'

'And who else knows about this?'

'Everybody. Pretty much. What else d'you think we talk about? Down in coach.'

'I didn't realize,' Francis said. 'I thought people were keeping off the subject.'

'It's tricky, though, isn't it? One of us has done it, and here are the rest of us, gossiping away and speculating, making that one person who *has* done it doubtless extremely uneasy.'

'Do you really think it's one of the group?'

'It seems unlikely, doesn't it, looking round. A perfectly civilized collection of well-to-do people, with only a couple mildly unhinged. And yet, one of us has poisoned an old lady in a sauna, and then apparently quite cold-bloodedly strangled a young woman in her bed. But who else could have done it? There's been no one coming in. No Russians spotted in the neighbourhood.'

'Fabio?' said Francis.

'Yes, he is pretty strange. If you lined us all up in a parade anyone would pick him out as the most likely to do something as horrible as locking someone in a sauna. But what's his motive? A long-standing hatred of snobbish old English ladies? I don't see it, really.'

Francis nodded. 'So who d'you see as "unhinged"?'

'Zoe's pretty crackers, wouldn't you say? Diana, in her way. Angela – have you spoken to her?'

'I've never got the chance. The ambient noise is always too loud. We grin at each other across the table.'

'You should sit and talk to her. Terribly sane on the surface. Rather nice with it. Extremely posh, in a quiet way. And then you suddenly realize she's mad as the proverbial hatter. Or perhaps it's just the tension of being here that's driving them all quietly nuts.'

'D'you think?'

'Don't you? As Liam keeps saying, it's like the Big Brother house. No cameras, but everyone surreptitiously checking you out twenty-four-seven. There's at least three who think I've done it.'

'Who?'

'I couldn't possibly say.'

'Oh, go on.'

'Maybe the doyenne of the group herself.'

'Diana?'

'She doesn't like me much anyway, after I got down to breakfast before her on the first morning. Yes. And those two Yorkshire ladies.'

'Why?'

'No idea. Because I'm a bit younger. Don't quite fit in. First timer. Why am I here? The same stuff they mutter about Liam.'

'Do they?'

'Yes. Why is he here? Which is a good question. Why *is* he here? Is he some rogue IRA man exacting a horrible revenge on the general's daughter?'

'That thought had crossed my mind.'

'But d'you think he'd have read out his poetry if that was the case? He's hardly keeping quiet about his sympathies in that area. Then again, he is a Northern Irish Catholic.'

'What's that supposed to mean?' Francis asked.

'You ever been there? Belfast. And environs.'

'No.'

'They're all like that. The Catholics. Fervent nationalists. If they're not actually Republicans, they sympathize.'

'So when were you there?'

'A few years ago. In my twenties. One of my disastrous love affairs. With an Irish hardman. He was proper IRA, as it happens. Some of his stories would put a serious chill up your spine. The only trouble was he was very sexy with it. Oh my God.'

'How long did that last?'

'A couple of years. On and off. He was never going to settle down with me, though, was he? I was the enemy. That's why he liked me. Nice little privately educated English girl. He absolutely adored the idea that I'd spent two years at Cheltenham Ladies' College. Fucking the enemy. That's what he used to say, even as he was doing it.' She let out a wild cackle.

'I don't suppose Liam knew him.'

'No, apparently not. Liam's from Derry. Colum was from *Belle-farst.*' She did the accent, and as she did, Francis got a powerful whiff of the place, and of her in the place.

Now he looked at her. 'May I ask you a question?'

'Of course. Not too personal, I hope.'

'It is a bit personal. When we went to Gubbio . . .' he began, then paused and watched her.

'When we went to Gubbio what?'

'Why were you snogging Tony in one of those baskets in the cable car?'

She didn't even blink. 'Was I?' she said.

'You were. You were coming down from St Ubaldo's, just before noon, and you and he were in a fervent embrace.'

She looked at him in disbelief. 'So where were you, may I ask? To see this?'

'Just below. On the ground. I decided to walk up the track.'

'That's nowhere near the cable car.'

'Yes, but I then made the foolish mistake of leaving it and taking a footpath up through the woods. I thought it was going to be a shortcut, but it wasn't, it took me out to a steep, shaley slope which I nearly tumbled down all the way to the town.'

'Christ. We might have had a third body.'

'Luckily I managed to spread-eagle myself and slow down on a rocky outcrop and crawl back.'

'Lucky you.'

'Lucky me, indeed. And the answer to my question . . .?'

Roz looked at him for what felt like a long couple of minutes but was probably five seconds. 'Tony's my married man,' she said, and she was, to give her credit, blushing.

She told him everything then. Or so it seemed. That they had come out here to be together for a few days away from his wife. That that's why she hadn't been at Francis's exercise on dialogue, because they had gone for a sneaky day out together. To Castiglione dell'Umbria. She hadn't cycled there. Fifteen miles, you've got to be joking. She laughed. She'd walked down the hill and he'd picked her up in his hire car. And no, of course he wasn't a counter-intelligence operative, that was just a joke. He was an antiques dealer. That's why he kept shooting off, looking at stuff in the local towns.

But why hadn't they come out as a couple? Francis asked. Because it would get back, she replied. Really, far away in Umbria, would news of a private arrangement such as this travel to wherever Tony lived in England? Steyning, Roz replied. Little place on the edge of the South Downs. Between Brighton and Worthing. Maybe yes, she said. Sheila was a maniac. The wife. She tracked down everything Tony did. Sorry, but with all due respect, actually without all due respect, since she didn't deserve any, she was a crazy bitch. Unfortunately, Tony didn't do the kind of work where he could make up a foreign conference that he had to attend. Or something of that kind. They had real problems even sneaking a full night away back at home.

So why a writing course? Francis then asked. Where you have, if you've come as individuals, to be apart? Why not a hotel, where you could be together? He'd never swing it, she replied. Why would he be in Italy in a hotel for a week?

'To look at antiques?'

'Nah. She'd insist on coming with him.'

But the clever thing was, the writing course was his birthday present. From her. His fiftieth. He had always wanted to write and now she was trying to help him make it happen.

Francis gave her a considered look. 'That doesn't exactly sound like a crazy bitch,' he said. 'A wife who would arrange a thoughtful present like that.'

'That's where you're wrong. That's exactly the kind of manipulative thing she does. All the time. To get him where she wants him.'

There was clearly not going to be any arguing with Roz about that. He let it go. So how had she managed to get Tony's wife to give him a present that would allow her, Roz, to be there with him? She hadn't, she replied. Tony had been given the present, five months ago, and then they'd had this mad idea that it might be fun if she came along too. 'It was like an idea we had in bed,' she said, giggling.

Francis nodded. He could imagine the scenario, perhaps a bit too well. 'So now you're both stuck here,' he replied. 'For who knows how long? Hopefully there's no danger that wifey – Sheila – will find out.'

'God knows. It depends on how soon the story gets out. To the press. With half the cooks living in the village up the road it's surely only a matter of time.'

'I'm sure they're all very loyal to Gerry and Stephanie.'

'Let's hope so. I'm surprised the police have kept it quiet.'

'They must have their reasons.'

'But it won't stay local, will it, with all of us here. Murder at the villa. Once it gets out, it'll be *Mail Online*, complete with a Cluedo-like list of suspects. That's what I'm dreading. Once Sheila sees that she'll dump the kids with neighbours and be out here. She's one of those people. Terribly controlling.'

'So they have kids?'

'Yes. Two teenagers. That's why he won't leave her. Yet.'

'I see. And when they're a bit older he will leave her, is that his story?'

'I can't wait until then. He knows that. I'm not going to be one of those mistresses that hangs around until it's too late. I want a baby. I'm forty-two. I don't have much time. This is what this week was supposed to be about. Him making a final fucking decision.'

Francis looked at her, wondered whether it was worth tackling her on her inconsistency; decided that on balance it was.

Inconsistencies were, by their very nature, suspicious. 'I thought you didn't like children,' he said.

'Other people's,' she replied. 'For a long time, I thought I didn't want one, that it would slow me down, that I wouldn't be able to travel, all that stuff. But then, suddenly, I do. It's crept up on me. With Tony. Sorry about that.'

'No need to apologize to me,' Francis said. Then: 'So has he? Made a decision?'

'He said he had. On that day. That we went to Castiglione. And then went on, after lunch, to see Piero della Francesca's pregnant Madonna in the museum in the pretty little town . . .'

'That Gerry talked about?'

'That one, yes. Monterchi. You know, if you're pregnant they let you in for free. We were in there, alone, and he kissed me and said that when I was . . .'

'Pregnant?'

'Yes . . . we'd come back. That's why I was so happy that evening.'

'I see.' It all began to fit now. The glowing woman, returning to the group discussion. And that's why Tony had looked so worried that evening, Francis thought.

'Thanks for telling me,' he said.

'You won't tell anyone else, will you?'

'Not if you don't want me to.'

'Please don't. It'll get back. Somehow. Sheila will turn out to know Zoe or something. It's a nightmare. Everything always gets back.'

'One other question,' Francis said. 'Why did you say, that evening before you went to Castiglione, "I'm not in the longevity business"?'

She laughed.

'It worried me,' he said.

'Did it? Good. It was supposed to. Oh, I don't know. I fancied leaving you with a cryptic remark. I thought you might think I'd gone off and topped myself or something. I wanted to get your writer's imagination racing.'

'Well, you did.'

'You need to watch out for me. I quite like winding people up like that.'

'Even when there's a double murder?'

'Give me a break. It was before all that. I wouldn't do it now. Now all I want is for this to end, so I can get back home.'

'What have you and Tony decided?'

'I don't know. I thought it was all in the bag and then this happened and now he's in touch with Sheila again and anything could happen. She might even turn up. Who knows? Perhaps that's what we need. A showdown. Her and me.'

Twenty minutes later they drained the last of their second glass of grappa, got up and put the light out in the side room. There was just one light left on in the hall. The railings of the stairs cast big shadows on the whitewashed wall. At the top, the long, tiled corridor was dark. Roz made a mock-scared face and put her hands around her neck. Francis laughed, though it was hardly a laughing matter. He reached for his mobile phone and clicked on the torch app, lit them round the corner and along.

'Good night,' she said, as she came to Fra Angelico and paused.

'But . . .' Francis began, and then, as Roz put her finger to her lips, realized his mistake. Of course. Tony's room. So they weren't disagreeing that much then.

'Good night,' he replied, and put his own finger to his lips in acknowledgment of her secret.

He walked to the end and let himself into his lonely room. Once inside, he clicked on the dim overhead light and turned the key behind him.

THIRTEEN

Tuesday 2 October

In the morning the sun continued to shine from a clear blue sky. Mockingly, even, Francis thought. They'd never had such a run of good weather, Diana said, in all the years she'd been coming. Usually there would be rain or a storm at some point. After Francis had finished his ham roll and coffee he paced gently up the drive to see if the young policeman was still there. He wasn't. There was a new one. An older man who looked as if he hadn't allowed himself to become a stranger to pasta.

The last breakfasters were still sitting round the long table when there was a familiar sound of squealing brakes and crunching – or rather, flying – gravel, and two police cars appeared down the drive, one marked, the other not. The doors opened and disgorged Moretti, Ceccarelli and prosecutor Sabatini, together with Lorenzo Ricci and two burly *agenti* in uniform whom Francis hadn't seen before. Without greeting any of the guests they headed straight in through the front door in a posse.

'Hey ho!' said Belle, who was slicing a pear into four neat quarters with a steak knife.

'Something's up,' Mel agreed.

'I would say so,' said Angela, nodding excitedly.

'More interviews?' asked Zoe. 'I blinking well hope not. I've told them everything I know, at least twice.'

The chit-chat continued and then abruptly stopped. For five minutes later the police reappeared with Duncan and Fiona. Neither of them were in handcuffs, but there was something almost caricatured about the way the two *agenti* were shadowing them. Duncan was then escorted into the back of the marked Squadra Volante car, with an *agente* on one side and Sabatini on the other. Moretti got into the front passenger seat and Ricci took the wheel. In the other car were Ceccarelli, in front, Fiona in the back, and the other uniform at the wheel.

'What the feck!' said Liam, voicing the group's thoughts.

The cars sped off and Gerry, who had accompanied them out, was left standing on the gravel.

'Gerry!' called Mel. 'What's going on?'

He turned towards his guests and paused. For a moment it looked as if he might ignore them and go back inside, but then he came over.

'They've arrested Duncan,' he said.

'What on earth are they thinking?' said Belle.

'I have no idea. They came up, found me, took me along to the room he's sharing with Fiona and then made a formal arrest.'

'In Italian?' asked Belle.

'In Italian, first, and then with an English translation.'

'Crikey!' said Mel, looking round. Roz and Francis, who had been reading in separate deckchairs in the sun, had now joined the little group around the table.

'Does this mean we can go back home now?' asked Belle.

'I'm afraid not,' said Gerry. 'You're all staying here at the villa for the time being, and the policeman will remain at the top of the drive. They need to question Duncan thoroughly, they said.'

'Surely they've questioned him thoroughly already,' said Zoe. 'We've all been grilled like kippers. What are they going to do? Put him in a cell and force a confession?'

'How very alarming,' said Angela. 'I do hope the poor man's going to be OK.'

'What have they got on him?' said Liam. 'That's what I'd like to know. They must have something. Because they can only hold him for so long until they charge him. I imagine that's the same out here, isn't it, Francis?'

Francis, too, was wondering what on earth Moretti and Sabatini were playing at. Did they know something he didn't? Had Sabatini managed to get privileged judicial access to the general's will and found out that he hadn't, after all, left Framley to the sister? Or had they some other concrete evidence that was driving this – a fingerprint on the sauna handle or some such?

He didn't know the answer to Liam's question. What *did* they need to hold someone in Italy? In the UK it was 'reasonable grounds', but arresting someone at home meant the police thought they were guilty of something, because they had to charge them within twenty-four hours or else let them go. He had no idea how it worked in Italy, except that the public prosecutor, in this case Sabatini, had a key role. He decided to play it straight. 'I honestly don't know, Liam,' he said. 'Presumably it must be much the same. This is Europe, after all. I don't imagine the rules allow them to hold him for any longer than they do at home.'

'I wouldn't be so sure about that,' said Diana. She had been unusually quiet for a change. She looked, frankly, shocked. Perhaps it wasn't in her lexicon that you could arrest a titled ambassador.

Liam was laughing. 'This isn't fecken' Saudi Arabia or somewhere, Diana,' he said.

'I appreciate that, Liam. But it's not home either.'

'Have they arrested the daughter too?' asked Angela. 'Duncan's daughter, I mean.'

'Fiona,' Francis said. 'I don't think so. She wasn't here, after all, when Poppy died.'

'Maybe they're in it together,' said Angela. Her skinny white eyebrows shot up as she broke into that mischievous, childlike smile. It was interesting, Francis thought, that this arrest, even if it turned out to be spurious, had allowed the elephant that had been lurking around the villa for days to be finally openly acknowledged. Murder most foul.

The answer to Angela's supposition came after lunch, when a taxi arrived in the drive with Fiona on board. She paid off the driver, then marched purposefully through the front door and up the stairs to her room. When she reappeared, half an hour later, changed out of her smart jacket and skirt combo into more relaxed shorts and top, the inquisitive prisoners of the villa gathered around her like desperate bees round a particularly sweet pot of Home Counties honey. One moment she had taken a deckchair on her own up by the table below the vine; the next, they all seemed to be hovering nearby. Not that she seemed to mind. She was, she said, as baffled as they were. The police had not explained to her, in any coherent way at all, why they were holding her father. He was being questioned, Moretti had told her. She was not allowed to sit in. She would either have to wait outside, in a dreary corridor in the *questura*, or return to the villa. And yes, unless they decided to release him, he would be spending the night in custody.

'They're contacting the British Embassy in Rome,' she went on, 'which is a bit embarrassing with him being ex-Diplomatic Service. The absurd thing is, Dad knows all the protocol anyway. Anyway, we've got him a lawyer and stuff. There's no bail in Italy, apparently.'

'There you are, Liam,' said Diana. 'It's an entirely different system. Even if they are, notionally, in Europe.'

A young man had appeared by the tall wrought-iron gates at the top of the drive, with a camera with a very long lens. He had been seen remonstrating with the uniform on duty, but hadn't been allowed in.

'Journalist,' Liam said. 'Has to be. The first harbinger of fecken' doom. I'll go and investigate.'

He returned triumphant. The young man was from the *Corriere dell' Umbria* newspaper and Liam had spoken to him. 'Just gave him a mini-briefing. Nothing he didn't know already. The poor fellow's travelled all the way out here, he needs something to take back to his editor.'

'Did you let him take your photo too?' Mel asked.

'Perhaps.'

'You did!' cried Belle. 'You are now the face of Murder Villa, do you realize that?'

'It's not funny,' said Diana. 'Now you've given him something, it's not speculation any more. It'll be a story. We'll be besieged. Camera crews, the lot.'

'They'll be here anyway. Do you really think he's going to come all this way and write nothing?'

'Don't you think you should have checked with the rest of us, before you released a statement on our behalf?'

Liam's good humour was fading fast. 'I didn't release a statement, Diana. On anyone's behalf. I just gave your man a short summary, on my personal feckin' behalf, of what's been going on here.'

Diana made the kind of face that made you glad you weren't her partner or child. 'On your personal behalf,' she repeated scornfully, pointedly leaving out the Irish expletive. 'Who knows what you've unleashed now. At least it'll be your ugly mug in the paper.'

Francis retired to the Wi-Fi bench with his laptop. He found

Il Corriere dell' Umbria (circulation 11,212) and its sister paper *Il Corriere di Siena*, but there was no mention of Villa Giulia yet in the surprisingly comprehensive online coverage. Once again he cursed his lack of Italian. There was a picture of an *ambulanza* on the front page and details of some *tragedia* involving someone *trovato morto*, but it wasn't either Poppy or Sasha. A scout around some other websites confirmed that the Italian legal process was somewhat different to the British. As well as the whole inquisitorial system, with the *procuratore* and all that, there seemed to be no formal charging by the police, instead a requirement that a judge confirm the holding of the suspect. There was no bail. Why was that? Francis wondered. Something to do with the mafia? With making sure the *polizia* could hold on to the big fish when they caught them? But how very inconvenient for the well-heeled lawbreaker. At home, if you were wealthy enough, you were almost always allowed to go home. And Angela was right: Italian jails were notoriously overcrowded, with three to six per cell.

Privately, Francis was worried. The police had made a mistake arresting Duncan. Though he too had had him marked as prime suspect for a while, now that his motive was gone, any suspicion attached to him had gone too. That little outburst at supper last night ('it's tantamount to torture') had only confirmed Francis's gut feeling: that the ambassador was innocent, and that on his return to Blighty he probably was going to be kicked out of the house and garden he loved. Moretti had had a bee in her bonnet about Duncan right from the start. Francis wouldn't forget the look on her face when she'd made up her 'little story' about the passionless marriage and the beautiful house. It had been like watching a child who thinks they're being super-clever. Once she had formulated her thesis, she had never quite, he thought, accepted Duncan's rejection of it.

All this, obviously, was unfortunate for poor Duncan, now presumably being put through the mill at the *questura* in Perugia, by a group of professionals who didn't believe him, but it was more unfortunate, if not actively dangerous, for the group left behind at the villa. The killer was still at large.

The only advantage of this situation that Francis could think of was this: perhaps with Duncan taken into custody, the real murderer would relax, would somehow give themselves away, even if it were only by the enthusiasm with which they wept crocodile tears for Duncan. Two things were for sure: 1) he was going to double-lock his bedroom door tonight, and 2) he was going to be watching every last one of them like the proverbial hawk.

If Francis couldn't go for a walk, he could at least enjoy the pool. He got his trunks and the last tranche of Zoe's memoir and headed down there. To his surprise, despite the sunny afternoon, he was alone. Perhaps the others were all cowering in their rooms.

Eventually, around four thirty, he heard the click of the little gate in the surrounding fence. He looked up, thinking it might be Liam, or one or both of the Yorkshire ladies. But it was Barbara.

'Oh, hi,' she said. 'I'm not disturbing you, I hope.'

'Not at all.'

She took a lounger two along from him and settled herself down. She had no book or magazine with her. She let out a loud sigh and closed her eyes. Francis continued to read, though the silence between them was heavy with possibility. Should he offer his condolences? Should he ask her how her day had gone? He didn't want to be intrusive; on the other hand, he didn't want to be unsympathetic. But it was Barbara who broke the spell.

'This is more like it,' she said eventually.

'Yes,' he agreed. Then: 'Difficult day?'

'Just a bit of one.'

She gave him a cracked smile and was soon off into a quiet rant about the police, the Italian authorities, everything she had to do, just to get her poor daughter released so she could fly her home. 'They're insisting on doing this autopsy on her, which I do totally understand. But it's not at all clear that they'll release the body even when that's over. She can't be registered dead until the body is released. And I can't book her on to a flight home until she's registered dead.'

Outside of this frustration, Barbara had a lovely gentle manner, though with her classically neat figure she was of a totally different body shape to Sasha. Francis found himself wondering again about the father and what his story was.

Anyways, she went on, somebody from the American Consulate in Florence was coming over to meet with her tomorrow, so maybe they could get things moving. 'I just feel at the moment like I'm the one they should be helping out, and they're not.'

'Aren't they at all sympathetic?' he asked.

'They are. Of course they are. *Condoglianze* and all that. But beyond that, they're not in the business of making it easy. See this person, speak to that person, go to this office, climb these ancient stone stairs to find another locked door, drive out to this police station on the edge of a trading estate, it's all a . . . a . . . fucking nightmare.'

With that she was suddenly in tears. Francis got up and went over to her. He sat down on the lounger next to her and took her hand. She continued to sob.

'I'm sorry,' she said eventually. '*Mi dispiace.*' She smiled through her tears. 'You shouldn't have been so sympathetic. That's what set me off. I'm much better when people are just being businesslike and annoying.'

'That's OK,' Francis said. He gave her hand a little squeeze and let it go. 'Perfectly understandable. Jesus, you've lost your daughter.'

'I know.' She stared out silently in front of her and for a moment Francis thought he'd gone too far. 'I can't believe it,' she went on. 'What am I doing in this place, with all these old ladies telling me they're sorry for my loss. Who are they all? What do they know? Do you know the reason Sasha was even here?'

'She told me she'd wanted to come to Italy ever since reading *A Room With A View.*'

'Was that the book? The main reason was that she'd had an abortion. After a silly one-night stand with some bloke she met on Tinder. '"Ethically polyamorous", apparently. But he ran a mile when he heard about the child. She was very cut up about it all, so when afterwards she suggested a break somewhere, I encouraged her.'

'Financially?'

'Yes.'

'I didn't know this,' Francis said. It made the whole situation almost unbearably poignant.

'Why should you? But the point is, am I really supposed to believe that one of them strangled poor Sasha? Which one was it? None of them look strong enough, except perhaps that big scary one.'

'Diana.'

'Is that what she's called? The one who greeted me when I arrived. With the Scottish accent. Who's always bustling around like some big old hen.'

'Diana.'

'Oh, she's perfectly sweet. They all are. But I just want to be left alone, really. I nearly checked into a hotel in town. But then I thought, no, I want to see them, I want to know what happened. To my poor, wonderful, little girl.'

Francis let there be silence. Then: 'She was wonderful,' he said. 'Truly, Barbara. She had real talent. I'm sure you know that. She wrote beautifully. Better than all of this lot, really. And she had another rare quality . . .'

'Intuition,' said Barbara, quietly.

'Did you know I was going to say that?'

'I thought you might.'

'Astonishing, really. She played this game the other night where she did character analyses of a couple of us. And they were so spot on. And she was so young. I was amazed. We were all amazed.'

'Twenty-four. She just had her birthday a month ago. Twenty-three years since I found her, rolling around in her cot in her foster mom's backyard.'

This was a surprise.

'You adopted her?'

'Me and my then husband did, yes. We couldn't have kids of our own.'

'I see.' Francis was tempted to tell her his own story, how John and Susan Meadowes had rescued him, too, from a foster carer at the age of fourteen months, but decided against it. This was not, as they say, about him.

'So bright-eyed, such a clever little thing. And even though she'd been through God knows what before we found her, she always had the sweetest disposition. And such natural talent. She was one of those kids who could turn their hand to anything. Her drawing was wonderful. She quickly picked up the piano and passed all her grades. Then she moved on to the clarinet and was in school orchestras and things. But her writing was always special. She was always inventing stories, even from a very young age. Long, twisty, imaginative stories. About trolls and dragons and fairies and all sorts. We were so proud of her. Had such high hopes for her. She won competitions at high school.'

Francis was longing to ask about her father. But the last thing he wanted to be now was intrusive in the way that people so often said he was, when really he was just curious. So he said nothing. He sat there on his lounger, looking out over poor Barbara's head at the valley, the criss-crossing ridges of field and forest, the tiny orange dots of villas and villages, the little thread of grey tarmac road that wound through the middle, and in the distance the mighty blue-grey hulk of the Mountains of the Moon.

'You want to know about her father, don't you?' she said. 'Donald. We're not together, though we're still friends. He's a musician. You know the type. A talented man, but you know, not made for the long-term project of fidelity. So we went our separate ways when Sasha was about nine. In answer to your unspoken question, no, we didn't adopt any more. She was the only one.'

Francis didn't know where to look. But Barbara seemed better now. Her storm of emotion had passed.

Five minutes later they were joined by Mel and Belle, down, as they said, for an early-evening splash. 'Oh, sorry,' Belle said, as they came through the gate and saw the two-person tableau in front of them. 'We're not interrupting anything, are we?'

'No, no,' said Barbara. 'I was just going to get in the water. Have a little swim before dinner.'

'You know that Erica St John is joining us tonight,' said Mel.

'Who the heck is Erica St John?' Barbara asked.

'Some local artist,' Mel said. 'She was going to come last week and then . . . and then, well . . . she was cancelled. Due to events. But I think Stephanie thought we could do with some distraction. And entertainment. She'd be right about that.'

Erica St John was quite something. How old was she? Francis wondered. Late seventies, early eighties? She had clearly been a beauty in her youth, with those well-defined cheekbones. She had not tried to cling on to that, as some did, even some of those around her tonight, with their dyed hair and powdered skin. Erica's hair was as white as bone, her skin as wrinkled as a prune. She had a line of kohl around her lively dark eyes and the thin, amused strip of her mouth was crimson with lipstick – but that was it.

She arrived in a yellow Mini Cooper, driven by a short, tubby man whose name was Benjy. Benjy was younger and their relationship was not stated. Was he lover, companion, friend, butler, secretary? From the way she treated him he could have been any of those things. He was decidedly boho, with his bushy grey hair, his unkempt eyebrows above heavy black specs. He had a diffident manner, but it was, with his fruity, drawly, well-educated voice, the diffidence of the entitled.

Why had Stephanie invited them? It was a very odd call, particularly as Erica's new show – in Geneva, opening in two weeks' time – was called A Preoccupation with Death, and featured real human skulls set in found-object tableaux. There were 'canvas-sculptures' too, they learned. Because at one stage of her career Erica had been an abstract painter, like Gerry. Now she tore and broke her paintings or decorated them with broken shards of mirror or bone. Frames were no longer simple boring decorative oblongs that surrounded the image; they too might be smashed. One skull, spattered with blood-like red paint, had a length of fancy gold moulding jammed alarmingly into one of its dark eye sockets.

At least she was a distraction, Francis thought, as they took turns over the pre-prandial Prosecco to admire Erica's catalogue, where lavishly produced images were interspersed with the usual gobbledegook artspeak. Liam loved it – and her. Diana, you could see, was struggling (Francis imagined that Constable's *The Hay Wain* was more up her street). Mel and Belle made polite faces, as well they might, after a week of struggling to paint fruit and flowers and *alla prima* landscapes. Gerry was gracious, as one artist had to be to another, especially if that other was as successful as Erica was. Was he considering smashing up his moody abstracts too? Maybe that was the shortcut to the Biennale.

Duncan had not returned from Perugia. 'Sadly,' Stephanie said, 'he will not be joining us tonight.' And that was that. No further mention was made of the fact that he had been arrested, that he might at this very moment be in Capanne jail, in one of those cells that Zoe had talked about, shared with 'three to six' others; that two highly suspicious deaths had taken place within these four walls within the past week, that though Erica and Benjy had been allowed in for the evening, none of the rest of them were allowed out.

Fiona, too, was absent. After her long day with her father, she had decided to have soup and a sandwich in her room. But to Francis's surprise, Barbara was present. Why she wanted to face the four-course set piece again was a puzzle to Francis, even after the conversation they had had earlier. *I want to see them, I want to know what happened.* Perhaps that was it.

In the dining room, Francis found himself almost opposite Erica, who was between Liam and Gerry. Benjy was sitting next to him, and Stephanie beyond that. He had tried to escape down the other end, where Barbara was now between Mel and Belle, with Diana and Angela opposite her. But Stephanie had insisted, pretty much manhandling him up to be near their distinguished guest. On his other side he had Roz, who was rather naughtily right next to her lover again. What kind of a buzz were the pair of them getting out of that? Would she and Tony be playing footsie during the antipasto? Or were they about to put the cat among the pigeons by coming out as a couple?

For a moment, looking down towards the fire crackling in the wood stove, he caught Barbara's eye. Without smile or acknowledgment, she looked away. If she, too, was using the sympathy of the kind ladies to play detective, she wasn't going to mess it up. Perhaps she felt she had already told him too much.

It was a long evening, during which Francis learned quite a bit about the Tuscan/Umbrian expatriate scene. Erica and Benjy were full of gossip, and Gerry and Stephanie weren't holding them back. Dear Jonte was being as preposterous as ever in his *castello*. Sylvia's attempts at B&B were comic; the trouble was she was such a snob she couldn't really bear her guests. After the success of her book about moving to Tuscany, Georgia was trying to write a novel, but by her own admission she had no imagination. Geoffrey and Antoine had split up, Geoffrey had gone back to London and Antoine was bereft and back to his best friend the bottle, poor soul. None of these names meant anything to Francis – or presumably Liam – but in half an hour he got a better idea of Gerry and Stephanie's social milieu than he had in the whole of the previous week.

Francis wondered how Erica and Benjy would describe this

scene to the Jontes and Sylvias and Georgias and Antoines. 'One of them was the murderer, and we were sitting there eating and chatting as if there was nothing out of the ordinary at all.' Perhaps, indeed, that's why they'd agreed to come – to be at the fount of the best local gossip for years.

FOURTEEN

I n the morning, in any case, the story was officially out. Liam had got himself on the front page of the *Corriere dell' Umbria,* grinning inappropriately between the tall, ivy-covered gateposts of Villa Giulia. Below was the headline: MORTI MISTERIOSE NELLA VILLA INGLESE.

'I told you you'd be the face of Murder Villa,' Belle said, as Tony's iPad was passed eagerly around the breakfast table.

The breaking news had brought out other journalists too – and not, as Roz had predicted, just local ones. It looked as if the policeman at the top of the drive was holding back a proper press pack behind those wrought-iron gates. Francis didn't want to risk being photographed, so he hadn't gone up to have a closer look. Liam, who had sneaked up, thought there were at least twenty, with a couple of TV cameras too. He hadn't shown his face this time. For the moment all the posse were getting was footage of the *agente* and the gateposts.

But at nine thirty, the journos did have something to point their cameras at. Barbara White-Moloney leaving the villa in a taxi. As mother of a victim and a new arrival, she was obviously exempt from the rules governing the others. Francis watched the car go with some frustration. He had hoped to talk with her about what she had discovered, if anything, over dinner; what her suspicions were about the guests she had met. She had got up and left the table before the pudding had even been served, so he'd not had the chance last night. And now she was gone, having taken breakfast in her room, and marched out to her car without even a glance in the direction of the guests.

He was frustrated too, he had to admit, at being treated like all the others. In both his previous 'investigations', he had had a measure of freedom, if not special status. He had never been boxed in with the suspects like this. Had Moretti even been fibbing earlier, leading him to think that he was, himself, above suspicion? Surely the police didn't think he had anything to do with either of these horrid crimes? No. She and her colleagues, having expressed an early interest in his detecting skills, had decided for some reason of their own to clip his wings. In doing so they were making a mistake, because he was ninety-five per cent sure they were wrong about Duncan. He could see what they were thinking, of course, but they were stupid, not prepared to listen to the thoughts of someone who'd been here since before the first murder, who had chatted to all the guests individually at dinner, heard their life stories, and had much more of an idea of what might have motivated one of them to do these terrible things. He had, after all, come up with Framley Grange as a likely motive long before Marta.

At eleven a.m., the gates opened again, and a police car swept down the drive. But it didn't contain any of the important police personnel, let alone the missing ambassador; just two blue-shirted *agenti*, who marched into the house and returned with Fiona. Each was now carrying a heavy suitcase, while Fiona carried a light bag. Without a word to the others she was shown into the back seat and the car swept away, slowing through the jostle at the gate, the shouts, the flashing of cameras.

'And what does that mean?' asked Belle, of the three ladies sitting in the row of deckchairs in the sun. Mel was reading, while Zoe and Diana were hard at work, Zoe tap-tap-tapping away at her laptop, Diana writing some great screed with her pink fountain pen in a loose-leafed A5 notebook.

'I don't think they've arrested her,' said Mel. 'They'd have sent a more senior officer to do that.'

'But they haven't released Duncan,' said Diana. 'Have they? Or he'd be back. Wouldn't he?'

'Not necessarily,' said Liam. 'He might have had enough of us.'

'Maybe they're taking his daughter to witness his release,' said Zoe. 'It looked like both their suitcases going off with them.'

'Maybe they're taking his daughter to witness him being charged,' said Liam, who was sitting further off.

'If you want to join in the conversation you can always come over here,' Zoe called back.

'Maybe Liam's right,' said Diana. 'Maybe they are going to charge him. I mean he has the motive, doesn't he?'

'It doesn't really work like that out here, I don't think,' Francis said, turning, and then getting to his feet. He too had been sitting a little way from the group and hadn't been planning to contribute. 'It's not so much about formal charging as ongoing investigating. In any case Duncan doesn't have the motive. That's the whole point. The beautiful house goes to her sister. He gets chucked out.'

'So he says,' said Diana. 'But who's to know that's true. Has anyone here seen Poppy's will?'

It's not her will, you idiot. It's the father's will. The general's. It was made some time ago and as it happens I've ordered it online. I should have it in my fat little mitts in five days' time. If only it were sooner! was what Francis didn't say. Instead: 'It's the general's will they need to see,' he replied. 'Isn't it?'

'Quite,' Mel agreed. 'Hers won't be proved for some time.'

'So what are you saying?' said Diana. 'That the general left the house, in the event of Poppy's death, to her sister?'

'Exactly,' Francis said. 'That is what he, Duncan, alleges. Which is why it's a little odd that the police are continuing to hold him.'

'Unless they know something you don't,' said Diana.

'Indeed,' said Francis. He got to his feet and headed towards the hall. It was time to do something bold and act on his intuition, which was gathering force like a rising wind.

'They may have compelling evidence,' Diana called after him.

'They may,' he called back. He ran up the stone stairs and knocked on the door of Tintoretto. Gerry was there, and yes, of course Francis could use the printer. Alone in Masaccio, Francis took the last twenty pages of Zoe's memoir and threw them in the bath, then ran the taps. He watched with quiet amusement as the ink ran on the now soggy paper. Perfect!

Back down in the courtyard Francis walked up to Zoe and produced his roll of damp paper. Silly fool, he told her, he'd managed to drop these pages in the bath while he was reading it. Was there any chance he could borrow her laptop for five minutes to print off some new copies? As she could see, he was nearing the end.

She laughed. 'Reading it in the bath. You must be enjoying it. Are we near a final verdict?'

'We are.'

She handed over her Mac Air without a murmur. As he took it

from her, she was beaming; at him, and also round at Diana, Belle
and Mel.

'No, absolutely no need to come with me,' he said. 'I'll just
pop up to Tintoretto and get Gerry to print off the relevant pages.'

'Are you sure?'

He was. The unnecessary printout took three minutes. Then he
was back in the gloom of Masaccio, scrolling speedily through
Zoe's files. How carefully would she hide this key and private
document, her daily journal? he wondered. It certainly wasn't
apparent in the basic list of files. But then, when he pulled up
Recent Files, there it was, right at the top of the list. 'Journal'. Its
actual location was inside a folder marked 'Private Notes', which
itself was inside a file called 'Personal'. Nothing like signalling
your intentions. Francis's own journal was called 'xyz', and lived
in a file called 'Rejected accounts', within a file called 'Tax
anomalies', which itself existed within 'Business'. He always
cleared Recent Files at the end of any session that involved confi-
dentiality. Poor, dear, tech-challenged Zoe. 'Journal' was hardly
the best hidden file ever.

He opened it and had the very briefest look. Oh my giddy aunt
. . . it was all there . . . more than even he could have imagined.
She had detailed everything. Every day since they'd been here –
and before. He copied it quickly on to a memory stick and then
ran back downstairs, ostentatiously clutching the newly printed
pages of memoir.

'There you are,' he said, handing back the laptop.

'That was quick,' said Zoe.

'Wasn't it? I shall look forward to giving you my full verdict
later.'

Back in his room he plugged in the memory stick and hunched
over his computer. God help him, his intuition had been spot on.
Not only did he now know who was responsible for all this crazy
horror, he had proof. Dates, times, actions, not to mention all the
guilt and revulsion that had inevitably followed. Motivation, too,
rooted in the very memoir he had been reading. Zoe had changed
the names of the private figures, of course she had.

He closed down his laptop and walked down the stone stairs as
calmly as he could. He was excited now, but he needed to pace
himself. He sat on the wrought-iron Wi-Fi bench and looked out

through the window at the sunny courtyard. Even if the police had treated him badly, he could hardly withhold this information, could he? He pulled out his phone and texted the number Moretti had given him.

Please come immediately – and alone. Crucial new information indicates identity of murderer. When you arrive it's important you make no signal that I have been in touch. Best, Francis.

He could only trust that Marta would do the right thing. There was of course a slim chance that some weird protocol would mean that she would insist on arriving with two police vans and screw everything up. But he had confidence in her. More so than in the others. The flashy gents. Ricci, in particular.

He got up and went into the side room to make himself a coffee. With a barista's care, he took the handle of the shiny chrome portable filter, twisted it out of the machine and knocked the black sludge of the last cup's used beverage into the bin. He held the filter under the coffee hopper, pulled the lever to release a neat shot of ground coffee, pushed it up against the tamper to make a nice smooth surface, then twisted the portafilter back into the machine.

'Nice action, bud.' It was Liam, right behind him.

'I love this machine,' said Francis, smiling round at the Irishman as he half-filled the steel jug with milk from the fridge. 'You want a coffee?'

'I can do my own. You've only got the one-cup filter there anyway.'

'So I have. I'll froth you some milk.'

'Thanks.'

Outside they stood side by side in the warm sun with their cappuccinos. The ladies had now got up, as one, to go in and make their own coffees and teas. 'I wonder how the ambassador's getting on,' Liam said. 'Perhaps they're still holding him. Why would they send a car for Fiona otherwise? She came back in a taxi yesterday.'

'Maybe they are.'

'Would they be right, though?' Liam went on. 'Aren't they barking up the wrong tree?'

Francis turned to eyeball him. 'What makes you think that?'

'Instinct.' He paused and fixed Francis with his plaintive brown eyes. 'It takes a lot to kill someone, you know. Either you really have to hate them, or they've got to be causing a serious block to your future success or happiness, I'd say.'

'Sounds like you know what you're talking about, Liam.'

He shrugged. 'Then again, there is revenge. After the fact. That's a very powerful motive. But I don't see that in Sir Duncan.'

'Who do you see it in?'

'Now that would be telling.'

'Don't they always say that revenge is a dish best served cold?'

'They do say that.'

'I expect you've seen that, where you come from . . .'

Liam sipped his coffee, almost daintily, and looked out over the courtyard. 'There was a war going on in our little statelet, Francis. They gave it another name, but that was what it was – a dirty little war. Being, as I am, a poet, an observer, I never got involved, myself, directly. But you're right, I knew plenty who did. So I've seen murderous passions in action. Very much so. Never a pretty sight.'

'Was that a problem, staying neutral?'

'I was never neutral, Francis. I just didn't get involved.'

'What are you two chaps looking so serious about?' It was Belle, with her own frothy cappuccino. 'Come on. We may be trapped, but we're trapped in a beautiful place. Perhaps we should all have a game of cards or something.'

Five of them – Francis, Belle, Mel, Zoe and Liam – sat at the long table playing Black Maria, a whist variation that Belle recommended. Diana didn't want to join in – she was still writing busily in her notebook and anyway she had things to do upstairs, she said. As for Angela: if anyone wanted to set up a bridge four she'd be interested, but no, she didn't think whist was quite her thing.

But they hadn't got through more than a couple of hands before the wrought-iron gates swung open and a marked Squadra Volante Alfa Romeo was nosing down the drive. It was Marta Moretti, thirty-five minutes after she'd been summoned. Apart from the handsome young *agente* who was driving, she was on her own.

She climbed out and looked slowly round the sunny courtyard.

Today she was wearing a rather fetching pale green leather skirt. She walked over to the card players and stood watching.

'*Buongiorno*, Marta,' called Liam.

'*Buongiorno.*'

'*Siete soli?*'

'*Per il momento, sì.*'

'*Dove sono gli altri?*'

'*Lavorando sodo, in città. Mentre voi giocate a carte, vedo.*'

'*Non abbiamo nient'altro da fare.*'

Marta laughed. As did Belle.

'Are you sharing the joke with the rest of us?' said Zoe.

'I was just asking the *commissario*,' Liam said, 'why she was on her own today and wondering where the others were. And she replied that they were all working hard, as you'd expect, while you lot were enjoying yourselves playing cards. To which I replied, "There's feck all else to do here. Given that we're trapped in the villa, not even allowed to go for a walk in the valley."'

Marta didn't comment. 'So Francis,' she said, 'it was you I came to see. If you don't mind me interrupting your game for a few moments.'

'Not at all.' He threw down his hand and led her into the house. She refused a coffee and they went together into the library.

'Thank you for your discretion,' Francis said, closing both doors behind them. He gestured for her to sit, then followed suit. They sat facing each other in the gloom, each on a shiny leather armchair. Outside the bright sun played on the leaves of the trees.

'So what are you so keen to tell me?' she asked.

'I'll explain in a moment, if I may. How have you been getting on with Sir Duncan?'

She paused and considered him for a few moments, as if wondering how open she ought to be with a man who might have some answers for her. 'There have been some interesting developments,' she replied.

'You're holding him on suspicion of murder?'

'No, as it happens, our investigation of him is concluded. He's been released. He's currently sitting in a nice hotel in Perugia with his daughter.'

'You what? I was assuming a tiny cell with six other reprobates.'

Marta laughed. 'I think for a British ambassador we might have managed . . . at least . . . *l'isolamento*.'

'So, how . . . why . . .?'

'We were fortunately able to fast track access to the general's will and his story stands up. As you thought it would.'

'Framley Grange was left to the sister?'

'Precisely.'

'You had better luck than me. I'm still waiting for my copy.'

'*Questo è presumibilmente lo svantaggio di essere un dilettante.*' She smiled, then: 'This is presumably the disadvantage of being an amateur,' she translated. Francis wasn't even clear why she'd bothered with the Italian, except to subtly remind him who was in charge. 'No,' she went on, 'without a motive, in fact with an anti-motive, I think Sir Duncan is in the clear. But I believe you thought that anyway.'

'Not to start with, no. But yes, once he said he was losing the house, it didn't strike me as likely that he was involved. Also, just the way he was reacting, in conversation, at dinner. I got the feeling, even under that old-school exterior, that he was genuinely upset.'

Marta nodded. 'This is the advantage you have over me. In being here, talking to them all at all hours. So what is it you want to tell me?'

'So now you've eliminated Duncan,' he replied, 'I'm imagining you might be stuck. With no leads?'

'I'll be honest, Francis. We need a result. Quickly. Look by the gate. It's not just the *Corriere dell'Umbria* any more. They're all here. *La Repubblica, La Stampa, Il Corriere della Sera*. TV networks. Other Europeans and Americans, too, this morning. Because you are British and American this story has an international dimension. And maybe, too, because we are from Perugia. Some of those foreign journalists have never forgotten the Amanda Knox story. Already the reference has been made. The Americans are just waiting to have another go at us for being inefficient, corrupt, all the things they said when they disagreed with our procedure before . . . and our conclusions . . .'

'You really think so?'

'I do. More urgently, Ceccarelli's boss had the Interior Minister on the phone from Rome last night. In strict confidence, if we don't have some sort of solution by tomorrow he'll be sending someone down to take the case over.'

Francis looked down at his shoes, which badly needed a polish. He was keeping her waiting. Why, he hardly knew himself. Except perhaps to get back at her for the offhand way she had treated him on Sunday. Given the circumstances, he was in danger of being petty, not to say spiteful, not to say negligent. 'OK,' he said, after a few moments. 'So what do you think about Liam?'

'Liam?'

'As a suspect?'

The policewoman sat forward. You could sense her excitement. 'I think,' she said, 'we think – he is one of the suspicious ones.'

'So you haven't eliminated him?'

She shook her head. 'Obviously I would rather not say.'

'For a while,' Francis said, 'even when I was still thinking it was probably Duncan who had committed this crime, I had Liam in my mind as a possibility. There's this Irish connection, which you know about . . .'

'Poppy's father . . .'

'The general. Who was a significant player in the Northern Irish Troubles of the 1970s. I looked him up. He was a colonel then, based in Belfast. He would surely have directed a number of operations against the enemy, the IRA. Who knows exactly what happened, but this was a war – there were deaths on both sides. I'm sure he remained a target for the IRA until his death. It would take a particularly vengeful kind of IRA man to go after his daughter, but such people do exist. The Irish have long memories.'

'So you . . . and Diana . . . have told us.'

'And who's to say that Poppy wasn't at some level involved herself, in that she was in her twenties in the 1970s, which is when all this happened.'

'You mean . . . Poppy was a fighter in the British army?'

'No.' Francis laughed. 'Though I wouldn't have put it past her claiming to be. But I've checked her out too. She was never anything directly to do with the Army. But she was close to her dad. He was out there. So maybe there is some story there.'

'So you're saying that Liam was an IRA member? But I thought they laid down their arms.'

'Technically so. At the time of the Northern Irish Agreement, in 1998, there was a ceasefire. The IRA stopped fighting, and many of their prisoners were released. But there were others, diehard Republicans, who didn't give up on the cause. They moved into other organizations. There was one called the Real IRA. It's not important, except that if you were thinking of Liam as a possible murderer, that would all fit.'

'But you don't think it does?'

'No. He is too open about his sympathies. He reads poems about his dead father, who was an IRA fighter. Also, he's too . . . off the wall, if you understand me.'

'Off the wall?'

'Crazy, mad. He's a big supporter of the legalization of drugs. All drugs, not just the soft ones. He'd like to see them for sale in the local chemist. He has other controversial opinions too, which he's very honest about. And also, not to be discounted, he loved Sasha. They had become such friends. In a very short time.'

'So you don't, in fact, think it was him?'

'No.'

'So then . . .?' Marta gave him her nicest, most amenable smile.

She was being very patient, and Francis was, perhaps, being a bit of an arsehole. But he had worked through everything in his mind, and he wanted, if not exactly to show off, at least to share; to find out how much she had found out; whether her track of suspicion had in any way matched his. After that he would take her to the murderer.

'For a while,' he went on, 'I was suspicious of Roz. She was behaving oddly and kept disappearing. She confessed to me one evening that she was having an affair with a married man. I even thought for a while that she might be Duncan's secret mistress, that the pair of them had been working together, that she too wanted to inherit the beautiful house. But then, when we had our day out in Gubbio . . .'

'The day we searched the villa?'

'Yes. By chance I caught her in a very intimate embrace with Tony. On the cable car.'

'Tony!' Marta laughed. 'I thought he was *fin*— er, gay. He is so tanned and . . . fit for his age.'

'Who would have thought it, eh? But he is, it turns out, her lover. Did she tell you she was involved with a married man?'

'No.'

'Well, she is. And this is him. Tony. For reasons of their own they decided to be on this course together, but not together, if you follow me.'

'Pretending to be single?'

'Yes.'

'For some sexual thrill perhaps?'

'Maybe,' he said. 'Or maybe just because he's terrified of his wife finding out about them somehow.'

She nodded, with understanding. 'So what about him? Tony?'

'He is a man of mystery. He said at the start of the week that he would have to kill us if he told us what he really did for a living. It seemed like a joke . . .'

'Yes, one of the others told us this. Diana. She didn't see it as a joke. She was very concerned about him.'

'Was she?' Francis said. 'That's interesting. But though he had access,' he went on, 'to both Poppy and Sasha, I couldn't see a motive. My only thought was that he might have been working for someone else. Someone who would benefit from Poppy's death. Who wasn't here.'

'Such as?'

'The sister. Minty. We know there was no love lost between her and Poppy. Minty had always coveted Framley Grange. She also passed the test of knowing that Poppy and Duncan would be out here, in this place, at this time. So if you are squeamish and well-off, why not employ someone else to do your dirty work for you. Well away from home.'

'So you suspect Tony – of that? Being a proxy killer?'

'No.'

'Why not?'

'First, because of Roz. I can understand – just – bringing your secret mistress on holiday with you, and staying in separate bedrooms, being quiet about being a couple. Because you're terrified that this liaison might get back to your wife. But to do that when you're planning a contract murder . . . it seemed unlikely.'

'Unless all that was a front. To put you off suspecting if anything went wrong.'

'I thought of that, too. But then I found out what Tony does do for a living. He's an antique dealer.'

Marta laughed. 'An antique dealer, no!'

'Quite successful, it seems. He's made enough money to make contract killing an unlikely hobby.'

'So you have eliminated him too. Who does that leave? Your hosts, and a collection of nice old ladies.'

'Our hosts, yes. Gracious Stephanie and irreverent Gerry, the frustrated artist. Ideally placed to kill their guests, in that they would know all about the mechanics of the sauna, how to get the handle to fall off "accidentally". They also, obviously, knew that Poppy would be coming here this week. But what did they have against her, that's the question. Yes, Poppy had irritated Gerry with her remarks about abstract art, but that's hardly a motive for murder, is it?'

Marta laughed. 'Maybe in some places.'

'In any case Poppy had managed to annoy everybody, pretty much. It seemed that that was what she did, even needed to do. Find people's weak spots and poke them. Anyway, Gerry has his hands full. Literally. He's having a passionate affair with the cook.'

Marta's eyes widened. 'Benedetta?'

Francis nodded.

'How do you know?'

'I have seen them together. He isn't very careful, meeting up with her at night. He still thinks Stephanie doesn't know, but she does. As do all the staff. Which is why they give her the cold shoulder half the time, if you've noticed. She's a married woman, and that counts for something out here. No, I'd say Stephanie's just biding her time before she sacks her and confronts Gerry. I suspect that moment would have come this week, at the end of the season. But here we are. The food is one of the things that everyone talks about here, and Benedetta has, famously, "golden hands".'

'*Le mani d'oro . . .*'

'She is the reason the lunches and dinners are so delicious. Quite apart from the opinion of the guests, there's a food blogger staying. Roz. Didn't she tell you? Her Civil Service role is only her day job. Her passion is her food and travel blog. Which is quite widely read, it seems, and Stephanie and Gerry know all about it. So, I hardly thought, with all this going on, that our hosts would add murder to their to-do list, even if they had a motive.'

'So who does this leave?' asked Marta. She counted on her fingers again, muttering, 'Five old ladies.'

'Don't forget Fabio and Benedetta. And the other cooks.'

Marta smiled. 'I don't think so. What is Poppy to them? Just another foreign guest.'

'Quite. Though Fabio might fit the bill in other senses.'

'How do you mean?'

'He has the demeanour, don't you think?'

'How do you mean?'

'If you were to pick a murderer from an identity parade of all of them . . .'

'He would be the one?' She laughed. 'Maybe.'

'And it was he who turned on the sauna, early in the morning.'

'At Poppy's request.'

'The maintenance was his responsibility.'

'He told us several times that the handle was completely OK. That he regularly checked it. When he'd last looked at it, he said, the screws were all in place. In any case, what on earth would be his motive?'

'Working for someone else?' Francis suggested. 'Sister Minty? He could use some extra money, I'm sure.'

'And how would sister Minty have made contact with him?'

'She might have come out earlier, in the summer, with her children.'

'Did she?'

'Not that I could discover, no.'

Marta was studying him, head on one side. 'I have an *agente* outside, a constable, ready to help me arrest someone. If your reasoning convinces me, Francis. You are not telling me this is Fabio?'

'No. I'm just taking you through my thought processes. Fabio couldn't have done it anyway because he wasn't here on the morning when Sasha died. So you're right, we're left with five old ladies, three of whom are regular visitors to this delightful place. Why on earth should any of them set on a new arrival and kill her? Or if one of them did lure her out here, how and why did they do that? It does all seem most unlikely, even though Diana does always look rather murderously at anyone who gets to the breakfast table before her. Particularly anyone new.'

Marta laughed. 'You see. That's just the sort of insight you can only have if you're staying here. No one has mentioned this fine detail in interview.'

'Five old ladies,' Francis repeated. 'One of whom is over ninety and apparently sweet as pie.'

'Sweet as pie. As in a pie you might eat?'

'Yes. Did you never hear that expression during your time in Romford?'

'I didn't. Perhaps the pies weren't so nice there. So what are you saying? The sweetness of the pastry conceals a bitter heart?'

'No. I have chatted to Angela several times and though she, too, clearly disliked Poppy, she was far too well-mannered ever to say so. As far as I can ascertain, she had never met her before this holiday. There is no motive that I can see. Even if there were, can we imagine this frail, if straight-backed, old lady mustering the strength to strangle a strong young woman like Sasha?'

'No.'

'So we come to the two Yorkshire ladies . . .'

'Mel and Belle.'

'Now they have never been here before, which in a funny way makes them more suspicious than the regulars. They are also great friends and have known each other since they were teenagers. Say, for some motive we have yet to discover, they did have it in for Poppy and found out somehow that she was coming here, it would be all too easy to sign up to the course too. They have already told us they only booked a month or so ago. As we've discussed before, bumping someone off away from home has its advantages. Belle knows Italy, speaks Italian fluently, might know that there are no coroners out here and that *necroscopi* don't always call for autopsies . . .'

'You are still saying that it's easier to get away with murder here in Italy than at home in Britain . . .'

Francis shrugged. 'No. But they might think that. Or maybe they just think it's easier if they've got Poppy away from her friends and her routines at home.'

'So . . . what? It is this pair you are accusing?'

'I kept them in the frame for a long time. Partly because they seemed so unlikely, and from my previous experience it is the unlikely ones you need to watch the closest. Also, partly, unfairly, because of a certain look that Mel has . . .'

'Eyes close together . . .?'

Francis nodded. 'Among other things. All most unfair, I admit. I've never subscribed to the theory that your physical characteristics describe your character. But partly, also, because I found out that Poppy, before she met Duncan, had spent some time in their part of the world.'

'Yorkshire?'

'Yes. Belle lives in Knaresborough, which is not far from Harrogate, where Poppy lived for a while. Poppy did interior decorating, as did Mel and Belle. Was that a coincidence? Also, this is a well-to-do part of the country, but it's not London, where there are jobs galore. Perhaps they quarrelled over work . . .'

'This hardly seems like a motive for murder. Years later.'

'I agree. It really was, I think, just a coincidence. If Poppy even had a business up there. She was quite a fantasist. Maybe she did a couple of jobs for friends and then exaggerated it into something more. And there was no cover-up about them not having known each other. They hadn't known each other.'

'So you are letting these two off as well?' Marta asked.

'Yes.'

'So, you are left with . . .?'

'And then there were two,' said Francis. 'Zoe . . .'

'. . . and Diana.'

'Both formidable women.'

'They are.'

'And you think it is one of these two?'

'I know it is one of these two. But it's a little more complicated than that. Because these two, Zoe and Diana, are regulars here. They are not the closest of friends, but they have both been coming for years. So we are thrown back to that original question of mine. Why would a regular – or two in this case – want to lure someone new out to the villa to kill them?'

'What are you saying? They are both guilty?'

'No, no. They are not both guilty. But yes, they were working together.'

'I don't understand.'

'Earlier in this holiday, Zoe gave me her memoir to read.'

'Her memoir?'

'An account of her life, memories, characters, adventures . . .'

'Ah, her *memorie* . . .'

'Is that the word? Her autobiography.'

'*Autobiografia*, yes.'

'I groaned, inwardly, because often these manuscripts that your students give you are pretty dreadful. You are obliged to wade through them and then find something nice to say, something you almost certainly don't believe.'

'I'm sorry, I don't quite follow . . .'

'I'm getting there. Anyway, the good news is that this memoir of Zoe's is surprisingly good. She's Jewish, as I'm sure you know. She is wealthy now, but it wasn't always that way. Her family escaped with nothing from Poland at the start of the last century. Her grandfather was a poor tailor in Whitechapel. It's an interesting read, a classic rags to riches story, full of entertaining detail about that colourful Jewish milieu. Now by the time Zoe came along, the family were well-established in the UK and on the up. She was able to go to college, the Royal College of Music indeed, and join a lively London scene in the early 1960s.'

'Swinging London?'

'A bit before that, but heading that way, yes. To cut a long story short, she met a man. A handsome and talented musician, whom she fell in love with. He was in fact the composer Robert Heddon – have you heard of him?'

'No.'

'He's well-known in England. He wrote a famous piece for piano and saxophone called *Rural Idyll*. It's the kind of thing people play at weddings and funerals. Anyway, she and Bobby were together for a while, and then along came a younger woman. A *femme fatale*, if you will. In Zoe's story, even though this younger woman knew they were happy together, perhaps even because they were happy together, she stole Bobby away. Zoe, being young, optimistic and in love, hoped he might come back. But even when this younger woman dumped him, a couple of years later, it was no good. Zoe had by then met the man who was to become her husband. He was nice, decent, stable – and

Jewish to boot. She didn't feel she could leave him to return to someone who made her heart beat that much faster, but . . .'

'Might break it again too.'

'Exactly,' said Francis. 'And the name of that *femme fatale* was . . .'

'Poppy?'

'Poppy Pugh-Smith. Born to privilege, beautiful, spoilt, one of those people who didn't care what she did.'

'And that's all in the *autobiografia*?'

'It is. Although Zoe changed her name. If I'd been sharper I might have recognized Daphne Cassock-Jones earlier, which sounds like a made-up name, but then so many English names do. At one point, just before you dismissed me, I was going to tell you to read it. Then, I'm afraid, I took umbrage and kept the information to myself. As I did also about another story of love and betrayal, which happened thirty years later, in the late 1980s. This time to our last suspect . . .'

'Diana.'

'The more prosaic Diana MacDonald. Happily married to a man she lived and worked with twenty-four-seven. They ran a fabric importing business together, specialising in designs from Africa and the Far East. And all was well, until one day, along came a client, a younger woman, who lured him away. Diana always thought that the main attraction for this younger woman was that the man was out of bounds. Because two years later, she was off, but again it was all too late. Diana couldn't take him back, even though there was no one else. For her, the betrayal was too much. He found someone else, but she, Diana, never forgot the woman she called "the floozy". Never forgot, and never forgave.'

'Are you telling me this was also Poppy?'

'It was.'

'A client, you say. So she *had* been an interior decorator?'

'Apparently so. For a while at least. But down in London by now. So how and why,' Francis went on, 'did she end up here, at remote Villa Giulia, with these two women whom she had wronged in love? Both Zoe and Diana were regular visitors to the villa, as we know. One night, a couple of years ago, they were telling each other stories after dinner. They were talking about coincidence, and what a small world it could sometimes be, and Zoe came up with a story about how she had recently gone on a weekend course in memoir-writing in London and found out that one of the other participants was a woman she had crossed swords with years before, when this woman went off with a man Zoe had loved. Zoe had two points to make: a) that it was bizarre that she should run into this woman again, and on a memoir-writing course of all things, when she, this woman, the *femme fatale*, and what she'd done, took up at least a chapter of her memoir; and b) that she was surprised this woman had no idea who she was, or of how she had affected her life. Even when she'd asked her leading questions, she hadn't taken the hint. Poppy Pugh-Smith was not just a *femme fatale*, but *une femme qui ne se souvient pas*.'

'A woman who didn't remember.' Marta laughed. 'Or maybe didn't even know.'

'That is possible too. Anyway, at this point in the story there had been loud shrieks from Diana. It was really no surprise to her, she said, that in the world as it is, you might run into someone whose life had crossed with yours years before. But what was a very strange coincidence was this. This very same Poppy Pugh-Smith had ruined her life as well. It was she who had seduced Diana's husband, David. And then, after a short two years, thrown him over. But once betrayed, like Zoe, Diana could never go back. And not just because Poppy had, to her certain knowledge, nick-named him "David the Dreary". She just couldn't forgive him. Or her.

'The coincidence was so strange, Diana thought, that it seemed – somehow – *meant*. It was almost, she thought, as if they were supposed to be having this conversation, on this terrace, on this warm September night. The two ladies decided they had to do something. How about this, Diana said. How about trying to get Poppy out here, next year, to this very place, and then confronting her. Making her aware of the harm she'd done, the hurt that her actions had led to. There were surely others, too, victims of her casual promiscuity, her attraction to established couples; maybe they could find them – somehow – and get them out too.'

'This sounds a little . . . would you say . . . crazy. Would you really go to such lengths, for a lost love, so many years later?'

Francis shrugged. 'You're right. They are a little crazy. Both of them. Diana, in particular, is a woman obsessed. At home we say,

"Hell hath no fury like a woman scorned". It's a quote from one of our famous playwrights . . .'

'Scorned?'

'Rejected, turned down . . .'

'*Respinta.*'

'I imagine.'

'It's a good one.'

'They were lucky,' Francis went on, 'in achieving their first objective, getting Poppy out here. Zoe had her email from the *Guardian* course and managed to persuade her that if she wanted to continue to improve her memoir-writing in a beautiful place she should consider Villa Giulia. Was it a little naughty of Zoe to drop in the names of some of the more celebrated tutors they had had at the villa over the years, not to mention some of the more distinguished guests? Perhaps it was. But never mind, Poppy took the bait and wrote back. This sounded perfect, she said, because she was trying to get her husband interested in writing a memoir of his life as a diplomat, and this seemed like the ideal introduction.

'The other half of the plan was harder to action. Short of advertising, how were they going to find other women – and perhaps men – whom Poppy had wronged? Diana was convinced there were plenty. If Poppy had done this twice, and thirty years apart, surely she had done it other times? Maybe what they needed, Diana suggested to Zoe, was a two-part process. Get Poppy out here, not reveal themselves or their interest, and then encourage her to tell stories. Then they could find out exactly what she had got up to. The confrontation, involving other victims, could happen later, either here or perhaps, under the guise of a reunion, back at home.

'Unfortunately for Poppy,' Francis went on, 'Diana had other plans. Perhaps the whole idea of the "confrontation" had been a ploy to get Zoe to write to Poppy, and encourage her to come out here. At any rate, before they had done either of the things they had discussed the year before, and perhaps again this year, Poppy was dead in the sauna. Zoe was horrified.'

'Diana had meant to kill her all along,' Marta said. 'How did you get them to tell you all this anyway?' she added.

'Neither of them have told me anything,' Francis replied. 'But

Zoe let me know, let us all know, early on, that she keeps a journal, and I've been reading that.'

'She's confessed to all this in her journal?'

'No confession. As she sees it, she herself has done nothing wrong. Other than go along with Diana's idea of a confrontation. But her journal details the horror she's been feeling, knowing that Diana was very likely responsible for the death in the sauna, and then of course the follow-on strangulation of poor Sasha.'

'So where is this book? Can I see it?'

'It's not a book, I'm afraid. It's all on her laptop. Buried in a file that she thought no one would find to read.'

'How did you get access?'

Francis explained. 'So there it all was,' he went on, 'in front of me in writing. The original plan. The shock at what happened last week. Zoe's fear of talking to Diana about it, in case Diana should turn on her. Her failure to understand what happened to Sasha. If that was Diana's doing too – why? Had Sasha found something out? And then threatened to turn her in? She was scared she herself might be implicated. Because of their plan; and because she knows. She's in a panic.'

'And what about Mel and Belle. Do they know too?'

'No. They appear to know nothing. Zoe thinks, meanwhile, that either Diana had planned this all along or Poppy must have said something that tipped her over the edge. And then, when she knew she was taking a sauna every morning she couldn't help herself.'

'But what about the poison? She must have planned a murder if she brought cyanide with her. It's not something you'd easily buy in Castiglione dell'Umbria.'

'I agree.'

Marta said nothing. For all of five seconds she stared at the floor, taking this all in. Then, like someone waking from a dream, she jumped to her feet. 'God help us,' she said. 'We need to move. This woman may not even be safe.'

'Zoe?'

'Yes. And Diana. Where is she? We need to confront her right now.'

FIFTEEN

The door to Michelangelo – Diana's room – was locked. Francis shouted for Diana but there was no reply. Marta too. Then they looked at each other and had the same thought. Did they even have time to fetch Gerry and get the master key?

'It may be too late,' said Francis. 'We'd better break it down.'

He threw his upper body heavily against the door, but it proved stronger than he'd imagined. The villa was old. There had presumably been times when it wasn't just occupied by a bunch of arty types who trusted each other enough not to lock their rooms.

'You OK?' said Marta. 'That looked painful.'

'I'm fine.' It had bruised his shoulder a bit, but in the circumstances he was good for one more go. Tellingly, there had been no cry of protest from inside. Either the murderess was cowering, waiting for the inevitable end, or something worse had happened.

Francis took several paces back and ran at the door again. There was a heavy thud, and the sound of splintering wood, but the lock held firm. There was still no sound from within.

'I think we'd better try and get the master key,' said Marta. 'The danger is you twist the lock and then even with a key we can't get it open.'

'OK.' Francis turned, and raced along the corridor to Gerry and Stephanie's room. That too was locked.

He ran downstairs and out into the courtyard.

Three ladies and Liam looked up from their card game.

'Are you all right?' asked Zoe; she looked terrified, Francis saw.

'Have you seen Gerry?' he asked. 'Or Stephanie?'

'Stephanie went into town in her car,' Belle said. 'But I think Gerry's up in the studio.'

Francis sprinted up the gravel driveway. Halfway up towards the main gate he turned right into the studio. There was no one in the outer room, just an array of big colourful drawings of

flowers laid out on the table (Belle does Georgia O'Keeffe). But
in the inner room he found Gerry, standing with a brush in his
hand, staring thoughtfully at a huge canvas. This one was green
and pale blue, with touches of pink, altogether more optimistic
than the dull grey and brown squares in the villa corridors.

'Gerry, sorry to interrupt. We urgently need the key to Diana's
room.'

'Michelangelo. Is she all right?'

'No. I don't think so. You need to come now.'

Gerry put down his brush, resting it carefully on the edge of
his box of oils, which sat on a raised island in the centre of the
floor. Then he turned and followed Francis down. As Francis broke
into a trot, he did too. In a minute they were at the door to
Tintoretto. Gerry dived in and returned with the master key.

'I'm sorry,' Francis said, as they arrived back at the battered
door of Michelangelo. 'We tried to break it down.'

Marta, standing waiting, was on her phone. '*Sì, immediata-
mente*,' she was saying, and then another burst of Italian. Francis
caught '*non mi interessa*' then something like '*chiamarmi se vuole*.'
She clicked off. 'Sorry.'

Gerry had the key in the lock. 'I haven't used this for years.
Let's hope it works.' He turned the key, the lock clicked back.

Gerry pushed the door open, gestured politely for Marta to go
first. The two men followed.

'*Madonna Mia!*' cried Marta.

Diana was hanging from the heavy brass chain that held up the
little chandelier, a leather belt around her neck, her fine features
distorted in a ghastly rictus of shock, as if at the last moment
she might have regretted her theatrical finale. Below her, on the
tiled floor, one of the antique chairs was on its side. Near it was
a champagne flute, the tulip glass smashed, the neck intact.

'Christ,' said Francis, feeling a rush of nausea. There was no
inappropriate hunger this time – instead he found himself dashing
for the *en suite* with sour vomit welling up in his mouth. He
reached the toilet and threw up. 'Christ,' he repeated, as his breakfast and the dark coffee that had washed it down splashed into the
white bowl. He shivered, and reached out for a handful of toilet
tissue from the nearby roll. He wiped his mouth, got to his feet,

and returned to the room. He was desperate for water, but he didn't quite trust the supply away from the drinking water tap in the kitchen. This was just the kind of big old house to have a dead rat in one of the tanks.

Gerry and Marta were standing their ground, staring at the dangling corpse. Even in death, Diana was nicely turned out, in a pullover and skirt combo, with smart black leather boots underneath. The belt, Francis realized, was the one she had bought in Gubbio. So had she planned this even then? Even before Sasha? Or had she improvised?

'Sorry,' he said to the others.

'Please,' said Marta. 'It's a perfectly normal reaction. I am only used to it because . . . I have seen this kind of thing before.'

'What on earth happened?' asked Gerry.

'She took her own life,' said Marta.

'I can see that. But why?'

'She was the one,' Francis explained to him, 'who killed Poppy. And also Sasha.'

A terrible thought had occurred to Francis. Perhaps the piece of writing Diana had been working on so studiously for the last couple of days was her suicide note; perhaps it was here in the room.

It took him no longer to find it than it had to find Zoe's journal. It was sitting in an envelope decorated with a pretty floral design which was propped up on the dressing table by Diana's beloved lipsticks. On the front it read, in capitals: GERRY AND STEPHANIE.

'It's addressed to you,' he said to Gerry. 'D'you want to open it?'

'Please,' said Marta, intervening. 'I must take this. Just wait one moment.' She pulled out a pair of thin white plastic gloves from her jacket pocket and slid them on. 'We can read it together,' she continued, taking it from Francis, 'but it is obviously important evidence. We cannot have any other fingerprints on it, for example.' Carefully, she eased the flap of the envelope open and pulled out the piece of paper inside, which she held by one corner.

'This is some *nota di suicidò*,' she said, studying it.

It was. Four pages pulled out of the A5 notepad, carefully

covered in Diana's clear, swirling hand. 'Shall I read it out loud?' she asked Gerry.

'Please,' said Gerry, and Marta began.

> Dear Gerry and Stephanie, I am so very sorry to have to do this, in my favourite room in your lovely villa, where I have spent so many happy September holidays. As you know, for almost twenty-five years now, I have come here every summer, and right from the start the experience, very different of course to the adventurous holidays David and I used to have, racing in our open-topped MG down the Route Nationale in France . . .

And so it went on, in Diana's classic rambling style, to explain what Francis and Marta already knew. That Poppy had been Diana's nemesis, thirty years ago. That Diana had never forgiven her. That she was very sorry but what she and Zoe had planned, which was a confrontation, was never going to be enough for her. That she had never originally intended to shut Poppy in the sauna, she had intended to poison her, with cyanide, which she had understood from her researches on the Internet to be the quickest and most efficient way to kill someone, with the advantage that it was hard to trace, not that she was bothered about that. But that when she realized Poppy took a sauna every morning after her swim she couldn't resist the idea that had come to her, of trapping her in there. It had been so easy to tamper with the door, just loosening the screws of the internal handle, so it fell off when you opened and shut the door. Without a screwdriver, you couldn't put it back, though if Poppy had been more of a handywoman, like her, she could have held it in place with one hand while she turned it with the other. But Poppy wasn't clever like that. Others, menials, men, had always done that sort of thing for her.

Marta paused and raised her eyebrows. 'She really didn't like her very much, did she?' she said. She took another pair of thin plastic gloves from her pocket and handed them to Francis, nodding for him to slip them on. Then she passed over the letter.

'Your turn,' she said.

Francis took it, and read aloud to his audience of two.

I'm terribly sorry, but I just wanted the silly bitch, for five minutes, to feel a tiny dose of the daily pain that she inflicted on me for thirty long years. Was that so very terrible? I am not a bad person, nor even a particularly vengeful one, but sometimes I do feel that people should be made to understand the *consequences* of what they've done.

Her underlining of 'consequences' was so hard it had torn the paper.

Funnily enough, because David was working in London when he met Poppy, she never met me. I looked very different in those days – my hair was dark for a start, so I doubt she had any idea who I was, especially since I reclaimed my maiden name a couple of years after the divorce. Locked in her gilded cage of self-obsession, she had no idea who Zoe was either. Or what she'd done to ruin her life, years before. And the lives of who knows how many others. She was blissfully ignorant of what was about to happen to her.

But I did want her to know what I'd done. I didn't want to miss out on that. So once I knew she was in there, and yes, my plan had worked and the handle was on the floor, I knocked on the glass door of the sauna and told her that David had been my husband, and that Robert Heddon, another of her conquests, had been Zoe's beau. 'Didn't you realize?' I cried out to her. And then I left her.

I knew that no one else was likely to hear. The villa walls are thick and Fabio was down at the pool as usual, checking the chlorine content as he did every morning after Poppy had had her swim. It was a routine that takes him half an hour. So I knew there was plenty of time.

How did I poison her? That was easy too. I'm always a bit early for breakfast, as I like to be first down. So I knew Poppy liked a little warming espresso after her swim and before her sauna. She was always hopeless with the Gaggia machine, so it was easy for me to offer to help her, as I had done on previous occasions. And on that last morning of her life add a little something to the mix that she wasn't bargaining for. She did complain that the coffee was a little bitter, but I told her they'd changed the brand of beans. Ha ha ha!

There was one thing that I didn't tell Zoe. Or any of you, because I don't believe in sharing all your unhappiness all the time with everyone you meet, like the younger generation seem to do nowadays, bleating their every little personal upset out on Facebook and Twitter and what have you. Personally, I think you should have one person who is very close to you, with whom you can share the most intimate details, and that's enough. Of course, if that person has been taken away from you, in the cruellest possible way, then maybe you have to keep your troubles to yourself. Exercise a little stoicism, a neglected virtue, in my opinion. Of course, my local GP knew, dear Henrietta, and the consultant at the hospital, lovely Dr Gupta, but otherwise the fact that I have only three months to live was not one I wanted any of my friends – or you – to know. The cancer that I had five years ago, and got over, as I thought, has returned, this time to my bones, so the diagnosis is not a good one. Dr Gupta has in fact given me until Christmas. So I particularly enjoyed this year, knowing that it would be my last at glorious Villa Giulia. And maybe I am just a silly, superstitious old woman, but it was as if God knew it too, giving us the most perfect weather I've ever had out here, day after day of glorious sunshine.

I'm sorry about Sasha. Clever little thing, she realized that it was me who'd killed Poppy, so she had to go too. A little bit too psychic for her own good, wasn't she, with her oh-so-clever character analyses. I knew after I'd spoken to her that evening that she knew it was me who had done away with Poppy. All I can say in my defence is that she would have known nothing about it. She had a nice strong sedative – Propofol – before I twisted that fuchsia scarf of hers around her pretty neck. The mushrooms were a red herring – or rather, a pinky-orange herring! Perhaps it was selfish of me, but I wasn't prepared to face the music for what I see as justice, even if others might see it as a crime. I didn't want to undergo any of that police palaver that Francis loves to write about. I just wanted to leave on my own terms, in my own time, with the sunlight coming through the curtains in my favourite room. A final glass of lovely Prosecco, and then a leap into the unknown. Well, I've always believed that murderers should be hanged, so you can't accuse me of inconsistency.

So farewell, my dear September holiday friends, and Francis our tutor too. I enjoyed meeting you and chatting with you about my writing style. With the best will in the world I am never going to be Chekhov now, am I? But perhaps, in my funny old way, I have managed to put your advice about writing, Francis, into my final act in this beautiful, though often cruel world. I have, I hope you will agree, *shown not told* my anger, which has simmered quietly all these years. And if you love yourself, as I am not ashamed to say I do, I have *killed* my second most important *darling* – myself. Someone else killed my *most important darling*, thirty years ago, even if he did, at some pathetic level, go on living. In fact that fucking bitch worse than killed him, because she also killed any idea I had had of him being the decent, upright, loyal, faithful, fun man I had always believed he was, prior to that. For society's sake, I had to stomach that terrible betrayal and pretend it didn't really matter to me. But it did. Oh yes, it did. And this week I was finally able to serve my revenge as it should be, like the delicious Villa Giulia lunch prepared every day by dear, kind, beautiful Benedetta and her team – cold.'

'My good God!' said Marta when he'd finished. 'She's a psychopath. Sasha . . . was just . . .'

'Collateral damage,' said Gerry grimly.

SIXTEEN

Francis was on his way home. The minibus had brought them on motorways across Italy, past Arezzo away to the left, and Florence away to the right, and dumped them in the satellite car park at Pisa, from where you had to take a new shuttle train into the airport, a kilometre or two away. Francis had helped the three old ladies with him, as they struggled with their heavy luggage up and down lifts and tried to work out how to buy a single shuttle ticket with a foreign credit card. Eventually he had got them to Departures and handed the redoubtable Angela over to a young woman with film star good looks who was working for Special Assistance, a service that didn't seem to cover the area where Angela had really needed Special Assistance, i.e. the satellite car park. He then left Mel and Belle in the easyJet queue while he checked in with British Airways.

He had stumbled through the indignities of Security, his trousers falling down as usual, and had his hand luggage checked over by a Giotto madonna in uniform, who seemed tempted to confiscate the large lump of *parmigiano* he'd bought in the grocery in the airport concourse, but had taken no interest in his clear plastic wash bag, which could have contained, in the one-hundred milligram shampoo bottle, enough cyanide to knock out the entire plane. Now he was settled with a cappuccino in the one little café that the Pisa Airport planners saw fit to maintain airside.

As he chewed through his *bombolone* to find the sweet apricot jam at its centre he felt relief flood through him. He was finally away. From Villa Giulia, which had changed from *paradiso* to *inferno* in such a short time. Touch wood, Marta Moretti wasn't suddenly going to appear through the dangling leather bags and hanging *panetonnes* that surrounded him to question him one last time. He was free of the frankly haughty grilling of Sabatini and Ceccarelli, who had told Francis that he should have shared his suspicions – his *knowledge*, as they said – with them from the first moment he had them. He had almost been made to feel he'd been aiding and abetting Diana, though his realization that she was indeed the murderer had come late in the day, and certainly after the last time they had questioned him.

They had been even harder on Zoe, who was still at the villa, *aiutando la polizia con le loro indagini* (helping the police with their enquiries), with the clear and heavy threat that non-cooperation would lead to her being investigated herself. Fortunately the British Embassy in Rome had provided Vittoria, a charming and competent young woman who was fighting Zoe's corner for her. Even though the murderer was dead, this was still a murder enquiry. Had Zoe, in her panic, been committing *soccorso e favoreggiamento* (aiding and abetting), lying about Diana? Or could you argue, as Francis had with Marta, that she had been running scared of her, terrified for her own life? It was certainly enough to make you doubt the wisdom of ever keeping a journal. Francis felt a little guilty that he'd dumped Zoe in it so comprehensively. Then again, the journal was key evidence, even if superseded by the comprehensive confession of Diana's farewell letter.

As for the others, the questioning had been perfunctory. Duncan and Fiona hadn't even been brought back to the villa, and neither Francis nor any of the others had seen them again. Barbara White-Moloney, too, had stayed in Perugia and was now free to organize the repatriation of poor Sasha. Francis had been sad not to set eyes on her again; if he had known that his poolside encounter was to be the last time he would see her, he might have said even more.

Tony and Roz had departed too, apparently to some hotel in Perugia – and who knew what lies Tony was sending back home to his wife? But he was certainly happy to use the murder enquiry as a smokescreen for his ongoing affair. The murder-in-the-sauna story had now been reported not just across Italy, but worldwide, though British and American newspapers and TV stations had, fairly obviously, taken the keenest interest. But once the gruesome details of Diana's suicide had been made public, by the police, with some colourful elaboration from Liam, who had chatted indiscreetly to the journos at the gate, the media had done with the story. There were no suspects to fret about, no suggestion that

Mark McCrum

the Italian police had mishandled things, no criticisms of the country's inquisitorial justice system. The vengeful Englishwoman was the villain, and that was that. Done and dusted.

Marta Moretti had held true to her promise and taken all the credit for the resolution of the inquiry herself. It was just a shame that Liam had seen fit to inform the gathered journos that the crime had been solved by the writing tutor, an Englishman, who already had form for that sort of thing. This indiscretion had led, fairly inevitably, to Francis's photo being plastered all over the *Mail Online*, with side pics of the Mold-on-Wold festival and – God help him – the *Golden Adventurer* at sea. He was glad he was still out of the country, and could only hope he'd be left alone when he got home. On the other hand, as a writer in the over-crowded contemporary market, he was hardly going to be churlish about his media profile being raised. The irreverent Irishman wasn't with them today, which was a relief. Rome was apparently a cheaper and quicker option to Belfast than Pisa.

And here indeed, speak of the devil, were the last two, Belle and Mel, approaching from the leather goods concession, where you could buy a beautiful Italian bag for several times the price it had been in the market stall in Gubbio.

'Hello, Francis,' said Belle.

'Or rather goodbye,' said Mel.

'We thought we'd just come and give you a farewell hug,' Belle said. 'Our flight's been called.'

Francis got to his feet and put his arms around her. He had grown fond of dear scatty Belle, who wore her vulnerability so bravely on her sleeve. He imparted a kiss to her strangely smooth cheek, then turned to Mel, who stood waiting in line, Gandalf's little red-cheeked helper, with her incongruous carroty hair. His hug for her was less warm, despite his intention to treat them both the same.

'Safe journey,' he said. 'I hope Brian hasn't blown the kitchen up.'

'Oh, I expect he has,' Mel replied, her thin lips twisting into a genuinely warm grin at this attack on her other half. 'Doesn't bear thinking about.'

'Maybe we'll see you another year,' said Belle hopefully.

'If they go on with it. D'you think they will?'

Mel shrugged. 'Who knows. Once they've got over the shock. Maybe the publicity'll help them, you never know. People can be very ghoulish.'

'Bye then,' Belle waved. 'Look after yourself, Francis. Don't forget to kill those darlings.'

'I won't.' He laughed.

Watching Mel's compact oblong frame depart through the milling throng of travellers, pulling her neat little wheelie case behind her, he wondered whether she'd known more than she'd let on; to him, to the police, and to everyone else. Had it just been Zoe who'd been in on the murder, or had Mel known about the 'confrontation' too? There had been that guilty-looking trio up at St Ubaldo's – and he'd never quite felt it was just the ices they were guilty about. She was one of those folk who looked after number one, was Mel. She certainly wouldn't have done anything so stupid as to keep a journal, would she? But Francis suspected that a) she knew more than she'd told; b) she could have helped Zoe with the *soccorso e favoreggiamento* if she'd wanted to.

There were those that got away with things, weren't there, and those that didn't, and a third category too – those that for some reason didn't allow themselves to get away with things; who had to see what they saw as justice done in some way, even if that brought their own house crashing down around their ears.

Hm, nice thought, Francis told himself; though if he had written that in one of his drafts, he would almost certainly have ordered himself to scratch it out.

'Excuse me?'

Francis looked up to see an elegant sixty-something blonde lady approaching, smiling purposefully.

'Are you that detective chappie?' she asked, in confident English tones. 'Francis Meadowes.'

'No.'

She held up her *Daily Mail*.

'You look awfully like him. And here you are in Pisa Airport. Pisa, Perugia, it's not far.'

'I'm sorry, I have no idea what you're talking about.'

'Oh come off it, it must be you. Give us an autograph. My husband loves detective fiction.'

He met his tormentor's beady eye. She had rumbled him.

'OK then,' he said. 'Here's the deal. I'll sign a bit of paper. And you buy one of my books when you get home and stick it in the front.'

She cackled, proprietorially. 'I knew it was you.'

She brought out a thick notebook. 'I've just been doing a cookery course. Near Cortona. Such fun. Learning how to make pasta properly. Here we are, a blank page.'

Francis nodded and signed.

'Oh, thank you,' she said. 'Tim will be thrilled.'

'I'm glad to hear it.' He gave her a thin, unencouraging smile.

But: 'How do you do it?' she went on. 'Work out who's done it, better than the police? Although, I don't imagine the Italian police are up to much, are they? They made a right pig's ear of that other case in Perugia a few years back, didn't they? The poor English girl and the American with the Italian boyfriend, what was her name?'

'Amanda Knox. And the victim was Meredith Kercher. To answer your question, I suppose I pay careful attention to detail. And now I must apologize, as my flight has just been called.'

God help him and curse Liam. This was not what he'd asked for. He sincerely hoped it would all blow over and he would be able to return to peaceful anonymity. The last thing he wanted was to find he'd turned from a minor crime writer into some sort of celebrity detective, whom people actively sought out with their hard-to-solve cases.

ACKNOWLEDGEMENTS

I am grateful to Kay Dunbar and Stephen Bristow, originators of the Ways With Words festivals, who first encouraged me to teach creative writing on their wonderful courses in Devon and Italy, where I made a number of good friends (none of whom bear any relation whatsoever to the characters in this book). Also to Danuta Kean, who suggested I teach *Guardian* masterclasses in memoir and so meet many other fascinating people with stories to tell. Thanks also to the kind friends who read an early draft of this manuscript and offered encouragement and useful suggestions: Katrin Macgibbon, Stephanie Cross, Lin Hughes, Jackie Nelson and Ben Craib. Nadia Bonini corrected my inadequate Italian and picked me up on other inaccuracies (who would have known that Italian ambulances are routinely manned by volunteers?). Nick Farrell, Italian correspondent of the *Spectator* and biographer of Mussolini, made other useful suggestions. Alessandro Buscaglia was extremely helpful on the details of Italian police, judicial and medical procedure and both patient and scrupulous in his replies to my repeated questions. Further reassurances were kindly provided by Michele and Susan Delicato. My agent Jamie Maclean was his usual speedy and supportive self. Thanks to publisher Kate Lyall Grant for continuing to believe in Francis, to editor Sara Porter for a beady eye and sharp questions and copyeditor Anna Harrisson for fine-tuning. Finally, of course, to my wife Jo, for looking after me and being always, as a reader, impressively impartial.